How could I tell them that our lives were about get even more dangerous and depressing…

Kelly's, Chloe's, and Gareth's disembodied voices disappeared and were replaced with the oppressive silence again.

After what felt like an eternity later—although rationally it was probably only five minutes—Ophelia settled next to me in the sand beneath the house.

She combed through my hair with her fingers while she spoke. "What's up, buttercup? Having nightmares?"

"Living nightmares."

"About Marshall? Kelly said something about you screaming about Marshall."

I shuddered. "I hate when he talks in my head. It's like he's prying into my thoughts with knife-tipped fingers and he can see everything I know and everything my subconscious protects me from."

"Are you sure you weren't dreaming?" Her tone gave away that she wanted desperately to believe I was indeed imagining it.

"They're all trapped. He doesn't know where. He's worried about the Gifted being divided in the war. He says it's coming soon. We're not ready." By the end of my rambling, my voice had diminished to a whisper.

Ophelia wrapped her arms around my shoulders and squeezed them gently. "I can't pretend like I know what to do, but we'll just have to figure it out when the time comes."

"I don't want to tell Brandon," I sobbed.

I buried my face in her shoulder as hot tears streamed down my face.

Sable Mosley is what the government calls Diseased—she starts fires with her mind—and their assassins hunt her relentlessly…

When Sable and her friends, who also have supernatural abilities, find themselves shipwrecked, it seems like all there is left to do is to wait for the Diseased Affairs and Operations to find and kill them. Then a ghost from the past comes to their aid. However, Sable and her friends don't stay safe for long. The DAO captures them, demanding to know what the Bond is. Sable thinks it has something to do with her and Brandon, but she doesn't know exactly what. Can she find the answers and save her friends and herself? Or will the DAO destroy them all?

KUDOS for *The Catalyst*

In *The Catalyst* by Marissa Bauder, Sable and her friends are back and still running from the Diseased Affairs and Operations, DAO. Sable, Brandon her boyfriend, and their friends are rescued for a while but the DAO is never far behind. And soon the group is back in danger. When part of the group is captured, Sable and Brandon have to come up with some way to pull off a rescue without getting what's left of the group killed or captured. The story has a strong and complicated plot with plenty of action and suspense that will leave you screaming for the next book in the series. ~ *Taylor Jones, Reviewer*

The Catalyst by Marissa Bauder is the second book in Bauder's *Diseased* series and, like the first one, Sable and her friends, all with paranormal abilities, are classified by the government as diseased and hunted like rabid dogs. The government wants to either use these people as weapons, or else they want to eliminate them all. But these special kids don't want to be used as weapons. They just want to be left alone to live their lives in peace. Unfortunately, the government isn't going to let that happen. Like Bauder's first book, *The Diseased*, *The Catalyst* is fast-paced with a solid plot and plenty of surprises to keep you enthralled from the first page to the last. ~ *Regan Murphy, Reviewer*

ACKNOWLEDGEMENTS

Thanks to the team at Black Opal Books for guiding me in the editing process and for publishing my books.

I would also like to thank Cassie Wolfe for the amazing cover art. Your talent blows me away and it's an honor to have your work connected to mine.

This story wouldn't be half of what it is without the assistance of Aneta and Travis. Your suggestions and enthusiasm for this story have kept me going, even when times were tough.

Lastly, but certainly not least, thank you to my family and friends for your support. I wouldn't be the writer I am today without your encouragement all these years, I love you all.

THE
CATALYST

THE DISEASED SERIES

MARISSA BAUDER

A Black Opal Books Publication

GENRE: YA/PARANORMAL THRILLER/PARANORMAL ROMANCE

Published by Black Opal Books **http://www.blackopalbooks.com**

DEDICATION

For Grandpa Harry and Grandma Mare. Even though it's not your favorite genre, you're still my biggest fans. I love you.

CHAPTER 1

Sable

The crash of waves against the shore slithered into my consciousness. Behind my closed eyelids, the sun shone red. My boyfriend Brandon's chest rose and fell steadily beneath my cheek, his warm breaths hitting the top of my head in lazy puffs. It was like we were on the deck of the *Kandis Amelia*, sleeping in each other's arms until the sun completely made its way over the horizon. The sharp stinging pain in my ribs reminded me where we really were—stranded on the coast of an uncharted island in the Pacific.

We had been steadily putting distance between us and the Diseased Affairs and Operations' speed boat. A nasty storm rolled in, the wind whipping my chocolate brown curls out wildly in all directions. Rain had poured down from the sky in sheets, and hit my skin like tiny needles of ice. I couldn't believe the size of the swells. Even the bravest of surfers would never attempt them. When I was younger, I'd seen footage of this type of weather from Florida. Hurricanes looked terrifying, and I never wanted to be in one. I had the feeling this storm was part of a hurricane.

Shaw, our renegade band's leader of sorts, made the decision to abandon ship. Three lifeboats were aboard the *Kandis Amelia*. The nine of us all fit in one with some room to spare. I hoped the crewmen on the *Kandis Amelia* would fit into the other two. I never did see if they escaped. We watched in horrified awe as the ocean claimed her. It seemed like someone should've played *Taps* or something, but no one made a sound. I imagined the noise of glass being shattered, representing our broken hearts. The only home we had in the world was gone.

The tiny lifeboat capsized over and over again. During one of the upheavals, the oar lock jammed into my side, bruising my ribs. Somehow, we managed to keep ahold of the boat, whether we sat in it or floated on it while it was upside down. After what seemed like days, the battered boat banked on the shore of the island we occupied now. Our only hope of rescue was if the DAO came looking for us, or our corpses. I wasn't sure which one they'd be looking for or which one I wanted them to find.

Tentatively, I opened my eyes to see what our surroundings looked like in the calm. The rising sun created romantic oranges, pinks, and purples in the sky. A steady breeze whipped the water toward the shore and bent the trees away from it. White sand and shiny seashells comprised the floor on which we slept. In another circumstance, this setting would be quite pleasant. Now it seemed like its loveliness mocked our dire situation.

I craned my head up to see where everyone else was. Ophelia, my best friend, was curled up next to my self-adopted brother, Fang. Brandon's sister Chloe and her best friend Kelly slept side by side. Leilani, our newest edition, slept near them. Gareth, another recent addition, slept near Ophelia and Fang. Shaw slept closest to the shore.

As I leaned forward to sit up, a sharp stabbing pain lanced through my side. My breath hissed out from between my clenched teeth. I cradled my ribs gingerly, not wanting to inflict more agony.

"Sable?" Brandon's voice was harsh from his being exposed to the elements. I looked down at his face and offered him a weak smile. His electric icy blue eyes locked on my emerald ones before darting to my hand that still clutched my ribs. His brow furrowed and his jaw clenched, a silent show of concern.

"I've had worse." That was true. Just three weeks ago, I'd been shot in the hip.

"Doesn't matter." He sat up and gently lifted me onto his lap. It never ceased to amaze me how strong and yet so gentle his arms were at the same time. "As much as I hate to admit it, it would be nice to have Roger skulking around right about now."

Roger was Diseased, a person who was born with special psychic abilities, like us. His particular Gift was of healing, which is how my prior gunshot wound was mended. The thing with Roger was that he played both sides, mostly aiding the DAO but throwing us little lifelines here and there. I nodded in agreement.

The others remained asleep, and Brandon and I sat silently together, watching the sun rise. As I gingerly curled my body into his chest, I took another sweeping glance over my companions. We were all definitely worse for the wear.

I'd seen Fang and Ophelia look worse when we were imprisoned in an insane asylum together. That's how we'd met. Everyone else looking so ragged shocked me, though.

Fleetingly, images of a sitcom where a random group of strangers were stranded on a deserted island flashed through my mind. The idea made me giggle aloud, which instantly had me wincing. *Note to self:* never *injure your ribs again.*

Brandon's hand twitched against my thigh. I knew he was badgering himself about being powerless to heal me. I didn't blame him, but telling him so would do no good. If there was one thing I'd learned about Brandon, it was that he fiercely protected those he cared for. Being unable to do so tortured him. I placed a soft kiss on hinge of his jaw.

"Good God, we're shipwrecked and all you can think about is making out?" Chloe's words dripped with their usual disdain whenever she referenced Brandon and me as a couple. He settled me onto the sand next to him and smiled. Then he stood and walked over to where his sister sat.

"Ah, damn! I got sand in my eyes!" This declaration came from Gareth. It wasn't long before everyone was awake and assessing our surroundings and each other.

Fang plodded over to me. He limped slightly, and I frowned.

"What's the trouble, Miss Sable?" Fang always called me "miss." It was part of his Southern gentlemanly charm.

"You're hurt."

"Ah, it ain't that bad. I'll walk it off in a day or two. How are you?"

"My ribs are banged up, but otherwise I'm good." Really, I was surprised I made it through the shipwreck and the storm with my spider bite lip piercings intact.

Fang's brow crumpled at the mention of my ribs. "I don't envy you that, Miss Sable. They'll heal with time, but it ain't an easy fix, I'm afraid."

I smiled. "Don't worry, I'm tough as nails."

Fang chuckled, the sound deep like rolling thunder.

"Everyone, gather around." This command came

from Shaw. Fang helped me to my feet. As I stood erect, I hissed in a breath and wrapped my arms around my waist, clutching at my ribs.

"Take it easy," Fang soothed as we made our way toward Shaw.

When everyone was settled in front of him, Shaw looked each of us over with laser sharp precision, his blue-gray eyes cool and calculating. "All right, how many of you are wounded?"

Fang, Leilani, Gareth, Kelly, and I raised our hands. Shaw cursed under his breath.

"All right, what's the damage?"

"I sprained my wrist," Kelly reported.

"I twisted my ankle," Fang supplied.

"I got a bump on the head, but it's nothing serious," Leilani stated.

I sighed. "My ribs are bruised, or maybe broken, I don't know."

"I have sand in my eyes," Gareth moaned.

Shaw's glare froze on Gareth and a muscle ticked in his jaw. Gareth was generally the one making wise cracks in the group, but his timing wasn't always appropriate. He offered a sheepish smile to Shaw.

"So only a few major injuries. More than I would like, but better than all of us getting hurt," Shaw concluded.

"So what do we do now, just wait for the DAO to come find us?" I asked.

"Ophelia, have you seen anything recently?" Shaw inquired. Ophelia's Gift was the ability to see the future. She shook her head.

"Until I can come up with a plan, go gather firewood and search the beach and the water for any food sources. Sable, you sit this one out. Fang, don't strain yourself. Kelly, use your telekinesis to move things."

I felt useless as I watched everyone else depart to complete their assigned tasks.

The sun burned bright in the sky as I walked along the shoreline. The surf spilled over and rushed back across my feet with the recession of the tide. Tide pools revealed a colorful array of seashells, some with hermit crabs inside. Every once and a while, my gaze would stray over to Shaw, who paced impatiently in the sand. I'd seen him use this practice on the *Kandis Amelia* many times. All he was missing now was a mug of coffee in his hand.

Slowly but surely, everyone began returning to our desolate camp. Ophelia, Brandon, and Fang carried large palm leaves and thick branches. Chloe and Leilani carried berries and nuts, using the lower half of their shirts as baskets. A cloud of sticks surrounded Kelly as he emerged from the tree line, and Gareth followed behind him with firewood stacked neatly in his arms. Without any instructions from Shaw, the seven of them began making lean-to shelters, shelling nuts, and organizing the firewood into an arrangement fit for a funeral pyre.

In a desperate need to contribute *something*, I sat down with Chloe and Leilani and removed the meat from the shells of the nuts. We worked together in silence. Chloe cracked the shells with the knife she perpetually kept strapped to her waist on her gun holster, and Leilani and I removed the meat. Every once in a while, I would catch Leilani gazing longingly at Chloe. I wondered if Chloe ever noticed, but decided it wasn't my place to point it out to her.

The same day I was shot, I learned that Chloe had romantic feelings toward me. It still conjured up a whirlwind of emotions every time I thought about it. It wasn't that I had an issue with her sexual preference, but the fact that I was dating her brother made me feel uneasy about her unrequited affections. It must be awful to watch someone you're infatuated with be all romantic with someone else, especially someone close to you like your sibling. I made a mental note to try not to show so many public displays of affection in front of her. Had Brandon ever thought about that?

"Hello, Earth to star gazer!" Chloe snapped her fingers in my face, pulling me out of my musings.

"I'm sorry, what?"

"Shaw wants you to light up the firewood so Brandon can cook the fish Fang caught," Leilani explained apologetically.

"Sure, yeah." That was my contribution to our little band of freaks. I started fires with my mind. I closed my eyes and visualized the pile of dried wood smoking, with flames licking at the sticks on the bottom of the heap. When the crackling of flame consuming wood sounded in my ears, I opened up my eyes. "Why star gazer?"

"You're the one with stars tattooed on the side of your eye, aren't you?" Chloe snapped.

As irritating as her perpetual hostility was, I had to admit her nickname was clever.

Just as we finished shelling all the nuts, Brandon— our resident chef—finished with the fish. He must've had a blade strapped to him somewhere to be able to clean them. Did everyone still have a weapon but me? Flat stones Ophelia found served as our plates. A chunk of fleshy white fish and a handful of the berries and nuts were served to each of us. I wondered how it was that none of our meal managed to be poisonous, but between Fang's vast knowledge base gained in the Navy and Brandon's culinary prowess, I was fairly confident none of us would keel over and die from the meal.

After dinner, everyone was exhausted from the events of the day. Fang, Brandon, and Gareth built five stick and leaf tents. Shaw took one for himself, which left two to a tent for the rest of us. Ophelia pulled Gareth into one with her. Kelly and Chloe took another. Fang offered Leilani his and said he'd sleep outside, but she said he didn't have to, so he joined her inside. That left the last one for Brandon and me.

We'd only ever slept in the same bed once before, when we were on a rescue mission to get Kelly and Chloe back from the DAO and ended up bringing Leilani back with us as well. Butterflies fluttered in my stomach, which were quickly batted away by the sharp pain in my side when I sat.

Brandon kissed me on the cheek. He lay down next to me and eased my head onto his chest. "There."

I smiled. "This would almost be romantic if we weren't here with seven other people and I wasn't banged up."

"I'll keep that in mind for our honeymoon one day."

"Honeymoon? You just assume I'm going to marry you, Brandon Harper?"

"It's never a good idea to assume, but I have it on good authority that you're wildly attracted to me, Sable Mosley."

"Love and attraction are two entirely different things," I objected.

"I know."

A small smile played on his lips until he caught me staring. Then a full on grin took over before he kissed me.

A breathy sigh escaped me as I melted into him the way I always did when we kissed. Before I could get too involved in him, he pulled away from me and shook his head.

"Not until you're well."

"That could be weeks!" I protested.

He groaned. "I know."

"So what do we do now?"

"Sleep."

"How utterly boring."

He chuckled as he eased me down so that my head rested on his chest and I was nestled into the crook of his arm.

After a few minutes in silence, the rise and fall of his chest slowed and evened out. I looked up at his face, but I couldn't see much at the angle I was at. I traced my fingers along his jaw. A little stubble was growing there. I'd never seen him with facial hair. What would that look like if he grew it out? I tried to picture it, but I was never good at visualizing stuff like that. After all, I wasn't an artist.

Brandon stirred at my touch, so I gingerly removed my fingers. His breathing evened back out. So, I hadn't woken him up after all. Since it was completely dark now and there was nothing else to do, I fell asleep, too.

CHAPTER 2

The roar of a boat's engine startled me awake. I sat up too quickly and my splintered ribs screamed in protest. What air was left in my lungs rushed out between my clenched teeth in an angry hiss. Then it occurred to me that Brandon was no longer beneath me. As I crawled out of our makeshift hut, I squinted against the sun's blinding reflection off the water.

Shaw stood on the shoreline, two sticks with pieces of shredded red material tied to one end in each of his hands. He waved his arms up and down slowly, trying to signal the passing boat that we needed rescuing. Brandon and a shirtless Kelly stood a few yards behind Shaw, all of their backs to me.

"Brandon, wake up Sable. Kelly, round up the remaining firewood," Shaw barked. The boys turned to set off on their appointed tasks.

I sat on my knees and braced my palms on my thighs. Before I could decide the best way to stand up while inducing the least amount of pain, Brandon's strong hands wrapped around my waist. I allowed him to support my weight, and then it was just a matter of straightening my limbs out.

"Thanks." I winced. The stinging pain from my careless movements when I woke up was dulling to an aching throb.

"You sleep okay, baby doll?"

It wasn't a name he used for me often, and I swooned every time he said it. I nodded and offered him a small smile. He kissed the top of my head as he led me down the beach toward Shaw.

By the time we made it to the shore, Kelly sprinted out of the foliage behind the huts. A cloud of sticks and dried up palm fronds zipped along in the air behind him. He skidded to a halt next to Brandon and me and the debris fell unceremoniously into heap behind us.

I knew what Shaw wanted me to do without him telling me. We needed a bigger signal than the ones he waved in vain. I closed my eyes and pictured the sticks and leaves burning, small flames at first, then growing into an ever larger raging inferno. The scraps Kelly managed to find on such short notice would soon burn away, and we'd lose our smoke signal. I concentrated on diminishing the flames until there were just enough to keep the smoke billowing into the sky. It would've been faster to set myself ablaze, but when I was engulfed in flames, there was never any smoke.

When I opened my eyes, I saw my audience had grown from three to eight.

"Good work, Mosley," Shaw grunted.

He wasn't a warm and fuzzy kind of guy. That sort of praise from him was like getting a bear hug and a broad smile from my father. My heart skipped a beat at the thought of my father. He and my mother admitted me to the asylum where I'd met Fang and Ophelia after I'd set my bedroom curtains on fire during a bad dream. I hadn't seen them since.

The roaring of the boat's engine grew louder as it approached the shore. As it came ever closer, I noticed it was a pontoon boat. Flaxen waves billowed out in all directions from the boat's wheel. The rest of the driver remained hidden from view. Anticipation permeated the air around us. Had we found a means of rescue?

The pontoon boat cut its engine about five yards from shore. After the anchor was dropped, the boat's driver dove into the water. When she resurfaced and began walking towards shore, Brandon sucked in a breath. I whipped my head to my left to see what provoked this reaction. His eyes were wide and his lips parted just slightly. I looked over at Kelly and Chloe. A radiant smile broke across Chloe's face. Kelly looked stunned.

She was gorgeous, there was no denying it. Even with her golden hair plastered to her face, arms, back, and chest. I imagined her hair was the same length as mine. Her eyes were as clear an aquamarine as the water she emerged from. A white string bikini with gold accents showcased her perfectly proportioned hourglass figure and complimented her sun tanned skin. A glittering pink gem hung from her navel. Women like her belonged in the ads in magazines.

"Melody Wilson? Is that really you?" Brandon called as the bombshell approached the shore.

Wait a minute. He knows *her?*

"Brandon Harper! I thought I recognized you. And Chloe! It's been ages!" she gushed. Her accent was unmistakably Australian.

Shaw nodded. "You're looking well, Melody."

"Shaw! It's so great to see you all!" Then she hugged him. *And he hugged her back.* A bizarre mixture of jealousy and bewilderment bubbled up in my chest. Now Brandon, Kelly, and Gareth were all gawking at her. I could practically see the drool running out of their mouths. Chloe still had the uncharacteristic smile plastered on her face.

Just who was this Melody Wilson?

"Brandon, who's your friend?" My words dripped with acid. I mentally slapped myself for it.

He blinked at me after a moment when my question finally sank in. "She used to live on the *Kandis Amelia* with us. About two years ago, she went back to Australia. Her mentor and Shaw are old friends, I guess."

Melody smiled. "There's a lot more of you now than when I left. Who're the new recruits?"

Was she always this…bubbly?

Shaw introduced Fang, Ophelia, Gareth, Leilani, and me each in turn. Melody shook hands with each of us and hugged Chloe, Kelly, and Brandon as she reached them in line.

"What are you doing here?" Brandon asked her as they embraced.

My stomach knotted when they did.

"I should ask you the same thing!"

Were they ever going to let go of each other?

"The *Kandis Amelia* got caught in a storm and wrecked. We're marooned here."

"Well, I come to this spit of land to think, mostly. Daydream sometimes. It's about forty kilometers off the coast of Sydney."

"Are you still staying with Agatha?" Shaw asked.

Finally, Melody and Brandon released each other. The knot in my stomach loosed, too.

"Yes, in a house in the country. The DAO found her penthouse in the city, so we fled."

"They have the DAO in Australia?" Leilani questioned.

"The DAO is international," Shaw answered.

A tremor of fear ran down my spine at that information. The action caused a stabbing pain to lance through my ribs. I gasped and winced.

Brandon's eyes clouded with concern. "Sable, are you all right?"

I nodded. There was nothing he could do to fix it anyhow.

"You lot better come with me. Agatha will be pleased to see you, Shaw." With that, Melody began making her way back to the pontoon boat. She glanced over her shoulder once, to make sure we were following her, and then continued toward our destination.

"Crikey, that's one beautiful sheila," Gareth crowed. He attempted an Australian accent, but it came out sounding more Irish than anything.

"You can say that again, just without the crappy accent next time," Kelly agreed.

"Piss off," Gareth muttered.

Brandon took my hand as we waded into the water. The dried salt water made our clothes crusty. Being back in the water did little to revive them. I wondered how much it was going to hurt my ribs to swim as the water climbed from my knees to my waist. Thankfully, I didn't find out. Fang had me climb onto his back and he swam me to the pontoon boat. Upon our arrival, I saw that the name *Cha Cha* was applied to its side with thick black block letter decals.

Once we all boarded *Cha Cha*, which fit all of us comfortably, we began our voyage to Sydney. Chloe stood at the wheel with Melody and they spoke animatedly with each other. It amazed me how radically different this Chloe was from the one I knew. She was never this cheerful, not even with Brandon. Was this girl's Gift the ability to make everyone insanely happy? No, that couldn't be. She didn't make me happy. But why did she irritate me so much? Sure, she hugged Brandon for far too long, but she'd been nothing but pleasant to all of us. The whole situation made my head hurt.

I didn't realize I fell asleep until Brandon woke me up. He whispered in my ear, "Sable, we're at the marina now. I'll help you up, don't move."

I could tell by the sound of his heartbeat and the rise and fall of his breathing that my head was on his chest. A smile crept across my lips as I gazed up into his eyes. They were as pale blue as the afternoon sky.

He returned my smile with one of his own as he gently positioned me so I sat upright next to him. My back was stiff, but I refrained from stretching to spare myself the pain.

"How far out of Sydney do you live?" Chloe asked Melody as we pulled up to the dock. Brandon, Shaw, and Kelly sprang into action, tying the vessel to the metal posts of the dock. Fang dropped the anchor over *Cha Cha's* side railing.

"About an hour and a half," she answered. Then she turned to Shaw. "I've got a Land Rover but it will only seat three of you. There's a car rental place about a half a kilometer from here. I can take a couple of you there to pick out your transportation."

"That's fine. Fang, come with us. We'll be back soon. Everyone stays on the boat until we return," Shaw instructed.

Brandon sighed as we watched Shaw, Fang, and Melody drive away. "I guess you can go back to sleep."

"I'm all right. I can't sleep all the time."

"Something wrong?"

"How do you mean?"

"Well, you're frowning a little bit, almost like you're pouting. Usually that means something's bothering you."

"Well, I was wondering—" *What exactly was the nature of your relationship with Melody?* "What is it with Melody and Chloe? I mean, I've never seen her like that, not even with you."

"Like what?" Brandon tried to suppress a chuckle, but failed.

"All…happy."

At this, Brandon laughed long and loud. Everyone stared at him with varying degrees of puzzlement on their faces.

Chloe raised an eyebrow in suspicion. "What's so funny?"

Brandon smiled. "Just discussing your change in demeanor because Melody showed up."

Chloe's eyes narrowed and her hands cemented to her hips. "Is that so?"

"You're not the only one, Chloe. There're a certain three young men with rampant hormones who seem to be affected by her, too," Ophelia observed.

Brandon, Gareth, and Kelly simultaneously blushed.

Ha! So I wasn't the only one who noticed! My internal happy dance was soon replaced by a wave of jealousy. I wasn't the only one who noticed that Brandon took particular notice of her. What was it about this boy that made me so prone to jealousy? I'd never felt that way toward anyone before he came along.

"Sable, can I see you over here for a minute?" Leilani piped up.

I nodded and stood slowly. We walked to the back end of *Cha Cha* away from the others, who were still discussing Melody.

"What's up?"

She wrung her hands together and stared at her feet. "I had an idea about your ribs. About how to make it less painful. But I don't know if it will work."

I cocked my head to the side and bit my lip. "Well, what's your idea?"

"Have you ever heard of people being cured by hypnotism?"

"Yes." I didn't believe it worked, though.

"Well, when people are under the influence of my venom, it's like they're hypnotized. I mean, it would require a great amount of trust on your part, but if I gave you just enough to convince you your ribs were fine, maybe you'd forget about the pain. You'd still have to baby the injury, of course, and there's no guarantee it would last very long, but if you're getting desperate, we could try."

The venom she spoke about was her Gift as a Diseased. Her saliva contained some sort of poison that, in small doses, rendered the victim helpless under her control, their will bowing to hers. In large doses, it was lethal.

When Brandon and I found Leilani at the DAO's headquarters in Washington DC, they were using her venom to control the other Diseased there. They administered her venom by means of injection. We didn't have any needles or syringes here.

"That means—that means we'd have to k—kiss?" I stammered.

She nodded and sighed reluctantly.

"Well, I appreciate the offer, but I think we should get another opinion on the matter first."

Leilani's eyes went wide at my suggestion, but a moment later she conceded. "Whose opinion would you like?"

I looked around at my companions and decided whose advisement would be best in this situation. "Ophelia, would you come here, please?"

Ophelia looked up from her conversation. "Excuse me, Chloe and gents."

The remaining four watched Ophelia briefly, as she made her way toward us, and then resumed talking to one another.

Ophelia smiled. "What's up?"

"Well, Leilani had this idea about using her venom to make the pain in my ribs go away," I explained. Ophelia's smile vanished. "Her venom doesn't have healing properties."

"It would be like a form of hypnotism. We both know Sable would have to have great faith in me to allow it," Leilani said somberly.

After a few long, tense moments of silence, Ophelia sighed and crossed her arms over her chest. "For Sable to even consider it means, she has to have a little faith in you, at least. From what I can gather, she's a decent judge of character. But be warned, Leilani, if you kill her—if you harm her in *any* way—you'll wish it was you in her place."

Leilani swallowed hard and nodded more vigorously than I think she intended. Ophelia's eyes were hard as diamonds and her lips pressed together in a thin line.

"Okay, Leilani, I'll try it. Ophelia, I'm trusting you to look out for me. If I seem unlike myself, do whatever you feel is necessary to bring me back to me." Ophelia offered a curt nod in agreement. I took a deep breath and attempted to steel my nerves before plunging into the unknown. "Well, there's no point in waiting I guess. Ready, Leilani?"

Leilani let out a heavy exhale and stepped toward me. Goosebumps broke out all over my skin. I closed my eyes and puckered my lips. She let out a soft chuckle.

"I'm afraid it's a bit more involved than that," she whispered.

Then her hands were on either side of my face, her tongue parted my lips, and we were kissing.

CHAPTER 3

Brandon

B randon, I think your girl's batting for the other team," Gareth said.

I frowned. "What?"

Gareth pointed toward the back of the boat. Ophelia stood with a rigid posture and frowned as she watched my girlfriend making out with Leilani. What the hell was going on? White hot anger speared through me.

"Sable!" I growled.

She ripped herself away from Leilani and stared at me, her eyes wide. Leilani wiped off her lips with the back of her hand. At least she had the decency to appear ashamed.

Gareth grinned. "What was that about? Harper here not giving you what you need?"

Sable rolled her eyes. My hands clenched into fists at my sides and a muscle ticked in my jaw.

"Leilani was trying to see if her venom could hypnotize Sable into thinking her ribs weren't causing her pain anymore," Ophelia explained flatly.

"Did it work?" Kelly questioned.

"Let's see."

The words barely left Chloe's lips before she pounced. It never ceased to amaze me just how fast she moved. I didn't even have time to protest before her stiletto heel connected with the space between Sable's two lowest ribs.

"That's crazy—There's no pain. Nothing!" Sable squeaked.

"You're still taking out your blind rage on innocent people?" The question came from Melody, who laughed while she asked.

Chloe's cheeks turned scarlet. "We were experimenting with the strength of Leilani's mind control," she mumbled.

"Who decided that's what you should be doing with your free time?" Shaw asked. Everyone fell silent then. "Very well. If you're all done playing, we have vehicles and we'll be traveling to Agatha's."

The two vehicles Shaw rented looked similar to Melody's Land Rover SUV. Shaw and Fang were driving them. Chloe and Kelly hopped into Melody's SUV, Ophelia climbed in with Fang, and Leilani, and Gareth rode with Shaw. I stood facing Sable with my arms crossed over my chest. She bit her lower lip on the side where it was pierced. She only did that when she was nervous. Well, I wasn't feeling charitable enough to let her off the hook about that kiss. I shook my head slowly once and climbed into Melody's SUV.

I regretted it as soon as I saw her face. It was like I shot her dog or something. But there was nothing I could do to change it now. Fang helped her into his SUV and Melody took off in ours.

Just as Melody said, the drive to Agatha's house in the country took about an hour and a half. I sat quietly while Kelly, Chloe, and Melody caught up. When Melody would try to engage me, I gave her one word answers.

She got the hint pretty quickly and pretended to ignore me for the rest of the drive. I saw her steal glances at me every now and then, and I was pretty sure she noticed me doing the same thing. It felt like forever ago that she left so suddenly. A pang of longing rose in my stomach.

Agatha's house wasn't quite a mansion, but it was very large. The structure looked like a colonial plantation house from the South in the United States. The walls were a mosaic made up of large stone fragments in different shades of browns and nudes. Six thick white pillar columns lined the front porch, which was as long as the house. Eight tall windows, half on the first story and half on the second, made the house seem open and inviting.

As our crew piled out of the SUVs, Melody ran inside to announce our arrival to Agatha. A few moments later, a round woman about a head shorter than Melody bustled out of the door behind her with a smile on her face. Her salt and pepper hair was pulled tightly into a thick bun on the crown of her head. She wore khaki pants and a blue and white checked shirt. Smoky gray eyes were set deeply into her tanned face. Lines crinkled around her mouth and at the corners of her eyes. She smiled broadly at Shaw as she approached him.

"Drake, it's been far too long!" Agatha exclaimed as she threw her arms around Shaw's middle.

He enfolded her in his arms as a grin broke across his face. How…odd.

"Yes, it has."

"Look how many of you there are! Melody only ever told me about three of you. And there's eight now? Incredible!" Agatha gushed.

Chloe rolled her eyes. "We've had a recent explosion in our population."

"Come inside, everyone! I'll have Harvey prepare rooms for you. Unfortunately, some of you will have to share rooms, as there're only six bedrooms," Agatha explained.

While she spoke, I noticed she didn't have the same Australian accent as Melody did. She still spoke like she lived in the States.

"Agatha, are you from Australia, too?" Sable asked.

"No, dear. I'm from the States originally. My family comes from Michigan. We're registered members of the Potawatomi tribe."

"How did you end up here?"

"That's a story for another time when everyone is well rested." Agatha beamed at us all, but lingered slightly on Shaw before she opened the door and made a grand sweeping gesture with her arm, inviting us inside.

The inside of the house was painted a creamy color of beige. A large dream catcher made with turquoise beads, deep green leather, and large golden colored feathers hung on the wall behind the small golden yellow couch, which was adorned in dark purple throw pillows. A matching armchair, ottoman, and loveseat were placed in the room. Each piece of furniture acted as a point in a triangle. Under the furniture sat a large ornate Persian rug with an intricate swirling pattern of greens and dark blues and turquoises. The rest of the floor was comprised of square shaped mocha colored sandstone tiles. An archway on the left side of the room on the back wall gave a hint to the formal dining room that lay beyond it. The archway on the right wall of the room revealed nothing more than a black cavern. As I took in my surroundings, I noticed movement at the top of the stairs.

"Madam, the guest rooms are readied for their inhabitants," a man called down to Agatha.

Sandy blond hair fell in loose waves to his shoulders. Light green eyes peeked out from under his prominent brow. Stubble a shade or two darker than his hair dusted his jaw and chin and above his lips. He wore navy colored slacks and a white short sleeved polo style shirt. A pair of black loafers was on his feet. He seemed as tall as I was, almost six feet, but I couldn't be sure since he was so far away.

"Thank you, Harvey. Now, Melody, would you help arrange our guests into their new accommodations?" Agatha prompted.

Melody nodded and we all followed her up the stairs, which three of us could walk up side by side. As we reached the second floor, Harvey pulled Shaw aside and led him to a room in the right wing of the hallway. The rest of us followed Melody to the left.

Chloe got invited to stay in Melody's room, and Leilani, Ophelia, and Sable were in the room across the hall and down a door from hers. A guest bathroom was directly across the hall from her room. Kelly and I took the room next to theirs and Fang and Gareth took the room across the hall from ours. Melody said a library occupied the space between her room and Fang and Gareth's room.

In the afternoon sunlight, a gleaming metal ladder shone brightly next to a door on the other end of the hallway.

"Melody, what's the ladder over there for?" Sable asked, pointing to it.

"That goes up to the widow's peak. Agatha has a telescope up there. She likes to chart the positions of the stars and the planets. She's fascinated with astrology," Melody explained.

"Don't you mean astronomy?" Gareth challenged.

"Well, she's interested in astronomy, too, but I meant what I said before. She's obsessed with astrology."

Melody's reply sounded sweet enough, but I detected a slight edge in her voice. Melody didn't like to be corrected.

It reminded me of the time when she and I were arguing about metric conversions. I knew them from converting recipes. She was furious when she finally admitted that I was right and she was wrong. I bit the inside of my cheek to keep from smiling.

"I think we all need some decent sleep before supper tonight. Thank you kindly for your hospitality, Miss Melody," Fang said while giving us all pointed stares.

Everyone took the hint and disbanded to their assigned rooms while muttering farewells to one another and gratitude to Melody.

Sable lingered in the hallway while everyone else shuffled into their rooms. Before I reached my door, she grabbed my arm. Fang gave us a knowing nod and shut his door. We were the only ones left in the hallway. Her face was pinched and pale. Even if she couldn't feel her injuries right now, they were still draining her body's energy.

I sighed. "You should be getting some rest, Sable, and I should, too."

"I can't sleep yet. Why are you mad at me?" she blurted out.

Worry and anger mixed inside me and blended about as well as orange juice and toothpaste. "Do you really have to ask me that?"

She stared at me sheepishly and bit her lip. "Was it because—was it because I kissed Leilani?"

"That's part of it. I mean, you asked Ophelia if she thought you should trust Leilani. Haven't I always taken care of you?"

Shit. I hadn't meant to say that last part aloud. What I wouldn't give for a cigarette right now…

Hurt pulled the corners of her mouth down. She wrapped her arms around my waist and squeezed me tightly. I couldn't bring myself to do the same. She shouldn't be worried about me. There were enough things for her to be concerned with besides my petulance.

"I didn't mean to make you think I don't value your opinion, but I thought that if this experiment was going to go badly, she'd know that before I even tried since she can see the future."

"For the record, I think it was an awful idea. We still don't know if we can really trust her."

"Brandon, she's been with us for a month now. Don't you think this is a little long to wait to brainwash someone?"

"I don't know." That was one of the many things I loved about Sable, that she could see the good in everyone. In that moment, I needed to hold her, but I had to be careful. I gently enfolded her in my arms, indulging in the softness of her, and kissed the top of her head. I breathed in her scent, which had more cocoa notes when she wasn't bathed in her usual faux vanilla and bruleed sugar perfume. "They really don't hurt, though? Your ribs?"

"For now, no, they don't. But I don't think I'll do that again when this wears off." She nestled her head into my chest and breathed deep. I thought that was her favorite place to be, pressed against me while I held onto her. She always seemed so serene in my arms. It was my favorite place for her to be, too.

I smiled at her and placed a soft kiss on her lips. "Not that I want you to be in pain, but I think that's a wise decision."

"Do we have to sleep? Can't we just stay here, like this?"

"Unfortunately, I think we probably do need to sleep. But I'll still be here when you wake up. We can do more of the making out—I mean making up—then."

She laughed at my not so subtle suggestion and kissed me. One peck on the lips turned into two. Then pecks turned into lingering kisses, and lingering kisses turned into our tongues colliding and rolling together. I backed her into the wall as her hands fisted in my hair. I gripped her hips and tilted my head to deepen the kiss. It was always so easy to get lost in her.

The sound of a girl clearing her throat made us spring apart. Sable was breathless. Dread hit me like a ton of bricks. Reality had a way of doing that to a guy. I guessed there wouldn't be a need to gently break it to Melody that I was involved with someone.

Melody smiled uncomfortably. "I was just, uh, going downstairs."

"We were just going to bed," I replied.

"Indeed," she muttered.

"Goodnight," I called after her as she skittered down the stairs.

"Night!" Her voice seemed to float up from the floor.

Sable sighed. "I don't know which is worse, being interrupted by her or by Chloe."

I chuckled and kissed her on the tip of her nose. "Well, I didn't get punched or yelled at this time, so I'll say Chloe is worse."

Being caught by Melody was so, so much worse.

Sable wrapped her arms around the my shoulders and placed a long lingering kiss on my neck. My pulse jumped and quickened as the fire she caused in me— which had nothing to do with her Gift—rushed through my veins. She shivered in that way that I knew wasn't because she was cold.

"What was that for?" I asked breathlessly.

She winked. "Later."

She turned and went to her bedroom door, then she paused.

"Goodnight," I whispered.

"Goodnight."

I went into my bedroom and shut the door. I wasn't surprised to find Kelly waiting for me.

"Don't ask," I warned as I plopped down onto the vacant trundle bed.

"So the ex-girlfriend knows about the new girl-friend?"

Of course, he asked. I sighed and nodded.

"Does Sable know about you and Melody yet?"

"No."

"Oh, man. What are you going to do?"

I buried my face in my hands. "I don't know."

CHAPTER 4

Sable

I grudgingly opened my eyes and rubbed the sleep out of them. After having the best sleep I'd had in a while, I was painfully aware of the stiffness of my clothes and my hair. I sat up in bed and looked at Ophelia and Leilani. They seemed to be asleep still.

Now that my eyes were fully adjusted to the darkness, I scoured the room for a closet. When I found it, I slid the door open as quietly as I could. I felt the fabrics hanging inside. One felt long enough to be a dress and I prayed it was close to the right size. To make less noise, I took the dress-like garment, hanger and all, with me to the bathroom.

On my way, I noticed the décor that I ignored earlier. The floors were the same mocha colored sandstone tiles and the walls were the same creamy beige color as downstairs.

A random assortment of abstract paintings adorned the walls. The one thing they all had in common was the signature of the artist—Melody Wilson.

The bathroom had her artistic touch, too. A wraparound mural of Sydney's skyline was painted on all four walls. I had to give the girl credit. She was an excellent artist.

Since I had sufficient light to see, I looked over the garment I grabbed. It was a pale yellow color that reminded me of the scrubs I had to wear while I was imprisoned with Fang and Ophelia in an insane asylum. The memory made a chill run down my spine and my stomach lurched. It was a size too small, but I thought I could squeeze into it. The neckline was square. It had no sleeves, but the straps on the shoulders were about three fingers wide. The length seemed like it would fall a little above my knees. There were darts sewn into the chest. The fabric felt like polyester. It was definitely more Jackie Kennedy than the rocker style I normally wore, but it would have to do for now.

A blond-colored wooden cabinet with glass doors that sat across from the midnight-blue-swirled-with-white marble sink held all different colors of towels. I picked out a smoky gray one. Then I peeled off my clothes and heaped them into a pile in the shower with me.

The warm water rejuvenated my spirit. It never ceased to amaze me that no matter how much abuse my body took, a hot shower could make it all feel better. The soaps were all scented like roses. I never was a fan of the flower—they were overrated. However, beggars couldn't be choosers, and I didn't have any other options.

After I finished showering, I washed my clothes with the rose scented soap and wrung the water out of them the best I could. I hung them over my arm so I could hang them up somewhere in my room to dry after I shimmied into the pale yellow dress.

Against my better judgment, I looked at myself in the mirror. The dress's style felt so foreign on my frame. It flattered my minimal curves, but contrasted strangely with my lip piercings and the stars tattooed on the outside of my left eye. I felt like I should be wearing pearls and pumps instead.

I sighed as I opened the bathroom door. I jumped back about a foot when I found Melody on the other side. Her eyes flicked from my face to the dress.

"I guess Brandon's got a thing for girls with tattoos," she muttered.

I knew she was baiting me, but I couldn't help myself. "What are you talking about?"

"Didn't you know? Brandon and I used to be an item until I came back to Australia." She pulled down the right side of her waistband of her baby pink designer sweat pants and underneath where a silver "86" was emblazoned on her pants, she bore a tattoo of a blue swallow. Without a prompt for more information, she continued, "I have a red one on the other side."

"How cliché of you."

"Well, not everyone has the desire to mar their face for the rest of their lives."

"I'll keep that in mind," I replied dryly.

"And what's that awful perfume you're wearing? It's practically making me gag!"

"Your body wash."

I didn't want to deal with her anymore, so I pushed past her and slipped into my bedroom. Leilani was still asleep, but Ophelia sat up on her bed. A knowing smirk played on her lips.

"So the battle for the heart of the boy begins."

"You saw this happening before it happened? Isn't that supposed to be one of the perks of your best friend being able to see the future is that she can warn you about crap like that?" I took the dress off and put the wet clothes back on.

Everything reeked of roses. I desperately wanted to run outside and bask in the fresh air, but I didn't want to give Melody any inkling that she got under my skin.

"No, I just heard the exchange. You guys weren't exactly being discreet."

"Do you think anyone else heard us?" I half whispered. The thought of Brandon overhearing the squabble was nauseating.

"If they did, they most likely wouldn't say anything. Unless it's Chloe. You never know what that girl's going to do."

"That's true. Do you think we should wake up Leilani? I know I could use some grub. Everyone else probably could, too."

Ophelia nodded and chucked her pillow at Leilani. It made a dull thump when it hit her face.

"Okay, I get it. Good morning to you guys, too." Leilani yawned as she stretched. After she finished waking up, she tossed Ophelia's pillow back at her. Ophelia caught it and dropped it behind her onto the bed.

"How're your ribs doing?" Ophelia asked me.

"Still pain free for now." I traced my fingers over my rib cage. There was no pain, only minor pressure. How long would that last, though?

"Someone mention food?" Leilani prompted as she stood up.

Ophelia and I followed her out of the door and into the hallway. The sound of Chloe and Melody giggling wafted down the corridor. A sudden urge to punch their door made my fingers twitch as we passed it, but I kept my hands at my sides.

The scent of chicken became more pronounced the closer we got to the dining room. Agatha was busy setting the table for twelve. Shaw sat to the right of the head of the table and made small talk with her while she worked. I wondered if she was cooking or if Harvey did that here.

"Aggie, are you sure I can't help you with something?" Shaw beseeched.

"Oh, Drake, you make me feel like such a young girl when you call me that! And I told you already, you're a guest in my home. The least I can do for you is make a nice table for you to eat some real food. It's enough that I'm letting that boy cook the meal for us. If it wasn't for Melody's insistence, I would've done that, too."

Of course, Brandon was the one cooking. He always felt at home in the kitchen. As I often did, I thought of Brandon as a little boy in the kitchen with his father, a trained chef. His father was the inspiration for Brandon's love of food. Then the mention of Melody spoiled my reverie. She'd lived with him, for how long I didn't know. That meant she'd eaten his cooking, too. Did he make her special things like he did for me?

No, that was a road I didn't want to go down. I didn't want to compare his relationship with her to his relationship with me. All that mattered was how we felt about each other. She was just another nuisance like Chloe.

"Girls, you're awake! My goodness, child, you look like someone just fished you out of a well!" The last comment Agatha directed to me.

"I just really wanted a shower and these are the only clothes I have, so I washed them and put them back on."

"Yes, we'll have to take everyone to town tomorrow and get new clothes. This is getting to be expensive, constantly restocking nine different wardrobes," Shaw muttered.

"You always were such a softie," Agatha gushed. Who was the Shaw Agatha knew? He certainly wasn't the same man the rest of us knew. Yet, he *did* take Brandon, Chloe, and Kelly in when they were small children. For all I knew, Melody could've been one of his adopted children when she was young.

"Are the others awake yet?" Ophelia asked.

"Fang is in the kitchen with Brandon, but I haven't seen the rest of them yet," Shaw answered.

Fang was in the kitchen? Doing what?

"We heard Melody and Chloe on our way down," Leilani reported.

"I'll send Harvey to fetch them when dinner is served. Please, ladies, have a seat," Agatha offered.

"I need to speak with Brandon for a moment. Where is the kitchen?" I inquired. Not that I wanted Brandon seeing me look like a drenched cat, but he'd seen me look far worse.

Agatha pointed to a door behind her I hadn't noticed before. "Through that swinging door there."

"Thank you."

Agatha moved to the side so I could slide behind her.

When I opened the kitchen door, the scents of all sorts of food greeted me. Brandon stood next to Fang at the stove.

Fang stirred something in a giant pot while Brandon's hands seemed to be in everything else. The kitchen was modest, with a brick oven in the corner. The stove was on the island, which had the sink and the dishwasher on the other side of it. It was the longest kitchen island I'd ever seen.

A deep freezer and a side-by-side refrigerator-freezer completed the appliances in the room. The wall opposite the freezers was covered in floor-to-ceiling cabinets. The dishes were kept on the wall with the door. On the opposite wall was where the pots and pans and other culinary tools were kept on racks and in drawers.

I smiled. "There're my favorite men in the whole world."

Brandon and Fang smiled back at me and continued their work.

"I trust you slept well, Miss Sable," Fang said, while adding spices to the pot he stirred.

"I did, thank you."

Fang chuckled. "Well, ain't you supposed to hug me now?"

"I would, but I'm still damp yet."

"It don't matter none."

I threw my arms around him and pressed my cheek into his back.

Fang cocked his head in Brandon's direction. "Ain't you forgetting someone else?"

I hugged Brandon, too.

He stopped what he was working on and wrapped his arms around my waist. "Did you take a shower with your clothes on?"

"Sort of."

"What's that scent? It's familiar but I can't put my finger on it—"

I sighed. "It's roses."

"Right, roses! Someone else I know always smelled like roses."

"Melody," I muttered acidly.

"Right." Brandon stepped back from me and offered me an awkward smile before returning to cooking.

I didn't want to fight with him about her, so I decided to change the topic before he had any other revelations about her. "So what's on the menu tonight?"

"We're fixin' a southern meal tonight. Well, as southern as you can get in Australia," Fang said thoughtfully.

"We're making barbeque chicken with Fang's own barbeque sauce recipe, fried green beans, mashed sweet potatoes with brown sugar and butter, and jalapeño cornbread," Brandon added.

I smiled. "Sounds delicious."

The menu seemed really rustic in comparison to Brandon's usually gourmet flare, but sometimes rustic was the way to go.

Agatha poked her head through the door. "How's dinner coming along, gentlemen?"

"Almost finished, ma'am," Fang answered.

"I'll have Harvey collect everyone from upstairs, then." With that, she was gone again.

I shrugged. "I guess I should go sit out there with everyone else." I gave both guys another hug and left a quick peck on Brandon's cheek.

"Save a place for me," Brandon called after me as I reentered the dining room.

I smiled inwardly as I sat next to Ophelia at the table. A few minutes later, everyone was seated at the table, aside from Fang, Brandon, and Harvey. Agatha sat at the head of the table with Shaw to her right and Melody to her left. I left a space open between Shaw and me for Brandon to sit, Ophelia sat next to me, and the chair next to her and the one directly opposite were open for Fang and Harvey, respectively. Chloe sat next to Melody, Kelly sat across from me, Leilani sat next to Kelly, and Gareth sat next to her.

Brandon, Fang, and Harvey brought out tray after tray of food. Lastly, Fang brought out two cast iron skillets with cornbread in them. When everything was arranged on the table, all three men sat down and food started being passed around.

"Melody, you were quite right about this boy's culinary skills. The food is positively delicious, Brandon," Agatha praised as she put a third helping of deep fried green beans onto her plate.

"The recipes are all Fang's. I just helped him execute them," Brandon replied modestly.

"Hopefully, our food will be just as impressive,"

Agatha said as she popped a bean into her mouth. "All right, as an ice breaker, let's go around the table and share what our Gift is. Drake, be a dear and start us off, will you?"

"All right, Aggie. I can sense the purity of someone's soul," Shaw shared.

I had the feeling if Agatha asked him to cut off his own foot and feed it to her, he would.

"And you, Brandon?" she prompted.

"I use electricity."

"I wield fire," I stated.

"I see the future," Ophelia said.

"I have kinetic shields," Fang replied.

"We'll excuse Harvey from this little exercise since he isn't Gifted. Garret, will you continue?" Agatha asked.

Harvey was *normal*? What did he think about being employed by Diseased people?

"It's *Gareth*, ma'am. And I have the ability to find anyone anywhere in the world."

"I hypnotize people," Leilani responded sheepishly.

I didn't blame her for not wanting to share the specifics of her Gift.

We still didn't know why when everyone else's Gifts were mental, hers needed to be both mental and physical to work.

"Telekinesis." Kelly kept his answer short and sweet.

"I dehydrate others," Chloe said.

"I create light in darkness," Melody shared.

"Ah, now it's my turn! I sense the bond between people. Now, don't we all feel a little more familiar?" Agatha seemed pleased with her little exercise. I was more interested in her Gift. What did bonds between people feel like? "Oh!" she said suddenly. "As much as I hate to run off from a lovely meal and conversation, Saturn is moving into Aquarius tonight and I simply must chart it out! Sable and Brandon, would you like to come with me?"

"Um, sure," I replied.

Brandon squeezed my hand under the table.

"Splendid! Off we go, then!" Agatha hopped up from her seat and practically jogged up the stairs to the metal ladder hanging on the wall. Brandon and I followed behind her, trying to keep pace with her.

The widow's peak was a cramped space with the three of us and her charts and telescope. While she adjusted some knobs on the telescope, Brandon ran his fingers lightly over my ribs.

"Still okay?" he whispered to me.

I nodded in response.

"Ah, my young ones, *this* is the real beauty of Australia!" Agatha cried with a flourish as she gestured the night sky.

Brandon and I craned our necks back and looked toward the heavens. It was more stars than I'd ever seen in my life.

It was truly breathtaking.

CHAPTER 5

I wasn't sure how long we stood on the widow's peak and listened to Agatha point out the constellations of the zodiac to us and explain their meanings. Some of it was interesting, but I really just wanted to get lost in the peace and quiet of nature. I had the feeling I wouldn't get such a spectacular view like this again for a long while.

As if she sensed my thoughts, Agatha rolled up her charts and placed the protective caps over the lenses of the telescope. "I'm turning in for the night. Feel free to stay as long as you'd like up here. Goodnight."

I swore I saw her wink before she descended the ladder.

With the telescope moved into its storage position and one less person, there was enough space for Brandon and me to sit together if I sat in front of him. He sat down first and gently pulled me down so I sat between his legs.

Laying my head against his chest, I savored the rise and fall of his breathing. I sighed contentedly. "It really is beautiful, isn't it?"

"Yes, you are."

I couldn't help but giggle. "Do those pick-up lines work on all the babes?"

He chuckled. "I don't need pick-up lines to get the babes."

"Well, you're stuck with me for now."

"Who said I was stuck?"

"That's good that you don't feel trapped in this relationship."

"Ah, so I *am* your boyfriend. I was beginning to wonder."

I twisted around so I could look at his face. A broad smile gleamed in the dark.

"Brandon, what am I going to do with you?"

"Keep me." He moved his arms from around my waist and held my face in his hands. He kept his left hand still and traced his right thumb across my cheekbone, then over my tattoo, then across my bottom lip, stopping on my piercings.

"I would never *not* keep you," I whispered.

His irises looked like circles of ice in the moonlight. Like always, his gaze pulled me into him, my lips meeting effortlessly with his. "Before I start enjoying this too much," he said in between kisses, "we should probably try and get some more rest. I'm not sure what Shaw has in store for us tomorrow."

"Shopping," I answered as Brandon helped me to my feet.

"Really?"

"That's what he was telling Agatha. I'll bet we train after that, though."

"Not you. Not with your injury."

"No, I guess not," I mumbled.

I never thought I would look forward to hand to hand combat and weapon training, but the truth was, it was the only constant thing in my life on the run. We trained every day. Well, every day before the shipwreck.

Brandon held me close to him and nestled his nose in

my tangled chocolate brown curls. This was one of those rare moments when we were alone that I wished I could freeze time and stay with him in that moment for the rest of forever.

"I thought we were supposed to be heading to bed," I reminded him reluctantly.

"We are," he agreed, but we remained in place. After a long pause, Brandon lifted my chin with his index finger so we looked each other in the eye. "Sable...you know I—"

"Oh, you guys are still up here! Agatha was just having me pass around night clothes for everyone. The view really is spectacular from up here, isn't it?" Melody interrupted.

"We'll be right down. Thanks, Melody," Brandon dismissed her.

A bubble of happiness swelled in my heart. Melody smiled and gave a little wave to Brandon before disappearing down the ladder.

Brandon released me and started toward the ladder.

"Brandon, what were you saying before Melody—"

"Don't worry about it, it's nothing. I'll tell you some other time. We have to call it a night."

Then he disappeared down the ladder. Did Chloe learn her impeccable knack for interrupting intimate moments from Melody, or was it that other way around? I let out a frustrated sigh and headed down the ladder, too.

Brandon kissed me briefly before going into his room. I pressed my fingers to my lips, trying in vain to make the feeling of his lips on mine linger a little longer.

When I woke up the next morning, it surprised me how fast I had fallen asleep. Leilani and Ophelia were gone. I stretched my muscles and went downstairs to find them.

The sound of crinkling plastic grew louder and louder as I reached the foot of the stairs. Sunshine streamed through the windows in the other room off of the living room, which turned out to be sort of a family room. This room was decorated with modern furniture and art deco pieces. I assumed Melody designed this room, too.

Everyone was passing around plastic covered garments.

I yawned. "Where did all this stuff come from?"

"Drake ordered it last night and I had Harvey pick it up in town this morning. I believe your pile is on the chaise lounge, dear," Agatha smiled.

I padded over to the chaise lounge and sat on the edge of it. The pile was pretty impressive. Shaw ordered everything, including extra lip rings and a toasted vanilla sugar scented bathroom set. I had no idea he paid that much attention to detail. Out of the corner of my eye, I saw Ophelia fawning over a new set of hair dye. The pink and teal streaks in her white blonde hair were severely faded. All the guys got new razors and Fang got a set of clippers so he could shave his head.

I gasped. "Shaw, how did you know to get all of this?"

"I told you before, Miss Mosley, I won't have my crew running around looking like vermin," he grunted.

I guessed that was his way of saying "you're welcome."

Agatha scolded him for his gruffness, but the smile never faded from her weather worn face.

Everyone went upstairs to freshen up. I couldn't be happier to have my signature scent back and to not have to stink like roses. I donned a black strapless cotton dress with silver eyelets down the front, which helped to simulate an hourglass shape, and distressed black lace trimmed the top and bottom. This was a more suitable to-the-knee-dress than the ugly pale yellow one. I finished off the look with black platform pumps with red roses snaking up the outsides of the shoes, and a silver necklace with a pale blue crystal star pendant and lip rings with matching pale blue crystals. The color reminded me of Brandon's eyes.

It was nice to see everyone decked out in their normal attire at breakfast. The spread was pretty simple, consisting of bacon, scrambled eggs, and toast with a dark salty spread on it. I didn't care for the toast much, but the eggs were good. Agatha put goat cheese in them.

"So what's on the agenda for today, Shaw?" Kelly asked as he finished off his bacon.

"Training. You're all sadly out of practice."

"Sable can't train. Her ribs are still bruised," Brandon pointed out.

"Right. With Leilani's venom coursing through her, I almost forgot," Shaw mused. "She'll spend the day with Agatha, then. Melody can come train with us, get back into the swing of things."

"Are we training independently or in pairs?" Brandon asked.

"You will pair up: Chloe with Gareth, Ophelia with Kelly, Leilani with Fang, and Melody with Brandon." Shaw stood up and waited for everyone to follow suit.

As everyone else followed after Shaw, Harvey began cleaning up the breakfast dishes and I followed Agatha upstairs to the library.

Instead of finding books lining the walls, there were rolls and rolls of parchment stacked in cubby holes. I guessed they were all stars Agatha charted.

The parchment she was working on the night before looked just like the rest of these. A large oak desk sat in the corner of the room buried beneath piles of unrolled parchment scrolls.

"Are we reorganizing the scrolls today?" I asked tentatively. I would almost rather be training while still in pain than do this sort of menial work.

"Not today, dear, but thank you for offering. Today, we'll be working on intensifying that fire power of yours."

"In a room full of paper?"

"If Drake trusts you, I trust you."

"Can't we do this outside?" I didn't want to ruin her charts. Even if she and Shaw both trusted me, I didn't trust myself to have that kind of control.

"If it makes you feel more comfortable, sure."

I followed Agatha back to the family room and out the set of French doors into the back yard. There was a building that looked like a double wide trailer home a few yards from the covered patio.

"What's that building over there?"

"That's where everyone else is training. Now, step out here into the sun and show me your fire."

I followed Agatha part of the way and stopped a few feet before she did. When she turned to face me, I closed my eyes and concentrated on the flames spreading out from my hands, up my arms, and consuming the rest of me. The tingling sensation that engulfed me when I was covered in flames took over my whole body. I opened my eyes and looked at Agatha. She seemed unimpressed.

Agatha crossed her arms over her chest, her mouth turned down into a pensive frown. "It's dull, your fire."

"I'm sorry?"

"Drake said something about venom in your system?"

"Um, yes." I didn't want to reveal anything about Leilani. I'd let Shaw clue her in about that.

"What is the purpose of this venom in your system?"

"I have bruised ribs from the shipwreck. It's supposed to make me feel no pain."

"Dear, Sable, you can't go through life numb. Feeling pain is how we know we're still living! We'll have to do something about extracting that venom. I thought your bond was unnaturally strong to that girl..." The last statement was muttered under her breath, but I chose to ignore it.

How did she mean to extract the venom from me? Flashbacks from my days as a glorified lab rat at the asylum haunted me. A cold sweat broke out on my back.

As Agatha walked toward me, with a bowl of paste in her hands, I stood frozen with fear. She balanced the bowl in one hand and took a knife off of her belt with the other. Her movements appeared in slow motion in my eyes, but I couldn't make myself move or cry out for help or breathe.

I found my voice again as the knife slashed up my thigh. As I fell to the ground, I screamed. Blood streamed from the gash into my shoe. I clutched at my thigh, but Agatha swatted my hands away. She wiped the knife off on the edge of the bowl and clipped it back onto her belt. Then she coated a wide paint brush with the goop in the bowl and hiked up my skirt so she could brush the salve on my wound.

"Sorry I had to do that, but I find it's better if you're not bracing yourself. Even if your rational mind knows no harm is intended, your instinctive mind is still operating on the defensive. Give it a few hours and that salve should heal the stab wound and your fractured ribs. The venom should be working its way out of your system about now," Agatha explained while she tended to the wound.

As if her words summoned it, a thick black tar like substance seeped out of the wound. I tried my best not to gag. Agatha collected the substance in the now empty bowl.

"What the hell is this?" I demanded as I watched the venom drain from me.

"I had to have access to fresh coursing blood for the salve to work. Of course, it mends topically, too, but for poison in your blood, it had to get into the blood stream."

"Is this voodoo or something?"

"I'm a descendant of a medicine man in my tribe. The secrets of all sorts of these remedies have been passed through my family for generations. I'm afraid the knowledge will die with me, though." A note of sadness tainted the wistfulness of her story.

"Couldn't you tell Melody?"

"As much as I like to think of Melody as one of my own, she is not related by blood. If I had a niece or a nephew, I could share it with them, but since I'm an only child and I have no children of my own, the family blood line dies with me."

A newfound empathy bloomed inside of me for Agatha. I thought being an only child was lonely, but to be the last one left in your whole family? I hugged Agatha and squeezed her tight. "Thank you for healing me."

"You're welcome, dear, but I must apologize to you again. The regrowth of your bones is going to be painful and difficult. If there's anything you can think of to comfort you, I'll be sure to get it for you or send Harvey to fetch it. I just ask that you let me know before nightfall."

"Brandon." The word slipped off my tongue before I realized I said it.

"Well, I'm sure that can be arranged. Now see? Your blood is running clean. It should stop actively bleeding in a minute or so. Then we'll see how brightly your flame truly shines." Agatha tossed the bowl of venom aside and smiled.

"I thought my ribs were just bruised?" I asked.

"If they were just bruised, you would be able to

move around better without resorting to that dreadful toxin you accepted into your body," she explained.

Once the wound stopped bleeding, I concentrated on the flames taking over my body again. My skin went completely frigid when the flames engulfed me. The tingles were what made the cold sensation. When the venom was in my system, all I felt was the tingles. The flames were uninhibited now, and they spread faster and faster until I was a ball of fire sitting on the ground.

"That's much better," Agatha mused.

At that moment, the door to the training trailer swung open and Melody yelped.

"Agatha, I'll put out the fire, don't worry!" Melody cried as she scampered toward the garden hose.

"Melody, it's quite all right—"

Before I had time to shift to my knees, I was doused with water.

"Oh, sorry, Sable, I didn't realize it was you," Melody said in a strained voice. She couldn't quite mask her fit of giggles. Chloe didn't even try to hide hers.

"That's a good look for you Sable. All washed up." Chloe joined Melody and the girls waltzed into the house together in fits of laughter.

Agatha knelt down next to me and brushed a wet clump of hair out of my eyes. "Sable, you must understand. Melody is not the deplorable human being she's put on display for you. Her heart was broken when she left Brandon, and it cut her deeply when she found him again and he was with someone new. The bond between the two of you…I've never felt anything like that in all my years. It's positively bone crushing in its strength!"

"What do you mean?"

"That's a story for another time, dear. Now don't try to stand up. I'll have that strapping young lad move you to the widow's peak so you can heal in peace. Only room for one or two visitors at a time. Now, what was his name again? Fang? That's an odd name for a man—"

"That's not his real name—"

"Ah yes, Fang! Would you be a peach and carry our dear Sable up to the widow's peak? I'll explain later on what's happened, but she's quite all right," Agatha called as she stood.

Fang walked over to us and scooped me up into his arms. When Agatha was out of earshot, he muttered, "That lady is damn near crazy, Miss Sable."

I smiled. "She's all right."

"You want me to find Brandon and have him keep you company?"

"Later. Right now I could use a little quality brother-sister time."

Fang chuckled as shifted me in his arms so he could climb the ladder one-handed. "Whatever you want, Miss Sable."

As I laughed, a throbbing ache lanced through my ribs. I sucked in a breath and swore. This was going to be a long day that turned into an excruciating night.

CHAPTER 6

Fang stayed with me into the evening. I vented to him about Melody trying to get her claws back into Brandon and he told me about what I missed in training. Apparently, Melody was skilled in more than just painting. She matched Brandon blow for blow and Shaw finally made them stop because neither one was gaining on the other. Fang had the feeling Brandon was holding back, though. When Brandon and I sparred with each other, he *never* held back. He said it was too important for me to know how to protect myself.

As the sun began to set, Brandon appeared with a grilled cheese sandwich with a slice of tomato on it, my favorite food. Ophelia and Kelly appeared briefly to wish me good luck and a speedy recovery.

"Brandon, can I talk to you for a minute?" Kelly asked as he began descending the ladder.

"I'll be right back," Brandon promised me. He kissed the tip of my nose before following Kelly down.

I knew it was impolite, but I couldn't help myself. I strained to hear their conversation. What did Brandon talk about with his best friend?

"Are you sure you're up for this?" Kelly started.

"I'm not just going to leave her up there alone."

"That's not what I'm saying. I just think you should have some backup or something. If I had feelings like that for a girl and had to watch her go through all that pain and feel helpless because there's nothing I could do to ease it, I think I'd be out of my mind."

"It definitely won't be easy."

"I can stay if you want, or Ophelia and I can switch off."

"Did Ophelia look for the outcome?"

"Yeah. Sable's going to be fine, but it's going to be hell getting there."

Brandon let out a long heavy sigh. "I was afraid of that."

"If you need us, come get us. Fang volunteered, too, but there's no way all three of you would fit in that small space. That guy is *massive*."

It was true. Fang was a giant wall of muscle and close to seven feet tall. My heart swelled with love that my friends cared so much for me and that Brandon's cared for him. The knowledge that this was going to be every bit as painful as Agatha promised it would be was terrifying. As if the thought of it was all the pain needed to be summoned, a stabbing pain shot through my chest cavity. I cried out and clutched at my rib cage.

"It's starting. I better get back up there. And Kelly, thanks, man."

His footsteps were loud on the metal ladder in his haste. The pain began to subside as he made it back onto the widow's peak.

"Sable, I'm so sorry," he breathed as he knelt next to me and scooped me up in his arms.

I curled into his chest like a frightened little child. "It's not your fault. You didn't break my ribs. I think a rock is to blame for that. Maybe some coral, I don't know."

"It's going to be okay." With some gentle maneuvering, he settled me between his legs so my head still laid on his chest. He covered me with the afghan Agatha brought up earlier, but I was already burning.

"You don't have to do this, you know." I wanted to give him an out. If our roles were reversed, I knew it would be agonizing for me to watch him writhing in pain.

"Where else would I be right now?"

I shrugged. "Maybe in the kitchen."

"Maybe," he agreed quietly.

"Brandon, this is going to get worse before it gets better."

"I know."

We stayed quiet for a long time. I nibbled on the grilled cheese sandwich between fits of anguish. Each bout of pain burned worse than the last. The fire inside me was trying to consume me, burning my organs and my bones but unable to escape my skin, further enraging it, making it hotter and hotter every time. All the while, Brandon held me close, stroking my hair and rocking me back and forth slowly.

I screamed into the dead of night, vaguely aware of the fact I was probably keeping everyone awake. As the sky turned from black to the deep purple just before the colors of the sky of dawn appeared, I was past the point of tears. My throat was hoarse from all the moaning and screaming. Brandon remained stoic, a trait I admired in him.

Every so often, he would whisper "we can do this" in my ear. I had no choice but to believe him.

At last, the pain was too much to bear. It would be easier to die than to endure this torture any more.

"Brandon, make it stop," I cried.

Tears trickled down my cheeks in steady rivers. So, I wasn't out of tears after all. Everything in my chest cavity throbbed, threatening to explode out of me and shatter my bones into a thousand pieces.

"I don't know how." The words caught in his throat and he choked on them.

"Kiss me."

"Sable—"

"Please, Brandon."

The simple request was his undoing. He shifted me so I sat sideways on his lap and his lips crashed into mine. One of his hands latched onto the small of my back while the other tangled into my hair. He was as needy and insistent as I was. I was trying to lose myself in him and shed away the pain. He was trying to take the hurt from me.

Something inside of me snapped and caused my back to arch involuntarily. I ripped my mouth away from his. A noise, I couldn't be completely sure came from me, rang out loud and long. I heaved in breaths like I would never have enough air to breathe.

"Shaw! Shaw!" Brandon bellowed.

Agatha was the first to make it up the ladder with Shaw following close behind her.

"I didn't expect this reaction at all. The light is almost blinding!" Agatha mused.

"What the hell are you talking about?" I panted.

"Sable, there's fire all around you—but the flames aren't orange, they're green. And Brandon—I can see the electricity popping off of you. It's so brightly white. Like Aggie said, it's almost blinding," Shaw explained.

"I told you there was something special about the two of them, Drake," Agatha stated matter-of-factly.

When Brandon and I were trying to be captured by the DAO so we could rescue Chloe and Kelly, we were kissing in the streets of a small seaside town. For some reason, I was engulfed in green flames. I didn't burn him or myself, but as far as we could tell, it was a onetime phenomenon. Now that it was happening again, and Brandon was affected, too, it had to mean something bigger was going on.

"Sable, look at me. Look into my eyes. You have to slow down your breathing or you'll pass out. We can do this."

Brandon took my hand in his and I stared into his eyes, just as he instructed me to do. In the instant our eyes locked, the pain drained away from me like someone pulled the stopper out of the bathtub and the water was sucked into the drain. The flames and the raw electricity faded away, too. So did my energy. My breathing returned to normal and I slumped back against Brandon.

Agatha knelt down next to us and put the back of her hand on my forehead. "Sable, how are you feeling, dear?"

"Beyond exhausted."

She poked around at my ribs, which were still a little tender, but now intact, and smiled at the success of her handiwork. "I think we all deserve a bit of sleep now. Come, there's a room next to the ladder you kids can stay in for the morning. Drake, you can stay with me or with Harvey, whichever you're more comfortable with."

I couldn't fathom how I was supposed to get down the ladder, let alone stand up. Turned out, I didn't have to worry about it. A small makeshift camp had been set up at the base of the ladder, consisting of Agatha, Shaw, Kelly, Fang, and Ophelia. Fang climbed up the ladder and carried me down, then laid me down in bed.

Before handing my care back over to Brandon, he kissed my forehead and whispered, "Miss Sable, you are incredibly strong. I am proud of you."

Agatha told everyone else they could visit when everyone was more rested and closed the bedroom door.

Brandon sat tentatively on the edge of the bed and

stared at me. I couldn't place the emotion brimming in his eyes—I couldn't make myself focus. The only thing I was sure of was that I felt like I could sleep for a million years.

"Brandon, come here."

He complied with my request, but kept his distance from me.

"Closer. I need you. Please, Brandon."

"I'm right here, I promise." He wrapped his arms around my waist and I laid my head on his shoulder.

When I woke up, I was in the same position I fell asleep in. All the pain in my body was gone. Moving slowly so I wouldn't wake Brandon up, I touched the spot on my thigh where Agatha stabbed me. The skin was smooth with no hint of a scar.

Then I studied Brandon's face. His hair was plastered to his forehead and sticking up in all directions farther back on his head. Dark purple circles hung beneath his eyes. His lips were pressed into a hard line and his brow was furrowed. This was not how he should look in sleep. He should be at peace when he slept.

I pressed my lips softly against the hollow of his throat. A quiet moan passed through his lips before he blinked his eyes open sleepily.

"What's wrong?" he mumbled.

"Nothing, dearest. Go back to sleep."

"Baby doll, I..." He fell back asleep before he finished his sentence.

It weighed heavily on my heart that Brandon sat through all that torturous pain the night before. I was grateful he stayed with me, but I felt guilty for being selfish and asking him to bear witness to that. Then an idea occurred to me.

I slipped out of his arms as gently as I could and made sure he was still fast asleep before sneaking out of the room. The rest of the house was quiet as I tiptoed down the stairs and into the kitchen.

My knowledge of cooking was minimal at best, so I decided to stick with what I did know—biscuits and sausage gravy. As quietly as I was able, I rummaged through the pantry and the refrigerator for ingredients. I was surprised how well stocked the kitchen was. Melody must have made sure Harvey stocked everything for Brandon. The notion left a bittersweet taste in my mouth.

As I mixed the dough for the biscuits, I said a silent prayer for Brandon to stay asleep until I was finished. While the biscuits finished cooling and the gravy thickened a little on its own, I made a pot of coffee and poured Brandon a cup. I broke two biscuits apart and put them on a plate, then ladled some gravy over them.

I carried my breakfast offering back upstairs to our temporary room. Since I couldn't juggle the plate and the cup in one hand, I had to set the coffee mug on the floor to open the door. Thankfully, he was still sleeping. I almost squealed in delight, but made myself stay quiet. I set the plate and the mug on the nightstand next to him and crawled back into bed.

"Brandon," I whispered as I kissed the hollow of his throat again.

"Mmm," he moaned.

"I have a surprise for you, wake up."

"What?"

"Come on, sleepy bear, rise and shine."

"Sleepy bear?"

"I know, my pet names need some work."

"Is that coffee?"

"Open your eyes and see."

Finally, he opened his eyes. He gave me a quick peck on the lips before turning over and finding his surprise.

"You brought me breakfast in bed?"

"I did you one better. I *made* you breakfast in bed!"

"*You* made this?"

"Don't sound so surprised. You're in danger of hurting my pride," I teased.

"It's not a question of your capabilities. It's just—no one's ever made me breakfast before except my parents when I was young. Why did you do this?"

"To say 'thank you' for going through hell with me last night."

"Oh, Sable!"

Before I knew what was happening, his arms were around me, squeezing me tight. I almost thought my newly repaired ribs would break again. My arms wound around his neck and I made a trail of kisses from the corner of his jaw to his lips.

He never did eat the breakfast I made for him, but I didn't mind. I could've kissed him for the rest of my life and been perfectly blissful.

CHAPTER 7

Brandon

Since Sable was allowed to rejoin training, it made the pairs uneven. Fang was on a different level than the rest of us, so he conditioned on his own. Shaw switched up the pairs: Gareth and me, Chloe and Leilani, Kelly and Ophelia, and Melody and Sable. I'm not sure what Shaw's reasons were for pairing those two together, but I knew it was going to be trouble.

For the first hour, the eleven of us trained simultaneously. I knew Melody would give Sable a run for her money. I also knew Melody would underestimate Sable. Gareth took advantage of my being distracted and punched me right in the gut. That should've brought my focus to my own sparring match, but I ended up on my ass more than I had since I was just a kid learning the basics. I couldn't help myself. Watching them spar was hot.

Then Shaw announced that we would spar for the others, one team at a time. Luckily, I kept my focus long enough to cause Gareth to submit in our match. Shaw nodded once, which was his general show of approval.

When Shaw said it was time for Melody and Sable to give their sparring performance, my nerves crackled with anticipation. They stood facing each other, waiting for Shaw to give them their cues to begin. He slammed his fist into his upturned palm like someone beginning to play Rock, Paper, Scissors. As soon as they heard the soft smack of flesh colliding with flesh, they sprang at one another.

Melody attempted to lock Sable into a choke hold, but she underestimated Sable's height. She was only two inches shorter than Melody, not five. Sable spun out of Melody's arms and tried to trip her, but Melody hopped out of the way. They dodged and wove around one another until they were a tangled mass of limbs and torsos on the ground. Then Melody pulled Sable's hair.

"You bitch!" Sable shrieked.

The mood shifted after that. It was a full-on girl fight. Normally, girls fighting are pretty sexy. This display made me want to vomit. They clawed, bit, kicked, punched, slapped, and spit on each other. I'm not sure how many blows they got at one another before Fang and Shaw pulled them apart. Melody's lip was bleeding and bruises were forming on the exposed skin on her arms. Sable's left eye was bleeding. Melody clutched a lock of Sable's hair in her fist like a trophy.

Sable struggled against Fang with all the strength she had left, but she was no match for his power.

"I'm ashamed of both of you. As a reminder of the stupidity of your actions, you'll heal as nature intended. Agatha will not be allowed to cure you of your wounds," Shaw reprimanded.

"But I think she broke my wrist!" Melody whined.

Shaw ran his fingers over both sides of her wrist, assessing the damage. "There's nothing broken, but I'm sure it's pained from that terrible form you had."

Sable smirked at his criticism of Melody.

"Don't be so smug, Mosley. You're damn lucky you

didn't break anything, either. I'm training you so you will be in control of your movements and anticipate those of your assailants, not so you can beat the crap out of each other to stroke your egos. That's enough for today. Fang, you'll escort Mosley to the widow's peak. Harper, you'll take Wilson to the downstairs study."

"Yes, Shaw," Chloe nodded.

"Not you. Your brother."

He might as well have punched me in the temple.

A triumphant grin spread across Melody's face as I put my arm delicately around her shoulders and steered her toward the door. Fang waited until everyone else left the training facility before he escorted Sable out.

"I hate her," Melody seethed.

I shook my head. "You hardly even know her."

"It doesn't matter. You know why I don't like her, right?"

I pushed gently on her shoulders to make her sit in the plush arm chair in the study.

"My guess is because she's my new girlfriend."

"It's more than that," she spat.

I raised an eyebrow. "Care to enlighten me?"

"Brandon, I was taken from you. I didn't know if I'd ever see you again. Then I find you washed up on some beach, and I'm thinking that that couldn't just be a coincidence, right? It meant we were supposed to pick up where we left off, doesn't it?"

Her eyes were bright with unshed tears.

I scrubbed a hand down my face. "What am I supposed to say? I'm sorry it's not the same, and for a long time, I thought one day it would be. Then I met Sable and she just—"

"I don't want to know. Look, I can take care of myself, okay? You can show yourself out."

I pretended not to notice the tears leaking from the

corners of her eyes. She was too proud to have someone comfort her when she cried, even when we were kids. Knowing that didn't make the knot in my stomach loosen any.

As I wandered toward the living room, I bumped into Sable at the foot of the stairs. Even banged up, the sight of her still made my heart race.

"Hey," she said shyly.

"Let's go for a walk. I need to tell you something."

I don't know what prompted me to tell her now. Maybe it was my subconscious trying to make up for hurting Melody. Or maybe watching Sable be tortured by Native American medicine while it healed her made me want to tell her. Whatever it was, I just knew I had to do it, and I had to do it now.

I led her out the front door and walked a good twenty feet away from the house before we started walking laps around the homestead. She was quiet, but I wasn't sure I would've heard her even if she was talking. I was too preoccupied with my thoughts.

How should I tell her? This was the first time I would ever say this to a girl.

On the fifth lap around, I finally had the nerve to say something. "I'm sorry."

I silently berated myself for another two laps before she broke the quiet.

"Why?" she prompted.

Another lap in silence.

"I could never guess this would happen."

Two more laps. Why was this so hard?

"You could never guess what would happen?" she asked.

"That Melody, of all people, would randomly find me on a deserted island. And that I would feel like this."

A look of horror arrested her features and she

stopped dead in her tracks. "Feel like what? Brandon, are you, do you want to—"

"No, Sable. God, no!" I turned her by the shoulders so she was facing me. Then I grasped her face in my hands and tilted her head up so she looked into my eyes. "I'm a little surprised Chloe hasn't rubbed it in your face—"

"Brandon, please, what are you talking about?"

I breathed a heavy sigh. "Melody was my first girlfriend. She was the first girl I ever paid attention to that wasn't my sister. And we were together until Shaw sent her here."

"How long was that?" Her voice was barely louder than a whisper.

"Almost two years. I had strong feelings for her. Really strong—"

"I don't need to know that."

"Right. Anyway, that's not the point. She'd been gone a year before I met you. And that first day I saw you in the asylum I knew there was something special about you. You know I was supposed to be looking for Ophelia. But I was just interested in you. In everything about you. And then they put you in that torture dungeon…"

We both shuddered at the memory of her stint as a lab rat at the hands of the sadistic Dr. Jude Pantiel. Everything I'd ever been afraid of before then paled in comparison to the sight of the lethal injection being put into Sable's arm.

"I didn't care about finding Ophelia any more. I just knew I had to get you out of that place. It was sheer dumb luck you begged me to drag her and Fang along with us. Then when the DAO wanted us to join them and Chloe left, I was sure I'd go with her, because she was my universe. But you asked me to stay with you. I just couldn't bear to tell you no. And when you were shot, before I found the wound on your hip, and I thought—"

She started chewing on her lip. I wished I was better at explaining things like this.

"I'm here," she whispered.

"I don't ever want to be without you. Not ever. And then Melody shows back up like a ghost from the past, and she wants to pick up where we left off. I've moved on, she hasn't."

"Why did Shaw send her away?"

"I don't know. I asked every day for three months, but he never told me."

Sable threw her arms around me and stared up at me. I still held her head firmly between my palms.

"If someone forced us apart, I wouldn't stop searching for you until I died," she promised.

"I've tried to tell you so many times, Sable. Something always got in the way. Usually, it was my sister. But I need you to know." *Here goes nothing.*

"What—"

"Sable, I'm in love with you."

Her eyes grew wide and she stood perfectly still. She wasn't even breathing for the first few moments. What was she thinking? Was it too soon to tell her? It felt like I'd been waiting for forever to say I loved her!

I dropped my hands from her face and grasped her hands in mine instead. I searched her eyes for some kind of sign of what was going through her mind. Her continued silence caused panic to quickly swell inside me.

"Sable, say something, please."

She just kept staring at me with those wide green eyes.

"Please," I begged.

In one swift motion, her arms snaked around my neck and she kissed me hard.

Oh, thank God!

I wrapped her tightly in my arms. Her body melted into mine as I deepened the kiss. Before I knew it, we were both breathing hard, clutching one another like we'd never see each other again.

"Brandon." She uttered my name like a prayer.

"Mmm," I murmured as my lips trailed hungry kisses from the hollow of her throat to her clavicle.

"I'm in love with you, too."

I swallowed her words with a kiss, and she curled her fingers in my hair. My hands slid beneath the hem of her shirt and I traced the vertebrae of the small of her back with my fingertips. She felt like the softest most expensive silk.

Everything about her was completely exquisite. My touch sent shivers up her spine and a mewl sounded low in her throat.

Suddenly, a new wave of fears slammed into my consciousness. Was this too soon? Did I push her to say she loved me? Was I overthinking everything? Was I not putting enough thought into it? I stopped kissing her and held her face in my hands again. I pressed my forehead to hers and whispered, "Is this okay? I don't want to screw this up."

She nodded and my lips crashed back into hers. My fingers traced up and down her spine ever so slowly, lingering over the closure of her bra before resuming their path. She started panting again, with more of the mewling sounds strangled in her throat. I wanted to stay wrapped together with her like this forever.

When I stopped kissing her again, she groaned in protest.

"If I don't stop now, I don't think I'll be able to later," I warned as I kissed her knuckles apologetically.

"Hold me for just a little longer. Please, Brandon."

I smiled at her and wrapped her in my arms, burying

my nose in her hair by her neck. This moment was perfect, and no one existed but us.

Then a scream of terror from the house ripped through our solace.

CHAPTER 8

Sable

Brandon and I sprang apart from each other's embrace and gawked at the house for a moment. Then our battle instincts took over as we leapt into action and sprinted to the back of the house. There was no sign of a break in from the rear. When we were a few yards away from the French doors, we slowed our pace to quiet our footsteps. It turned out, though, that that was unnecessary.

The racket in the house made my heart stop. If it were average burglars who intruded, there were more than enough people inside to subdue them. *How did they find us?*

Projectile glass shards shot toward us as a man dressed in sand-colored fatigues threw Chloe through the French doors. Brandon immediately engaged in combat. My movements made me feel like I was running through a lake of mud. While Brandon worked on taking out the guy who threw her, I fell to my knees to assess Chloe's condition.

"Chloe, are you all right?"

She winced as she rolled onto her side and sat up on

her knees. "Why are you wasting time with me? We need help inside. Go!"

Well, I guessed she was fine, despite the gash in her shoulder. I nodded and ducked through the hole in the destroyed French door.

An explosion of noise and chaos erupted around me. Loud bangs above me indicated the struggle took place throughout the house, not just the ground floor. I saw a flash of Fang throwing a couple of guys off of him in the formal living room. Brandon was already out of my sight.

An arm wrapped around my throat and squeezed sharply. I choked as I fought down the instant panic rising in me. That wouldn't help me get rid of this asshole.

"Ma'am, you are under arrest for harboring fugitives and illegally removing them from a government facility," the man rasped in my ear.

He must've been talking about when Brandon and I stole Leilani, Chloe, and Kelly from a DAO facility in the States.

I gathered all my inner strength and elbowed him in the groin. My aim was a little high. Half of my elbow came into contact with soft flesh while the other half hit hard plastic. My breath hissed out from my clenched teeth as he released me. In my best imitation of Chloe, I swung my leg around and kicked him in the chest. Since he was nursing the place where my first blow landed, he was unprepared for the second. He fell. I didn't waste time in seeing if he was still on the ground or if he was pursuing me. I had to keep running, keep searching for the others.

From what I could tell, we were outnumbered by at least four to one. While we could hold them off, I doubted we would win this fight. The sound of gunshots reinforced that idea. I surrounded myself in a cocoon of flames and barreled through the DAO agents.

"Enough!" one of the agents roared over the noise, a feat I was quite impressed with.

Someone screamed in my ear as a cold metal band wrapped around my throat. Shockwaves of electricity coursed through my body. I fell to my knees. Vaguely, I was aware that all of my comrades that I could see had similar reactions to mine. I wondered what they did to subdue Brandon since his Gift was electricity. Images of men in beige beating him and drugging him made the contents of my stomach roil.

"Now, I want you to take all the female Diseased in one van and all the male Diseased in the other," the man with the commanding voice instructed. All of the DAO agents wore masks on their faces, so the only distinguishing features they had were their differences in body type and height and their voices.

"Sir, one of the men is only human, not a Diseased," someone I couldn't see said. He was talking about Harvey.

"Cuff him and bring him in for questioning," the man called "sir" dictated.

I screamed in protest as I was prodded to my feet. Another wave of electricity ran through me, choking the air from my lungs. Clearly, they wanted us to go quietly. I couldn't escape them or help the others do so if I was dead, so I shut up.

Chloe, Leilani, Melody, Agatha, Ophelia, and I were herded into one van while Shaw, Fang, Brandon, Kelly, and Gareth were corralled into another. Harvey was taken away in an SUV with four DAO agents. We didn't have any agents sitting in the back of the van with us.

There were no windows in the back of the van, so we couldn't see where we were going or if the boys were going in the same direction we were. I looked around at everyone to see how they were handling our capture.

Agatha looked sad but distant. Chloe sat silently fuming. Leilani's eyes were wide with fear. Ophelia was only physically with us. Her vacant stare gave away that she was searching the future. As I looked at Melody, she looked glanced me. A mixture of fear and sorrow etched her features. What did I look like? It was probably better that I didn't know.

The drive appeared to be endless. We never seemed to stop for gas or at stop lights or anything. Where were we going? A deep blasting horn sounded as I was about to launch into hysterics. We were at a harbor somewhere. We were leaving Australia. The van shifted into "park." I waited for the DAO agents to collect us, but then the boat started moving.

"This is going to be worse than the Crazy Cannon Place," I muttered.

"What's the Crazy Cannon Place?" Leilani asked.

"The asylum where I met Fang and Ophelia and where Brandon and Chloe sprang us from."

"He likes a crazy girl?" Melody huffed.

"He *loves* me."

"What?"

I was sure that would be the only time Chloe, Melody, and Ophelia would speak in unison.

My cheeks got hot and I knew they must be scarlet at this point. I bit my bottom lip.

"When did this happen?" Ophelia demanded.

Despite our current predicament, she was practically giddy by this news. She really was a wonderful best friend.

"Just before the ambush at Agatha's. How did that start, anyhow?"

"They just came out of nowhere. Drake and I were in the sitting room having a cup of coffee and catching up, and then the DAO swarmed in," Agatha enlightened me.

"They're treating us like dogs! I mean, look at these shock collars!" Chloe growled as she yanked on hers. The action activated the current. She swore as she was electrocuted.

"They're afraid of us, dear," Agatha pointed out. "People fear what they don't understand. It's just our nature."

Agatha had to be the most serene person I'd ever met.

Chloe panted as she recovered from her disciplinary shock.

More time passed, but I couldn't tell how much. All I knew was that my stomach was eating itself I was so hungry. And I was worried sick about the boys. Where were they?

The deafening churning of the engines on the ship and the lack of sustenance gave me a migraine. At least at the asylum they fed us gruel. Who ever thought I would be appreciative of that slop?

Finally, exhaustion dragged me to sleep. My nightmares of what was to become of us made me restless. I dreamt of torture chambers and deadly experiments like the ones performed on me at the asylum. I woke up screaming and set off my shock collar.

"It's okay, we could barely hear you above the engines," Ophelia yelled in my ear.

I nodded, a silent indication I'd heard her speaking. My breath came in ragged gasps. Stupid nightmares and shock collars…

Finally, blessedly, the sound of the ship's engines grinding to a halt screeched and left silence in their wake. My ears still rung from the constant abuse of loud noise assaulting them. A short time later, the van's much quieter engine started again and we were on the move once more.

"Ophelia, can you see where we're headed?" I inquired.

"Somewhere in the States, but I'm not sure if we're in Hawaii or on the west coast somewhere. It's definitely south of Canada, though."

"Is that what you were looking for earlier?"

She nodded.

"Can you see where the others are?"

She grimaced and shook her head.

"Damn."

Silently, I prayed they were headed to the same place we were. I lost count of how many times I pleaded to God or whoever would listen for all of us to remain together when this hellish trip was through. Unconsciousness claimed me once more mid-plea.

"I said *get up!*" a man dressed in tan fatigues screamed into my face.

"What the—" I started to yell.

The shock collar cut me off. My assailant grinned as my body writhed from the electrical current.

"I didn't tell you to speak, just to get up."

Silently fuming, I obliged.

Agatha was being herded out of the van with me. Everyone else was waiting for us, each with their own escorts. The other van was nowhere to be seen. My heart sank.

Looking around at the others, it amazed me how a few days' starvation made them all look so frail. I imagined I looked just like they did—pale gaunt faces and hollow eyes with dark purple half-moons clinging beneath them, stringy greasy hair hanging in matted locks, and clothes fitting a little looser than they used to.

The landscape around us was as barren as our optimism. Everything around us was covered in dust. Mountains loomed vaguely in the distance, but everything around us was flat. The sun shone a blinding white reflection off of the pale sand. It made me squint.

"Where the hell are we?" Chloe grumbled.

"In the desert in Nevada. They're taking us to Area 51," Ophelia whispered.

"What's Area 51?" Melody asked.

One of the men in beige fatigues pulled a remote out of his pocket and pressed a button on it. All of our shock collars buzzed at once, rendering us all speechless and breathless again.

The man with the remote smirked. "That's enough conversation out of you."

I would have given almost anything to be able to light his fatigues on fire.

Five military vehicles pulled up to us. When they idled, we were ushered into them. Everyone was separated, except Leilani and me. We held hands the whole way to Area 51. She squeezed mine and I squeezed hers. I didn't know if we were trying to reassure each other or what the point was. Both of us were afraid of being imprisoned again.

I wasn't sure how much time passed before our vehicle slowed to a stop. The conversation between the driver and the soldier outside the vehicle was muffled. We weren't stopped for long before we were driving again. I assumed we were inside the military base now. My stomach dropped with the descent of the military vehicle. Eventually, the trajectory smoothed out. Not long after we began driving straight ahead again, the vehicle stopped.

More men in various military uniforms were waiting for us. While the soldiers inside the vehicle were pushing us out of it, the soldiers outside the vehicle caught us and began leading us deeper into the belly of the beast.

Cells made of frosted glass and reinforced with some

sort of metal bars loomed ahead of us. Without anyone saying a word, I knew these would be our new homes. As I was led past the first grouping of cells, a large dark colored fist punched through the glass and a roar of hatred and pain accompanied it. The sound became strangled as the now-familiar static of the shock collars thickened the air.

"Miss Sable…" the voice choked.

"*Fang!*" I screamed.

The force of electricity coursing through my body almost made my knees give out. They were here, trapped in the same place as us! Tears of joy streamed down my face as a hysterical fit of laughter took hold of me. Even the increase of voltage on my shock collar didn't quiet my manic cackling.

"Get them into cells *now*. Keep an eye on this one, she's going to be trouble," my escort instructed.

"Indeed she is," a familiar voice rasped behind me.

That voice…

My fits of laughter ceased immediately. All the joy I felt leached out of me. My spine turned into a steel rod holding me upright. The scent of cigar smoke wafted into my nostrils.

"Welcome home, my Diseased."

I spun around as best as I could with the soldier restraining me. My eyes locked with his. Commander Goldbrook smirked and blew out a puff of smoke as the soldier slammed the door to my cell shut.

CHAPTER 9

The walls of our cells were thick. Too thick to see each other through, too thick to hear each other clearly. My feet and hips were sore from pacing back and forth. The repeated shocks I received for screaming out to my brethren fried my vocal cords. What was going to happen now? Were we going to be stuck in the cells forever? Would we be experimented on? Would we be forced to become weapons and used in warfare? The stream of questions was an endless river which brought no answers with it.

Time becomes irrelevant when there's nothing to mark it with. Since we were underground, there was no visible rising and setting of the sun, just the constant glare of the overhead fluorescent lights. We were fed the same meal every day: a pile of mush guaranteed to provide us with enough vitamins, minerals, and calories that no one could accuse us of being malnourished if we escaped this place. I'd eaten nine piles of mush since I'd been here. As little as three days had gone by or as many as nine.

Most of my time was spent sleeping. My first instinct was to draw flaming pictures in the air when I was bored. Apparently, firelight was visible through the cell walls because I was electrocuted every time I tried. The realization sank in after my fourth attempt. Who could see the flames? How far did the light reach? I wish I knew Morse code. Then maybe Fang and I could communicate—

My God! Why hadn't I thought of that before? A barrage of thoughts flowed forth. Obviously, I couldn't ask for a book about Morse code. That would be too obvious. But how else would I be able to learn about it? I wracked my brain, straining to remember what I'd learned about Morse code in school. A phone rang outside of my cell and inspiration struck.

"Yes, Commander Goldbrook. The outbursts have ceased…Everyone seems to be adjusting to their new environment," one of our cell guards informed his superior.

"I want to speak to Commander Goldbrook!" I yelled. Was that ragged shrieking *my* voice? I banged my fists on the glass wall and made the metal bars on the opposite side of it rattle.

There was a pause, then the sound of keys jingling together and the tumblers on the lock to my cell scraping together. The cell door swung open and an irritated looking guard with a cell phone held to his ear stared at me.

"Haven't you learned to keep to yourself yet, Phoenix?"

Everyone in the DAO referred to us by our Gifts instead of our names.

"I want to speak with Commander Goldbrook."

"Commander Goldbrook doesn't have time for—" A grimace sharpened the annoyed look on the guard's face as he handed over his cell phone to me.

"What is it you have to say to me, little Phoenix?" Commander Goldbrook purred into my ear.

I swallowed the bile in the back of my throat before answering him. "I have a request. I want a book to read."

"Why would I give you something to read?"

"People in regular prisons get to read. I want a book, too."

"And what is this book you want to read?"

"I want to read a book about telegraphs. You know, like they used to use on ships."

I didn't dare breathe as his heavy pause dragged on between us. "Now why would you want a book like that?"

"I like learning about history. I remembered learning a little bit about it in school, when we were studying about the *Titanic*. I want to know why no one answered them."

Another drawn out pause. Could he already know what I was planning? Who was I to try to outsmart a man who was the head of a secret government agency? Tears pricked at the backs of my eyes as my hope abandoned me.

"All right, little Phoenix, I will allow you a book."

"Thank you, sir!" I said with a little too much enthusiasm.

The guard rolled his eyes and held his hand outstretched to me. He wanted his phone back. I spied the remote to the shock collars clenched in his other hand. I dropped the phone in his open palm as gingerly as I could. He slammed my cell door shut with a loud bang before continuing his conversation with Commander Goldbrook.

Eight more meals of gluey nutrient enriched slop were served to me before I got my book. I sat in the corner of my cell and read the book cover to cover before falling asleep. When I woke up, I read it again. It took reading the book ten times through and studying the sections about Morse code between six more meals for me to feel confident enough to attempt contacting Fang.

The walls of our cells were at least fifteen feet high,

but the walls didn't touch the ceiling. I could go the subtle route and bang on the wall, which would sound like a dull thud to Fang, if he could hear it at all. Then there was the more effective route. I could send up bursts of flames, which would surely get me punished. There was a good chance I'd be electrocuted for the thudding, too. My hand flittered unconsciously to my throat. Could my vocal chords handle any more damage? Probably not, but I had to try.

I raised my hands and dropped them to my sides several times before mustering up the courage to bang on the wall in front of me. The message was brief—the number eighty-eight, which meant love and kisses. Thankfully, my shock collar remained inactive. I paced back and forth and wrung my hands together as I waited for a reply.

No one heard me. Of course, they didn't. That's why the shock collar didn't go off. I sank to the floor and hugged my knees to my chest. A tear slid down my cheek, hot and stinging.

Suddenly, a rumbling came through the floor. It paused, and then it repeated. The third time the message came through, I was able to decipher it. *Who are you?* it asked. My heart beat faster in excitement. I banged out the Morse code for my first name and repeated the question asked of me to the message sender.

I held my breath as I waited for the reply. *Shaw.*

A maniacal laugh escaped me. From that simple answer, I knew we were all in this place together, possibly in the same room. Someone understood me. Shaw was the best one at making plans. No sooner had the laughter bubbled out of my chest, the shock collar buzzed a quick jolt into my system. It was a warning for me to shut up. But the soldiers hadn't heard our messages. Tears of joy streamed down my face, the loony smile left in the wake of my laughter splitting my chapped lips. I could only imagine how insane I looked. Surely, it would look like I belonged in an asylum now.

I banged a message back to Shaw. *What do we do?*

His reply was short and terrifying. *Melt the glass.*

How?

Fire, bravery, and strength.

It took me a few minutes to digest what he wanted me to do. Was my fire even hot enough to do that? I would definitely be electrocuted for that, and not the warning kind, either. Could I withstand that kind of pain while I drained every ounce of my energy melting my prison? And what about the metal bars beyond the glass?

When?

Now.

Now? My throat constricted and the muscles in my neck twitched beneath the shock collar. I inhaled deeply and closed my eyes. I needed something to focus on to make this fire hot enough. Like Shaw taught me to do, I focused on the flames beginning in my fingertips and spreading throughout my body until they consumed me. Then I projected the fire to surround me and pass through the glass walls. The exertion of pushing the flames through the glass made my muscles ache. Then the shock collar kicked in, causing me to seize up and my muscles to spasm uncontrollably. A cry of pain escaped me, barely audible past the flames and electricity popping in my ears.

I couldn't let the electricity take control of me. Electricity—Brandon—Images of Brandon gawking at me in the New England costal town while I burned green flames from his kiss, and when both our Gifts reacted on the widow's peak at Agatha's flooded my mind. Those moments felt like they happened a lifetime ago. Then it dawned on me.

I couldn't fight the electricity. I had to work with it,

use its heat and intensity to fuel my fire, just like Brandon's love fueled my drive.

I opened my eyes and found myself engulfed in a sea of green fire. My body twitched and writhed like a character in a horror movie. Well, if I didn't have control over my body, I had to have control over my mind. I closed my eyes again and focused on absorbing the electricity and using it to my benefit. The pressure inside my cell pushed in on me. I strained against it with all the strength I had in me. I opened my eyes again.

It all happened in slow motion. The green flames gave way to blindingly white ones that stung my eyes like staring directly into the sun. The pressure built steadily until I was sure I would implode. A crack formed in the glass in front of me. Suddenly, a shower of glass shards rained down on me. Muffled voices shouted as a siren began blaring and an overhead sprinkler system showered water down.

I accomplished my task, but what was supposed to happen now? My vision tunneled in as people began hovering over me. All of my energy was blasted away with the glass. My chest heaved as I gasped for air and caught sprays from the sprinkler system. Was I drowning? I submitted to the unconsciousness desperate to pull me under with it.

CHAPTER 10

I saw soldiers screaming and waving frantically at one another through the downpour of the sprinkler system. My comrades and other prisoners emerged from their cells looking like feral animals. Out of the corner of my eye, I saw Shaw directing people, or at least, I assumed he was. He was pointing and appeared to be yelling in the midst of the chaos. All I could hear was my heart pounding in my ears.

I stayed crumpled in a heap on the floor. Every ounce of my energy was gone. My mind screamed at my body to flee, but my body just couldn't respond. A soldier pointed his gun at me and fired, a snarl on his face as he pulled the trigger. How many times would I be shot this year?

The bullet bounced off of thin air and hit the ground. Strong arms banded around me. Before I realized what was happening, I was on Fang's back and we were running. His kinetic shield saved me from the bullet. I hugged him as tightly as I could in thanks. The vibration of his back alerted me that he was speaking, but I still couldn't hear.

Watching the prison break taking place while being bounced around on Fang's back was like watching one of those movies that was shot to look like an amateur filmmaker ran around with a hand-held cam recorder and submitted it to studios unedited. I buried my face in his shoulder and thought about what was happening. There had to be a reason Shaw wanted me to immediately break us free of our prisons. How was it that I managed to destroy the cells without destroying anything or anyone else? Where were we running to? How far behind us were the DAO agents? The torrent of questions made my head swim.

The muscles in Fang's back shifted. He was running on an incline. Surely we wouldn't be able to escape this secret military base. At least, not without killing anyone. Were my companions killing our captors? Shaw taught us in training we were supposed to disable our enemies, not exterminate them. He said if we killed them, we were no different than they painted us to be. He wanted to prove we were just like non-Gifted humans, that we weren't above the law. The other prisoners weren't exposed to Shaw's ideals, though. I was momentarily thankful my hearing was gone.

Abruptly, Fang glanced over his shoulder and stopped running. He let go of my legs and I did my best to wrap them around his middle so I wouldn't fall. His hands clasped the sides of his neck, fingers closing around his shock collar. My hands slid to his shoulders to give him space to work. The shock collar around my neck broke when I obliterated the glass cell walls. The veins in his hands and wrists rose up in his skin and his muscles tightened and bulged with his exertion. Finally, the collar snapped in half. He resumed his hold on me and kept running.

Chloe passed us, looking like a fairy as she darted around people. She yelled something over her shoulder and Fang nodded in response. He moved to the opposite side of the hallway from Chloe and pressed my back against the wall. I looked where we'd run from. A sea of soldiers in tan fatigues surged toward us. Why were we stopping now?

A solid wall of guns without people holding them appeared in front of the soldiers and began firing of their own accord. From behind the men ducking to avoid bullets, a blanket of blue-white lightning crackled across the ground, narrowly missing Fang's and Chloe's feet. Kelly and Brandon were all right! Tears pricked at the backs of my eyes, but I had no energy to cry.

Suddenly, the ground began shaking. I felt a shriek escape from my raw throat. Fang crouched low to the ground and centered his balance. Chloe followed suit. I couldn't recall hearing any reports of earthquakes in Nevada. So that must have been caused by one of the other Diseased imprisoned here.

When the earthquake subsided, most of the soldiers seemed to be immobilized, but not all of them. A handful of soldiers rose up from the heap on the floor and continued staggering toward us. Part of me was impressed by their commitment to protecting their country from what they'd been taught was a threat. The other part of me feared for our freedom and our lives. If we did manage to escape, wouldn't the desert claim us anyway?

Shaw, Brandon, Kelly, and a soldier closely followed by Leilani engaged in hand to hand combat with the remaining soldiers. She must have hypnotized the poor man. It was a good thing she was attractive so men and women alike would want to kiss her. She couldn't carry syringes of her saliva and needles around with her everywhere. Or maybe she should. If we ever escaped this place and the desert beyond, I'd have to mention it to Shaw.

As we started running again, the room went black.

Sparks showered from the overhead fluorescents as Brandon's electricity blew them out. Fang paused and turned around. A glow danced from side to side like a candle's flame in the breeze some distance away. As it came closer, the glow outlined two human shapes, one taller, one shorter. It must be Melody and Agatha. More figures followed behind Melody as she passed them. That still left Ophelia and Gareth unaccounted for. Where were they?

My consciousness faded in and out as our escape attempt continued. Fang seemed to run forever, his pace never slowing, even with my extra weight dragging him down. Thankfully, the rest of my comrades caught up with us. All except Ophelia and Gareth. My blood turned to ice as realization dawned on me. While the rest of our Gifts were valuable, being able to see the future and find anyone anywhere in the world were priceless gifts, especially to the DAO. If Commander Goldbrook had them, how would we find them?

Please, God, let them be safe.

Fang shifted me on his back as the floor's incline became steeper. We were almost free! This was a much shorter drive than it was a run.

My thundering heartbeat banged loud and clear in my ears, growing in volume as adrenaline surged through me. The proverbial light at the end of the tunnel was becoming less proverbial and more literal the more steps we took. Brandon ran past us, a glittering shock of electricity consuming him. A solid wall of blue-white light appeared in front of us. All my comrades skid to a stop as about twenty soldiers dropped to the ground, writhing in pain as the electric currents coursed through them.

Serves those bastards right after what they put us through.

Electric light gave way to natural sunlight as the

metal garage door slid up on its own. I suspected that was Kelly's doing. Brandon's light show disabled the electronic keypads which kept the doors locked. Shaw set to work hotwiring the Humvees parked in the garage. Leilani followed suit. Of all my comrades, Leilani was about the last one I would've thought had the knowledge to hotwire a car. Who knew what she learned in the DAO's militia, though?

Brandon jumped into the driver's seat of a running Humvee and waved Fang and me over to him. Fang set me down gently in the back seat. After offering me a weak smile, he closed the door and took a seat next to Brandon in the front. Kelly was in the back seat with me. He squeezed my hand lightly as we started driving forward. Shaw, Agatha, Melody, Leilani, and Chloe were in another vehicle. As usual, Shaw led the way.

Thankfully, my heartbeat quieted its frantic rhythm. The sound of my pounding heart was replaced by the engine's humming. Soon, voices accompanied the engine noise.

"What do you think happened to them?" Brandon asked quietly. His tone was too calm. We all knew well that his combat training was dominating his actions now, but inside he was distraught, just like the rest of us were.

"Considering they're still with Commander Goldbrook, nothing good," Kelly shuddered.

I'd never had the courage to ask Kelly about his time in the DAO. I wasn't sure he even remembered it since he was under Leilani's brainwashing most of the time he was there. But he had to remember. I remembered what happened while I was under her influence. I doubted it was a topic he'd enjoy rehashing, though.

Fang turned in his seat so he could see me better. "How are you faring, Miss Sable?"

A few choking noises managed to squeeze out of my

fried vocal cords, but no words. I grimaced and tilted my hand back and forth in the air to say "so-so." Fang nodded before turning back in his seat so he faced the correct direction.

"Where did Shaw say we was headed?" Fang asked.

"According the maps he managed to swipe, Vegas isn't too far from here, so I think that's where we're going," Brandon answered.

How much of this escape was planned before Shaw told me to set fire to the cells?

"We don't have any money, though," Kelly pointed out.

"You know he always has a way of accessing more," Brandon countered.

This was true. I knew Shaw was wealthy due to an inheritance from his deceased parents, but it seemed like it was an unlimited well of cash that people rarely dared to dream existed.

"He mention where we're staying?"

"You mean if we're staying on or off the strip? No idea. It's a fine line between blending in and overexposure. But I guess there're all kinds of random people there, so I don't think we'd stick out, necessarily."

"Even though we're all burned around the neck?"

Kelly made a good point. It was harder to make out on Fang's skin because it was so dark, but everyone except Brandon had a ring of angry red blisters that encircled our throats.

"I didn't think of that."

"Some protégé you are," Kelly ribbed.

"You're lucky you're back there and I'm up here or else I'd punch you," Brandon said wryly.

Boys, boys, can't we just have some peace for five minutes?

The atmosphere in the Humvee became heavy and

pensive as we all wondered what was next and how we were going to find Gareth and Ophelia. A familiar ache bloomed in my chest as I thought about them. Was this my life now, an ever revolving door of people I got close to being snatched away by people with sinister intentions and those of us left mustering up what was left of ourselves to go on rescue missions? What would happen when we couldn't save someone? What would happen when we couldn't save ourselves? How far was I willing to go for "the cause?"

Exhaustion replaced my earlier adrenaline rush, making my limbs and my head heavy. I blinked sleepily as we turned onto the highway. A mileage sign informed us that Las Vegas was fifty miles away and a town called Kingman in Arizona was one hundred fifty-two miles away. Surely a little sleep would do me some good. My eyelids fluttered closed as I wondered if the glittering lights of the Vegas strip would be as impressive in person as they were in pictures.

CHAPTER 11

As Fang carried me over the threshold of my hotel room, my eyes practically fell out of my head. Sure, I'd seen pictures of many of the hotels on the Vegas strip from my estranged parents' vacation photos, but I'd never experienced such opulence that the Bellagio Hotel boasted. I literally gagged as the desk clerk informed Shaw of the price tag for five rooms for four nights. Before that, I was wondering if staying in one place for that long was wise, considering we'd just escaped from a secret military base. Now, I wished I lived here.

A king sized bed sat directly in my line of sight, adorned with cream colored linens and more pillows than any one person would ever need. The walls were swirled with beige and mocha tones. Opposite from the hotel room door was a large picture window dressed with heavy dark brown curtains. A flat screen television hung on the wall opposite the bed.

Oh, the bed! Fang set me down gently on top of it. I could never remember a time when I slept on a mattress that was like sleeping on a cloud. A groan of appreciation sounded low in my throat. Fang chuckled as he smoothed the hair out of my face.

"I take it you'll be just fine then, Miss Sable?"

"After a hot bath, I'll be in heaven," was my garbled reply. My vocal cords were taking a long time to recover from their abuse.

"I'll take that as my cue to leave. If you need anything, Shaw and me are just across the hall."

I nodded and offered a weak smile. Fang returned my nod with one of his own before departing.

As much as I hated the thought of ever getting out of this bed, I very desperately needed a shower. A pang of loss hit me as I begrudgingly went to explore the bathroom. The accommodations in the bathroom were just as luxurious as they were in the bedroom. A large marble sink stood on the left wall. On the adjacent wall was a marble soaking tub. A glass walled shower and a toilet were on the same wall as the door. Linens lined the right wall.

Immediately, I turned the hot water knob on full blast in the soaking tub. I closed the bathroom door so the steam from the water would envelop me. As the water filled the tub, I removed my grimy white prison jump suit. I wished I could discard it, but it was the only clothing I had. This was becoming a too familiar scenario in my life, having only one set of horrendously ugly clothing. Part of me was sure Shaw would correct this problem in the morning, but I felt guilty counting on that.

I settled into the steaming hot bath water and let out a moan. My eyes closed as I leaned my head back against the edge of the tub. As the heat opened the pores in my skin and soaked into my aching bones, I considered what I might be doing if I was a normal teenage girl. I certainly wouldn't be running from the government and hiding out in a five star hotel. My parents would probably be asking me about what I wanted to do for my birthday. It was two weeks away now. I would probably choose the same thing I always did—dinner at an Italian restaurant with them. I never really had any friends I wanted to invite. I preferred being alone then.

Now I had no parents, but I'd gained a new kind of family. I had an older brother who would take a bullet for me, or stop it in midair, since he could do that. I had an incredible boyfriend I loved with all my heart. Shaw was like a wise old uncle who busted your chops to motivate you to be a better version of yourself. The rest, I guessed, were sort of like cousins. And of course, there was my best friend, the first and only best friend I'd ever had.

An icy shiver ran down my spine as I thought of Ophelia. Where was she? Was she all right? Was Gareth taking care of her? Could he?

I wasn't sure if the water in the tub had gone cold or if my dark thoughts made me feel chilled from the inside out. Either way, I didn't want to wash in lukewarm water. I pulled the drain plug out, causing a miniature whirlpool to form as the water drained out of the tub. Quickly, I washed myself in the shower. The last bit of water in the tub swirled down the drain with a loud gurgle as I stepped out of the shower.

As I finger combed through my hair, I wiped the steam fog off the bathroom mirror with my towel. While I didn't appear malnourished, I looked unhealthy. Part of that would rectify itself with a little makeup and grooming. The part that lingered was the angry red ring encircling my throat. I noticed that the burn marks from my shock collar were worse than the ones on the rest of my comrades. To the average passerby, it probably looked like I tried to hang myself and failed. A smirk played on my lips as I wondered vaguely if we appeared like some sort of sadist cult to strangers. I doubted Agatha could get some of her magic herbs in Las Vegas to heal us all. Perhaps if we were in New Orleans instead…

Just as I finished tying the belt on my plush Bellagio bathrobe, a knock sounded at my door. I padded over to the door with a longing backward glance at the bed. Gazing through the peephole in the door, I saw Brandon standing on the other side. I grin broke out on my face and I opened the door.

"Can I come in?"

"Would I have opened the door if I didn't want you to?" I rasped.

He smiled a strained sort of smile at me. "I suppose not."

I frowned after him as he walked through the doorway and settled into one of the armchairs sitting in front of the picture window. The door snapped shut behind me as I followed his lead and took a seat in the remaining armchair. We sat in silence for a long while. What was on his mind?

When I determined he wasn't going to start a conversation anytime soon, I opened the curtains and looked down at the Vegas Strip below. My room was high above the street, so the Strip itself seemed to be alive, swaying slowly to the glittering city's rhythm. The Bellagio's fountain was just finishing its latest round of synchronization of lights and music. Undoubtedly, people on the street were clapping appreciatively at the spectacle.

"There's so much going on down there," I murmured.

Brandon nodded in agreement.

"I'll bet there's more going on inside your head, though."

"You should rest your voice, Sable."

"Really, it sounds worse than it feels."

It was a small lie. It still felt like I was choking on acid, but Brandon didn't need to know that. Clearly, he felt guilty enough already, although I couldn't imagine why. If we'd been inside Agatha's house when it was at-tacked instead of a few yards away, we would still have been captured and imprisoned. I also knew Brandon took everyone's safety as a personal mission.

Deciding on a semi-brazen move, I got up from my chair and sat on Brandon's lap without asking. He stiff-ened at the contact with me at first. Just as I began to wonder if I should've stayed put, he wrapped his arms around me, crushing me to his chest, and buried his face in my neck. "Sable, I was so afraid you were going to die!"

I sucked in a breath and blinked. What was I sup-posed to say to that? I decided on a lame, "I didn't."

"Shaw shouldn't have asked that of you."

"We'd still be trapped if he hadn't."

He placed a soft kiss at the base of my throat, careful not to touch the burns. "My freedom, or anyone else's freedom, is not worth your death."

"What if death was my only freedom?" Wow, this conversation was becoming increasingly morbid by the minute. I'd have to steer this in another direction before Brandon lost all sense of his rationale.

He gasped. His eyes were wide and wild with anxie-ty. "Why would you say something like that?"

I smoothed my hand through his hair, brushing one of the curls at his temple back toward his ear. "I shouldn't have. Forget I said it."

"Sable—"

The only thing I knew to do to distract him from his troubled thoughts was to kiss him. Gingerly, I placed my lips against his and applied some pressure. His breath caught in his throat as I pulled away from his face enough to look him in the eyes.

We stared at one another. His tension from stress and fear evolved slowly into a magnetic charge between us.

Heat sparkled in his eyes, drawing me back to him. I kept my gaze locked with his as I pressed our lips together again.

His hold on me tightened as the hold on his control snapped. Kisses rained all over my face, my ears, my neck. He forged a scorching trail over my collar bone with his lips as my fingers tangled in the hair at the nape of his neck.

"Brandon!" I gasped as he lifted me off of the armchair and placed me on the bed.

The robe pooled around me, exposing my naked thigh. Shyness stole over me and caused my skin to feel hot and prickly.

He stood over me, his eyes hooded and bright with electrical current. My heart never beat so fast in my life. Slowly, so unbearably slowly, he climbed up my body, resting his atop mine.

Inside, I was burning with sweet agony. My skin was stretched tight over my muscles and bones, hyper sensitive to the slightest exhalation Brandon made.

He dipped his head low, placing a kiss on the corner of my jaw next to my ear. His whispered declaration set off an inferno inside me. "I love you."

We became a tangled mass of limbs, lips, and tongues. In that moment, he was more necessary to my existence than oxygen. Briefly, I blinked my eyes open and found us consumed in a cloud of green fire and blindingly bright white electrical current. I pushed on Brandon's shoulders, and he immediately withdrew from me.

"What's wrong?"

"We're going to burn this place down." Thankfully, I sounded more breathy than raspy.

"As long as I burn with you," he muttered as he kissed my cheek.

I smirked. "How very Romeo and Juliet of you."

"We won't become a tragedy of martyrdom."

"Good."

He lay down next to me and held me in his arms. I could think of nothing that personified perfection more than being in his arms on this heavenly mattress. I let out a contented sigh.

"Brandon, can I ask you something?"

"What?"

"Will you stay with me tonight? Please?"

He smiled as he drew me in closer to him. "I supposed Kelly wouldn't mind having the room to himself."

"You don't think he'll wonder about you being lost, will he?"

He let out a snort. "I doubt anyone would accuse me of being missing if you weren't reported as missing first."

My cheeks heated with embarrassment. "Are we really that awful?"

"It's not like they're watching or anything. Besides, the only one you'd have to worry about is Chloe."

"I think you would have to worry about her. I'd have to worry about Melody."

"Why would you worry about Melody?"

"She's not exactly my biggest fan."

"Don't worry about her. She's my past, and you are the one who matters to me now."

"I can sympathize with her, though."

He frowned. "What do you mean?"

"If I ever lost you, I would fight to get you back, too. I love you too much to just walk away from you and cut my losses."

"Thankfully, you'll never have to experience that first hand. I'm not going anywhere unless you don't want to be with me anymore."

I let out a humorless laugh. "That would never happen."

"Let's hope not."

The bone weariness I felt when we arrived in Vegas returned to me as the unreasonably comfortable mattress beckoned me to sleep. A yawn escaped me and I laid my head down on Brandon's chest.

"Let's go out for a night on the town." I could tell by the tone of his voice that he was grinning.

I smacked him on the shoulder. "Shut up."

"Would you at least let me suggest the use of blankets? They look pretty nice."

That was true. We covered ourselves with the soft bed dressings and resumed our position of my head on his chest. As I closed my eyes, I imagined Brandon and me walking hand in hand down the Vegas Strip, blending in as a part of the living ribbon winding its way between hotels, restaurants, casinos, and gift shops. It would be a small piece of normalcy amidst all the chaos perpetually surrounding us.

I wondered sleepily about Shaw's plans for us here, or if the purpose of our stint in one of the biggest tourist destinations was to come up with a plan about what to do next. What would we do? Again I wondered how it was we were supposed to rescue Ophelia and Gareth when they were the ones best equipped to find a missing person. My heart grew heavy as reality settled around me like an impending hurricane. It was nice to be lost in a reverie with Brandon, but there was still so much we needed to accomplish.

This was why Shaw made the plans. He was level headed and unemotional in his logic. It wasn't that he was uncaring, but his drive to complete a mission outweighed his emotional responses to anything. Yet, the way Agatha saw him—it reminded me of how I looked at Brandon. Perhaps she knew something about him the rest of us didn't. It was hard to say.

Despite my utter exhaustion, it took a long time before Brandon's steady breathing and quiet snoring lulled me to sleep.

CHAPTER 12

Bang! Bang! Bang!

"Brandon, get your lazy ass out of bed!" The demand came from Chloe.

As I sleepily blinked open my eyes, the corners of my lips turned upward into a smile. I didn't think there would ever be a time when I fell asleep with Brandon that Chloe wouldn't wake us up in a fit of rage.

The clock on the bedside table read 1:30 pm. When had we fallen asleep last night?

Bang! Bang! Bang!

"Sable, you should call hotel security. There's a crazy redhead outside your door causing quite a racket," Brandon yelled in the direction of the door.

"So help me, God, I will kick in this door—"

"Shut up!" I hissed as I threw the door open. Chloe pushed past me and strode into my room, heels clicking on the marble floor as she went.

So Shaw had had our wardrobe restocked. As Chloe made it her mission to beat Brandon to death with a pillow, I looked in my closet. A duffel bag and enough clothes, suited to my tastes, for a week were inside. Brandon's clothes were in my closet, too, along with another duffel bag. How had these appeared here? It unnerved me a bit that I slept so deeply I hadn't noticed someone enter my room and stock my closet. Had Brandon?

"Chloe, I can't get up if you're determined to pulverize me into this mattress!" Brandon protested. I knew he could easily outmaneuver his sister, but he would never lay a hand on her.

His logic seemed to jar Chloe from her rampage. She tossed her bright red locks over her shoulder and turned on her heel. Before slamming the hotel room door shut behind her, she informed us that we were to meet Shaw in the lobby in five minutes.

I dashed into the bathroom with the first outfit I grabbed out of the closet—a black T-shirt with red rhinestone lip prints on the front and horizontal tears up and down the back of it, a red satin camisole, and acid washed skinny jeans. A hairbrush, two toothbrushes, toothpaste, and a small makeup kit sat on the bathroom counter.

I brushed my hair, brushed my teeth, applied clear lip gloss, and rimmed my eyes with smudged black eyeliner in record time. I pulled my black high top Chuck Taylors on in the elevator.

As the elevator cruised smoothly down to the first floor, I studied myself in the reflection of the elevator doors. My hair fell around me in a fuzzy chocolate-brown curtain. I really needed to pick up a wide tooth comb somewhere. Otherwise, I decided I didn't look too bad for getting dressed and ready in four minutes. When we arrived on the first floor and the elevator doors opened, Brandon and I sprinted toward the lobby. I bumped into an older woman dressed in designer labels from head to toe in my haste. I apologized quickly, but my voice was drowned out by the yapping white Pomeranian in her arms. She scowled at me, causing Brandon and me both to laugh as he caught me by the wrist and dragged me in the direction of our destination.

"You're late," Shaw grumbled as we skidded to a halt behind Melody and Kelly.

"Sorry," I muttered.

"We have business to attend to," Shaw explained, before turning on his heel and leading us out of the Bellagio.

The streets were just as crowded and noisy as they'd been the night before. We walked in pairs, except Fang, who brought up the rear, following Shaw and Agatha to an unknown location. All the different smells wafting through the air from the many restaurants and buffets we passed made my mouth water and my stomach grumble. Hopefully, wherever we were going had food.

You would walk right past the smoke shop we stopped at if you weren't looking for it. The hole in the wall was called "Redman's." Why were we at a smoke shop? There was nothing to eat here! Well, nothing I wanted to sample, anyhow.

"Gus! It's me, Aggie!" she called into the cramped space. It was really a wonder we could get all nine of us in here. We were squeezed between a glass display case holding different smoking accessories and herb like substances and storage shelves with water pipes and other smoking memorabilia on it.

A weathered old man squeezed his way out of the back room door and scowled down at Agatha. His salt and pepper hair was fastened with leather cords with brown feathers on the ends in twin braids as thick as ropes that fell over his shoulders. Deep wrinkles carved lines in his dark face, making him appear as worn as the tan leather vest he wore over a dark green long sleeved cotton shirt. Brown suede beaded moccasins and stiff blue jeans completed his ensemble.

"You know you aren't supposed to come around here, Agatha," he wheezed, his deep set onyx colored eyes boring into her.

Agatha chuckled and patted him on the arm. He promptly crossed his arms over his chest. "You know I wouldn't have if it wasn't an emergency. Is he here?"

"Of course, he is. He never leaves."

Gus squeezed back through the back room door and waved a hand behind him, indicating that we should follow. How would we possibly fit in the storage room when the front room was so cramped?

The back storage room was as tiny as I imagined it would be, but the living space beyond it was surprisingly spacious. Sandalwood incense hung heavy in the air. I resisted the urge to choke on the overpowering scent. A futon and a trundle bed served as the furniture accompanying a television set that had to be at least twenty years old. A black bear skin area rug, complete with head and paws, took up most of the space on the floor. Two fluorescent strip lights provided the room's only light source.

Gus took a seat on the futon next to an unmoving man. He looked quite a bit younger than Gus, possibly middle aged like Shaw. A brown Fedora hat shrouded most of the man's features in shadow, but his sharp cheekbones were still visible. He put a tobacco pipe to his lips and lit it. The dried plant began to smoke and the mystery man inhaled deeply from it.

'Agatha, how nice of you to drop by. And you brought visitors with you this time. How charming.'

My jaw dropped open. I heard him speaking to Agatha *inside my head.* I looked at my fellow comrades to see if they experienced something similar. From their bemused expressions, I assumed they had.

"It's nice to see you, too, Marshall."

'I gather this isn't just a pleasant visit then. So

you've finally seen the inside of Area 51. I'm a little sur-prised it took Goldbrook so long to round you all up there. Then again, you do have a rather...spirited...bunch here.'

Marshall took another long drag from his pipe and blew the smoke out in rings. His subsequent chuckle was raspy, just like his speaking voice rasped in a way that made it seem like he was clawing through your mind.

"You could address us aloud, Marshall. Leave the children to themselves." Though Agatha's request was worded kindly enough, her tone was decidedly curt.

'You know I haven't spoken aloud in years, Aggie. I doubt if I still have a voice left to speak with. As for your children, *they seem pretty grown up to me. Then again, the Gifted children are often forced to grow up faster than the non-Gifted ones. You've come to ask for my as-sistance, is that right?'*

"If you already know what it is we came to ask of you, you should either accept or reject our request. Time is of the essence, now more than ever, and we've very little to waste," Shaw explained.

'I see that you've lost your psychics. Such a pity. They would have come in handy in these times of crisis. But that's why you want my help, isn't it? You want me to jump through a few minds, scramble some memories, and give you information of their whereabouts. That's a nice sentiment, but what's in it for me?'

Marshall let out a violent hacking cough before look-ing up at Shaw and smirking. A cloudy film covered his aqua irises. The part in his lips revealed decaying teeth. White blond stubble covered his chin and his cheeks. Plumes of dust wafted from his brown duster jacket when he coughed. How long had it been since this man moved from his futon? Everything about him made my skin crawl.

"What is it that you want?" Agatha asked.

'*When we find them, I want one and you can have the other.*'

"Absolutely not!" Shaw barked.

A throaty chuckle rumbled through my conscious mind. '*I'll let them choose which one wants to come with me. I can see how you're unable to choose between them. What's interesting, though, is that you're basing their value on the people they are and not the Gifts they possess or any other attributes. That's definitely not how I'd decide if I was in your shoes. These kids could really be great if you utilized them properly.*'

Various shouts of protest arose from my comrades ranging from astonished gasps to streams of profanity.

"So all those people who abused me to see what I was capable of are the ones who 'utilized me properly'? Shaw was being too soft when he taught me how to defend myself and how to extend the flames from my palms throughout the rest of my body? How would you have done it? Would you have thrown me out on the curb immediately because I wasn't good enough or would you put me through all kinds of hell for the sake of making me a better soldier?"

Me. And. My. Damn. Mouth. After all the times I'd gotten into trouble growing up for not being able to keep my opinions to myself, you would think I would've learned to rein it in a little. Apparently, that wasn't so.

The chuckle became grumbling laughter in my head. '*That's rather appropriate, a fiery attitude to go along with your Gift of being a Phoenix. I'd call you Spitfire instead of Sable if you were under my command. To answer your real question, which was not any of the ones you yelled at me aloud, I would not treat you like Doctor Pantiel.*'

A tremor ran down my spine at the unwelcome

memory of being a human test subject.

'*Yes, Spitfire, I can see all of that in your mind. Just because I operate differently from your beloved Shaw does not make me evil...*'

I was distracted from the dialogue in my head when I noticed everyone else paying attention to whatever Gus was saying.

'*You know, that's rude of you to tune out while I'm talking to you. Yes, you're the only one who can hear me right now. Gus knows where to pick up the conversation so the others aren't standing around in awkward silence while we have this little talk. Like I was saying before you stopped paying attention, different does not automatically equate with wrong or bad. Shaw and I mean to achieve the same ends, we just have different methods of going about getting what we want. Shaw uses able bodied youngsters such as you to be used as weapons when there is no other way out of a situation. I prefer a more offensive tactic. The situation as it stands calls for me to recruit people with their Gifts well established and under control.*

'*We are not freaks meant to be experimented on and controlled by the government, or by anyone else. We are an enhanced version of the human race. The non-Gifted fear their extinction is coming ever closer as the number of Gifted people grows. People fear what they do not understand, so they give us the derogatory label of* Diseased *and teach the rest of the non-Gifted population to fear us.*'

Since Marshall could apparently comb through my mind without consent, I decided to answer him in my head since Gus was still droning on with whatever he was talking about. '*So if you want the same thing as Shaw, that means you want us all seen as equals? The Gifted and the non-Gifted?*'

'*Ah, but we aren't equal. The Gifted are more. We cannot and should not have to pretend to be lesser beings to spare the non-Gifted's feelings of being inferior. It's…interesting…that Shaw would have you believe this is his motive. What it all comes down to is the guarantee of our preservation. We cannot allow ourselves to become snuffed out. He thinks merely preaching about equality will make the non-Gifted listen, make them trust us. I know better. I wasn't born blind and deaf-mute. I was made that way through experimentation to heighten my psychic sensibilities through the deprivation of my other senses. They must learn the error of their ways.*

'*Now, if I may address the rest of the class…*'

From the corner of my eye, I noticed Gus's mouth stop moving. What kind of link was between them?

'*Agatha, I will offer you a bonus piece of information if our trade is agreed upon. You want to know why the bond between Sable and Brandon is so uniquely strong? You're part of the way there to figuring out the answer. I commend you for being on the right track, but this goes far deeper than most anyone could conceive. Do we have a deal?*'

My heart stopped beating as I waited for Shaw to answer him. As much as I wanted to know about this bond between Brandon and me, it wasn't worth finding out if it meant sacrificing one of my comrades to this man who was clearly bent on getting revenge against the non-Gifted population.

If Brandon didn't have an ironclad grip on my waist, I surely would've collapsed to the floor.

"I'll do it. Now how are we going to find Gareth and Ophelia?"

CHAPTER 13

While Shaw, Marshall, Agatha, and Gus discussed a strategy of how to find our kidnapped comrades, the rest of us were instructed to make our way back to the Bellagio. We all took turns ranting about our strange encounter the entire way there. If I wasn't so heated by Marshall's opinions, I'd be more surprised that Chloe and I were on the same side of an argument for once.

"Where the hell does that guy get off saying all that crap? I've been on the other side of that training. I know what it's like for people to abuse you for your Gifts and not bat an eyelash. They call it 'justice' when it's really just imprisonment and exploitation!" Chloe raged. Leilani and Kelly nodded in agreement. They, too, had been puppets of the DAO.

"How are we supposed to buy that Marshall and Shaw have the same idea of how the world should embrace us? Clearly Marshall wants the non-Gifted to see us as superior. Shaw always taught us that we were equals to them. He said that some people had the gift of words, others the gift of numbers, and still others with the gift of music. Our Gifts just manifested in a more physical manner," Kelly noted.

We stopped outside the front doors of the Bellagio where the limousines pulled up to drop off their passengers. It would be too quiet inside the lobby to continue our conversation without being overheard. The Vegas Strip provided better concealment from eavesdroppers.

"There's really nothing we can do until Shaw and Agatha come back and tell us what they've worked out with that egomaniac. We might as well do something to relax," Melody suggested.

As much as I hated to admit it, she was right. I tried to sound neutral instead of annoyed when I addressed her. "What would you suggest?"

"Well, since Fang's the only one old enough to gamble, why don't we go swimming? The hotel has a heated indoor pool. I doubt a lot of people will be there in the middle of the day. My new wardrobe Shaw ordered has a swimsuit in it, so I'd guess all of yours do, too."

The idea seemed agreeable to the group, so we headed off to our rooms to change and planned to meet up with each other at the pool.

When I got to my room, I rummaged around in the dresser drawer with my delicates and found a black bikini with tiny silver lightning bolts patterned on it. Just like everything else Shaw ordered for me, it fit perfectly, accentuating what little curves I had. The depressing realization that Melody's bombshell body would look every bit as flattered in her swimsuit deflated my spirits a bit. I threw on a pair of black plastic flip flops and one of the Bellagio's bath robes and headed for our recreational rendezvous.

Fang, Brandon, and Kelly were already at the pool when I arrived. With a quick glance around, I noticed no one else was there. Melody was right about the rest of the tourists participating in other activities during the day. It was close to the dinner hour, after all.

Fang and Brandon were dressed in knee length swim trunks—forest camouflage and navy, respectively—while Kelly wore white square leg briefs with red piping.

"Kelly, where are your glasses?" I asked.

Brandon laughed. "He's dressed in that hot little number and that's all you notice is his lack of eyewear?"

"I have contacts in," Kelly answered.

He flushed a little, so I stopped my inquiry. But why would he choose to wear glasses when he had contacts? Wouldn't it be easier to train without worrying about breaking your frames or lenses?

My inner monologue ceased as Melody, Chloe, and Leilani entered the pool room. As I already knew, Melody looked like a total knockout in her very tiny candy apple red bikini that showed off the swallows tattooed on her pelvis. It was one of those swimsuits that a practical girl would wonder how that little fabric could possibly cost what the asking price was. Chloe looked equally fantastic in her '60s vintage style emerald green strapless one piece. Leilani's exotic islander features were equally stunning in a modern lemon yellow one piece that was slit down to her navel with a gold ring pulling the fabric together at the base of her cleavage.

"I'm not sure how he does it, but Shaw always manages to make us all look damn flawless!" Melody purred while twirling. I guess she didn't want to deprive us of the view of her rear.

"Well, let's get our swim on!" Brandon declared before doing a running cannon ball into the deep end of the pool. Water splashed high into the air before sloshing onto the concrete floor. Chloe followed her brother in, but opted to enter with a graceful dive instead.

I wanted my hair out of my face before I jumped in, too. I made quick work of French braiding my hair down the back of my head.

Brandon looked like I just performed an elaborate magic trick instead of a simple hairstyle. "How did you do that without looking?"

I shrugged. "Practice?"

His amazed stare turned into a smirk of satisfaction. What was that about?

Splash!

Fang pushed me into the pool. My head popped above the water a few moments later. I shoved a wave of water in Fang's direction as he jumped in after me.

The two hours we'd spent in the pool was the most relaxed I'd ever seen any of these people. We had chicken fights, Chloe made water balls and threw them at us, and we all raced laps against each other. Fang and I won the chicken fight. Leilani won the lap swimming competition.

Every now and then during our breather, a flitting thought of regret would pass through my mind that Ophelia and Gareth weren't here to enjoy this experience with us. They deserved this moment of carefree abandon, too.

When we were all sufficiently prune skinned and famished, we rinsed off in the showers located near the entrance to the pool room. I noticed Chloe peering at Leilani while I waited for Melody to finish using the shower. Chloe watched as Leilani combed her fingers through her hair and water from the shower ran down her curves in rivulets. It was the same way Leilani stared at Chloe when she thought no one was watching her. It was how I stared at Brandon.

As everyone crowded into the elevator to get washed and dressed for dinner, I pulled Melody back. Brandon shot a puzzled glance my way.

I waved at him nonchalantly. "We'll get the next one. Girl talk and all that."

I smiled as the elevator doors closed.

Melody crossed her arms over her chest and tapped her foot impatiently. "We don't girl talk with each other."

"True, but I need your help with something."

"Need advice about Brandon? Sorry, sweetheart, but you're going to have to figure that out on your own." Melody's tone was sweet and nauseating to listen to.

Since I still needed her help, I ignored her comment. "Actually, it's with his sister."

"I can't get her to like you, either."

The elevator doors opened and I followed Melody inside.

"I want you to help me set Chloe up with Leilani."

At least that shut her up for a minute.

"What makes you think Chloe would be into Leilani or vice versa?"

"Look, I've seen them checking each other out more than once. They deserve some happiness, too, don't they? I can talk to Leilani and you can talk to Chloe. Maybe we can fan the flames between them a little."

Melody sighed, resigned. "I guess if it gets her off her current dead end crush, it's worth a shot. All right, Sable, I'll help you. But it's for Chloe, not for you."

Bitch. "Thank you."

I knew Chloe's current crush was me, thanks to Brandon. Extinguishing her flame for me was a perk I hadn't considered before.

The elevator stopped at our floor. Melody pushed past me and sauntered toward her room. Fang was waiting for me as I stepped into the hallway.

"What was all that about, Miss Sable?"

I grinned. "Just trying to play matchmaker a little bit."

"You noticed how Kelly eyes Miss Melody, too, huh?"

My jaw practically hit the floor, causing Fang to

chuckle. I loved that sound. "I was trying to set up Chloe and Leilani. Kelly's into Melody?"

"Is it really that shocking? She's a nice looking girl. She may not treat you so good, but she's good to everyone else."

"But she's still hung up on Brandon. How would we convince her to consider Kelly?"

"Brandon might help. I reckon that might make his life a little easier if he don't have to worry about you and her not seeing eye to eye."

I stretched up on my tip toes and kissed Fang on the cheek. "You're always the voice of reason, you know that?"

He chuckled again. "I just been around and seen a lot is all."

We arrived at my room. Ever the gentleman, Fang waited until I was at my door before he left for his.

Playing Cupid for people left me feeling surprisingly light. As I scrubbed the stench of chlorine off of my skin and out of my hair, I decided I wanted to dress nicely for dinner. Hopefully there was a dress somewhere in my closet.

I kept it classic when I applied my makeup—nude eye shadow, black liner, black mascara, a pinch of blush, and ruby red lips. Finger combing through my hair while blow drying it left it coiled in tiny spiral curls cascading over my shoulders and spilling down my back. I squealed with elation when I discovered that there indeed was a dress in my wardrobe. It was a shade of purple so dark that it almost appeared black. The back tied up from the small of my back to the top of the dress with black satin ribbon like a corset. A sweetheart neckline without straps or sleeves completed the constructed look. The hem dropped just below my knees.

I blew myself a kiss in the mirror as I studied the

way the silky fabric clung to my frame like a glove would my hand. A pair of black stiletto cage heels completed my ensemble.

Everyone agreed to meet in the lobby so we could decide what to eat. I was the last person to arrive. A broad grin broke over Fang's face as I approached my comrades. Brandon gaped at me. I think Melody did, too, but I was too focused on Brandon to pay her any serious attention.

"Took you long enough," Chloe grumbled as I came within earshot of the group.

"Sorry."

I knew I didn't look very sorry. I couldn't stop smiling. The idea of my potential love matches combined with Brandon's still stunned expression left me practically incandescent.

Everyone else was dressed much more casually than I was. Leilani wore a dress, too. She looked much more laid back in her printed maxi dress than I did in this slinky number.

"Well, did you guys decide where we should go?" I asked.

"We were going to try out the buffet here," Leilani answered.

"Shall we?" Brandon stood and offered his arm to me. I took it and giggled. As we followed the others to the buffet, he whispered conspiratorially, "Fang filled me in on your love mission. Very nice."

"Thanks."

"And you look—wow."

Despite the fact that gravity kept my feet on the ground, I was floating on air. "So you're going to talk to Melody?"

"I'll talk to them both independently. Once Chloe is on board with the whole her and Leilani love connection,

I'll have her start working on Kelly. Not that I think he needs much convincing to begin with. He had the hots for her when she and I were together. He never said anything to me about it because he's too decent a guy, but I suspected it and Chloe confirmed it. That's hard to deal with when your best friend wants your girlfriend. Now my sister wants my girlfriend. I wonder if that means I have good taste or bad taste in women—"

I smacked Brandon's arm, half playful and half annoyed. It wasn't my favorite topic when he talked about him and Melody being an item.

"Ow! Okay, okay, I'll shut up! Or I can just talk about how gorgeous you look."

"Flattery won't get you very far, Mr. Harper."

"As long as it keeps my foot in the door, that's all that matters."

His grin always made him look so attractive. Not that he needed any help in that department.

We all stuffed ourselves at the buffet. The food reminded me of how Brandon cooked for us on the *Kandis Amelia*. I could imagine him cooking in a place like this after he made a name for himself in Paris, had his Gift not forced him to abandon his culinary dreams. My favorite dishes were the prosciutto wrapped asparagus and the miniature key lime cheesecakes.

After the great meal and the much needed leisure time earlier, I was exhausted. I dreaded having to wash my face before I got into bed. The linens were too fine a quality for me to mar with my laziness. I kicked off my heels when I got back into my room before I peeled off my dress and slipped on a comfortable tank top and cotton sleep shorts. Even though the mattress called to me, I made good on the promise to myself to wash away all my makeup before laying down on it.

I welcomed sleep with open arms. I sank deeper into

the mattress as unconsciousness beckoned me. Just when I hovered on the precipice of sleeping and wakefulness, a sharp rapping sounded at my door. I groaned in protest, but the insistent knocking continued.

"What?" I whined as I dragged myself out of bed and over to the door. Chloe stood on the other side, her hand suspended in midair as she stopped short from knocking on me now that the door was opened.

"Shaw and Agatha are back. We need to talk strategy."

It's funny how quickly tiredness abandons you when the idea of finding your missing best friend opens a floodgate of adrenaline.

CHAPTER 14

Brandon

The news that Shaw and Agatha returned with Marshall and Gus had us all on edge. This scenario was all too familiar to me now. Someone goes missing, chaos ensues, so on and so forth. It seemed like this was only a shock to Sable and Melody now. Melody had only been separated from us once. Sable had been through most of the same losses I had, but each new blow was as devastating as the first to her. For the first time since I'd left home, I wished for a stable life. No more running, no more hiding. Just peace, building a life with normal problems like deciding what kind of pet to have or even living paycheck to paycheck.

Chloe was a mere two steps ahead of me as my comrades gathered in an unoccupied banquet hall to discuss our plans for recovering Ophelia and Gareth. I took a seat in the middle of the table that occupied the majority of the space in the clean room. Sable sat on my right and Fang sat next to her on her other side. Shaw was seated at the head of the table with Agatha to his right and Marshall to his left. Gus was the only person to sit on Marshall's side of the table with him. Was this a silent statement of loyalty to Shaw by my comrades, or were they all just freaked out by Marshall and Gus, like me?

As usual, Shaw wasted no time in getting down to the important information. "Marshall has spent a long time searching. We believe Gareth and Ophelia are being held captive somewhere near Baja, but possibly in a nearby region in Mexico. He will be able to determine a more accurate location once we are closer to that area. I need everyone to get a good night's rest. This will be our last night in Las Vegas. Gus and I will be taking care of obtaining transportation after this briefing. Any questions?"

"Did you decide if we're losing Ophelia or if we're losing Gareth?" Chloe asked. She never was afraid to ask difficult questions.

"We're leaving the decision up to the two of them," Agatha replied.

Kelly sighed. "That doesn't make the situation easier for the rest of us."

'*Life, especially for the Gifted, is never easy*,' Marshall pointed out.

I resisted the urge to punch him in the face. He was the reason for this added stress anyhow.

"There's no way to make the situation ideal, but that might be the fairest decision for Gareth and Ophelia," I noted. Not that that made it right or good or whatever.

"Anything else?" Shaw asked. No one spoke a word. "Good. Now go get some rest while I secure the vehicles."

We filed out of the meeting hall with a somber atmosphere clinging to us. Everyone gathered in the elevator to return to our rooms.

"I know Shaw said we should be resting, but since it's our last night in Vegas, shouldn't we do something fun?" Melody suggested.

"Like what?" Kelly questioned.

She shrugged. "I don't know, sightsee or something."

"You kids go have fun. I think I'm gonna go hit the gym," Fang said.

He was right. What we really should've been doing was training, but everyone seemed so excited about going out, I decided not to mention it.

The elevator doors opened and everyone except Fang left for their rooms to get ready for a night on the town.

"You're sure you don't want to come?" Sable asked.

He winked. "You go make some romance happen."

"I don't know if it will work."

"I reckon you won't have an opportunity to make sparks fly while we're trying to rescue our lost brethren. Now's as good a time as any."

She hugged him and kissed his cheek. "You really are the best, you know."

"I don't know about all that, Miss Sable. Go on and have a good time."

He smiled broadly at her as the elevator doors slid closed.

I shook my head as I entered my room. With all this going on and Sable decides *now* is the time to play Cupid? It was equally endearing and frustrating. I knew her intentions were good, but there was so much else at stake right now. Then again, I fell for her while I was on a rescue mission myself. Maybe she wasn't being as ridiculous as I first thought.

Kelly and I rode down in the elevator together. I was surprised to see Sable waiting for us in the lobby. She looked casual and comfortable in her T-shirt with her favorite rock band's logo on it and Chuck Taylor high top sneakers. And those jeans that hugged her curves like a second skin with the rip artfully placed on her thigh. I wondered idly what her skin felt like beneath the worn denim fibers, but I quickly pushed it out of my mind. But that's how I loved her best, dressed down and herself.

Kelly smiled wryly as he took a seat in the armchair across from Sable's. "We probably have at least an hour to kill. Too bad we can't get onto the casino floors."

"While we have the time, I wanted to talk to you about something," Sable prompted.

"I'm going to get us some water while we're waiting," I said.

I winked at her before setting off for the bar.

I purchased three bottles of water for the same price I would pay for a cheap bottle of wine at a grocery store. As I headed back, I saw Sable staring intently at Kelly. What were they talking about? It wasn't the most honorable thing to do, but I held back and listened.

Sable laughed and rolled her eyes. "Anyway, do you like her?"

"She's a good person," Kelly replied.

"So I've been told." Bitterness dripped from her voice.

"Well, I could see her not being a fan of yours, or why you're not a fan of hers. Are you trying to distract her from Brandon with me?" His joking manner couldn't quite mask the vulnerability in his voice.

He was my first experience in hurting someone with a girlfriend. He backed off from Melody and let me go after her. That was one of my worst traits, being selfish. I was doing just about the same thing with Sable to Chloe, although I couldn't help that Sable didn't swing that way.

"No! Of course not! But you are attracted to her, aren't you?" Sable asked earnestly. My little Cupid, hard at work.

"To be honest, I've had a thing for her since she was with Brandon. She never even saw me, though. I tried not to make it obvious, but of course Chloe noticed. It put her in a hard spot, too, since she's so close to all three of us. She was kind enough to let me vent to her about it, but I tried to keep that to myself. Brandon's always been it for Melody, though. He was her whole world, just like he's yours and you're his. When you're that crazy about someone, you don't see anyone else around you. Sometimes, being a good best friend is a hard thing to do."

Unshed tears made Sable's eyes shine as she threw her arms around him. "Well, I think she sees you now."

I couldn't stand to see either of them torn up like that. Time to stop hiding and intervene.

"That's nice of you to say, but I don't think—"

"Man, if you're not trying to buy alcohol, it's hard to get someone to even talk to you!" I interrupted as I tossed a bottle of water to Sable and then one to Kelly.

She smiled as she removed the cap from her bottle. "I bet they'd give you a beer if you asked for it."

"Beer's not really my drink of choice," I confessed as I sat in the chair next to her.

"What is your drink of choice, then? Red wine?" she teased.

"Whiskey, actually," Kelly answered.

"Not that he's any good at shooting whiskey." This jibe came from Melody as she sauntered toward us with Chloe and Leilani accompanying her.

The other girls were all dressed up and wearing little cocktail dresses and heels. I really tried not to notice how short Melody's skirt was. I ended up noticing her chest instead.

A pang of guilt bubbled in my chest, but I kept noticing, anyway.

Shaking my head, I let out a low whistle. "Looking good, ladies."

"Shut up," Chloe replied.

"Did anyone decide where we're headed?" Kelly asked.

"Let's just see where our feet take us," Sable suggested.

"Says the girl who's not wearing heels," Melody muttered.

"I think a stroll doesn't sound like a bad way to start," I encouraged.

"All right, let's go then," Chloe ordered.

As the rest of our group made their way to the door, Sable pulled me back. "You don't have an issue with Kelly going after your ex, do you?"

"What?"

"Good! Then go tell Melody how amazing he is! I'm going to try to talk to Leilani about your sister. Let's make some magic happen!"

I laced our fingers together and led her toward the hotel's door. "What exactly brought all this on?"

She smiled innocently. "Just trying to spread a little cheer where I can."

"Right. Well, let's see if this works."

Before letting go of her hand and catching up to Melody, I left a chaste kiss on her lips. She grinned as I turned away from her. Then I caught up to Melody.

"Melody, can I talk to you for a minute?" I asked.

She batted her eyelashes at me. "Of course. What's going on?"

"Well, you know Kelly."

"Yeah, so?"

How did Sable make this stuff seem so easy?

"What do you think about him?"

"He's a good guy, a good friend. What's with all the questions?"

"You know he's into you, right? Since we were together, actually..."

She stared at me for a few moments before she spoke. I knew that was how she processed new information. "Seriously?"

"Yeah. I wouldn't tell you that if it wasn't true."

"How would you feel about it?"

"About what?"

"If I started talking to him—you know, as more than a friend. I mean, I guess you have Sable now and everything."

I grabbed her arm and spun her toward me. With her heels on, she was at eye level with me. "I wouldn't have said anything to you if I wasn't okay with it. You're a wonderful person and so is Kelly and you both deserve to find happiness. Give him a shot."

She sighed. "Okay, I believe you. I'll think about it."

"Thank you."

Chloe stepped up next to us. "Brother dear, can I have my friend back please?"

I smiled and held my arm out. "She's all yours."

I made my way back to Sable, put my arm around her shoulder, and kissed her temple. She leaned her head on my clavicle as we followed behind the others.

When Melody and Chloe started limping in their heels, we headed back to the Bellagio. We all got little souvenirs from our tour of Vegas. At the Paris hotel, I bought Sable a silver necklace with little charms shaped like a heart, a pair of lips, and an Eiffel Tower on it. She got me a brown leather braided bracelet with a sliver metal placard that had my name etched in hieroglyphs on it from the Luxor hotel.

We crept quietly through the hallway to our respective hotel rooms, hoping Shaw wouldn't hear. In the silence of the hotel room, my mind was anything but. There was too much going on. Aside from Sable's matchmaking, there were lots of unknowns. Where were

Gareth and Ophelia? What was Marshall's game? Which one of our comrades would come back, just to be lost again? What was this Bond between Sable and me? How was it supposed to help us? Did the DAO know about it, too?

Sleeping was anything but restful. Nightmares plagued me every time my eyes were closed. First was a dream about Sable being shot in the head. Then came a disturbing vision of Chloe being imprisoned by the DAO. Hordes of terrible things I hoped would never come true swam through my mind. Finally, I gave up on it and watched the sun rise.

Chapter 15

Sable

No wonder people in tropical climates wore hardly any clothes at all. The air was humid and hot. Despite the fact that Shaw found us a house on the coast of the Pacific Ocean in Baja, I was sweating at eight thirty in the morning. Not the kind of sweat where it rolled down your skin. It was just enough to make you sticky and uncomfortable. A quick dip in the water seemed like the perfect remedy.

The house Shaw rented for us was on stilts, like all the other houses on this stretch of beach. I climbed down the stairs as quietly as I could since most everyone else was still sleeping. We'd spent more time in a vehicle before than the five and a half hours it took us to get from Las Vegas to Tijuana, but everyone's heightened sense of nervousness drained their energy. Shaw sat on the balcony studying papers and drinking coffee. He nodded at me as I padded onto the sand.

There were a few people on the beach as I headed towards the water. A few sunbathers came out early to either get a good spot in the sand or to sunbathe topless before too many people were around to notice. A couple of guys were jogging with surfboards under their arms, but the swells weren't very high at all. There were a handful of people milling around in the water close to the shore and one woman combed the beach with her metal detector.

I hadn't realized how much I'd missed the smell of the ocean since the loss of the *Kandis Amelia*. One day when all of the running from the government was over, I'd have to find a house on the ocean to live in.

The water was cool against my skin as I walked farther into it. When I was up to my waist in the ocean, I ducked my head beneath the surface. I never could go swimming and not have my hair wet. It just felt weird. When I resurfaced, I kept everything below my shoulders in the crystal clear water. I used to think that ads for resorts in this area were manipulated to make the water look more enticing. The truth was that it really looked that jewel-toned blue color.

A wave crashed over my head and interrupted my musings about the scenery. I choked. My eyes and nose stung from the salt. Ophelia would've laughed at me and splashed more water in my face. I sighed as I looked back at our rented yellow house. Would I ever see Ophelia again? Even if we managed to find her and Gareth and break them out of whatever prison Commander Goldbrook had them trapped in, she might be the one to go with Marshall. Could she see us searching for them? Did she see the choice she'd have to make if we were successful? We'd been lucky so far in escaping the DAO but eventually, luck ran out. Frankly, I considered it a miracle that we'd escaped capture three times already.

My dark thoughts were interrupted as I noticed Agatha walk out onto the balcony. Was Shaw smiling? That was a rarity for him. I tried to remember an instance when he smiled since I'd met him. The only time I could think of was when I'd first met Agatha in Australia. He smiled when he first laid eyes on her, then he quickly regained his composure. I choked on the air in my lungs as Agatha bent over and kissed Shaw. It was quick, but it happened. How was it that she managed to get underneath that impenetrable exterior? Not even Brandon, Chloe, and Kelly could do that and they were like his children!

Suddenly, I had the feeling I was intruding on a private moment, so I turned around and focused on the horizon. My mind returned to the more somber thoughts of facing down Commander Goldbrook again. Seriously, how many times would I live through this scenario? I'd long ago surrendered to the idea that I would be on the run for the rest of my life. It seemed so redundant. Once again, I found myself longing for the monotony of the average high school teenager's life. There were hardly any unsuspected surprises to threaten your life. You knew someone else was taking care of the major responsibilities to keep providing you with the luxuries you were accustomed to.

On the other hand, Shaw always provided us with a roof over our heads, food to eat, clothes to wear, and the tools to survive being attacked by government assassins. Amid the chaos of the Diseased life, he gave us something to control. Our Gifts.

In spite of the humid air, I was glad the water was warm. If it were cold, the heat would leech out of my body and my internal temperature would become too low. I smiled to myself. At least I had a good excuse for using up all the hot water when I showered.

I dipped my head below the surface of the water. It would've been nice to have a pair of goggles to see the sea life. If I opened my eyes now, the salt would burn them. I imagined brightly colored schools of fish swim-

ming around me. Had there been any, I could've seen
them by simply looking into the water when my head
wasn't submerged.

Suddenly, a familiar yet muffled voice dragged me
from my musings.

"Sable?"

It was Brandon.

I popped my head above the water. He was on the
shore, making his way toward me.

"Is everyone awake now?" I asked.

"No. Just us, I think. And Shaw's reading the paper
on the balcony."

"Agatha's up, too. I saw her—come out and say
good morning to Shaw."

I decided not to tell Brandon about Shaw and Agatha's kiss. It wasn't my romance to share details about.

When Brandon reached me, he brushed a lock of hair
plastered to my cheek behind my ear. "You know, these
tropical surroundings look good on you."

I splashed water onto his torso and smirked. "Yeah?
And if I stay out here much longer, my beautiful alabaster
skin will blister and turn redder than the lobsters you
cook."

He laughed and encircled my waist in his arms. "Fair
enough. I remember when Chloe and I were little and our
parents took us to the beach. She always came home with
nasty sunburns because she's pale like you. I don't think
I've ever had a sun burn."

"Cry me a river," I replied sarcastically.

Brandon leaned down and kissed the tip of my nose.
Then he pushed me back into the water. I screamed as my
arms spun like windmills. The attempt at regaining my
balance was in vain. At least I splashed him in the face
when I plopped like a boulder into the ocean.

When I broke through the water's surface, he grinned

at me and folded his arms across his chest. A challenge.

Taking the bait, I dove at him. Of course, he dodged and I ended up back in the ocean. He was more agile than me, despite being taller and built bigger than me. This time, I dared to brave the assault of the salt water on my eyes. The stinging sensation was well worth being able to knock Brandon on his ass from behind. I laughed as we broke the surface.

We stayed suspended in the water from the shoulders down. It was one of those rare times that he and I were at eye level with each other. Usually, that only happened if we were lying down next to each other. As I gazed into his glacial blues, Brandon grinned at me.

"You're a pretty decent swimmer for someone who's Gift is fire."

"I had swimming lessons five summers in a row, starting when I was ten years old."

"It took you five years to learn to swim?"

"There was nothing else to do. I didn't have friends, we didn't have a pool, and the high school always offered swimming lessons for cheap. My parents took pity on me and kept paying for me to go. When I was twelve, the gym coach finally gave up making me do the exercises and going through safety procedures with everyone else and let me have the deep end of the pool to myself."

Brandon cupped my face in his hands. "You know, I'm glad your parents sent you to the asylum."

"Did you pick up Melody in a nut house, too?" I joked.

He smirked. "Nah, that's not usually where I pick up women."

"Do you usually meet women where Chloe does?" I countered.

"So that's why all of my former prospects haven't panned out!"

I attempted to push his head under water, but he stayed firmly in place. "Glad to know you're working at becoming a lady killer."

"As it turns out, I'm a one-girl kind of guy. And this one I've got now, she's a keeper."

"Is that so?"

Brandon drew me closer to him and pressed his lips to mine. I locked my hands behind his neck and angled my head to deepen the kiss. He tasted like salt and lemongrass and anise. These carefree moments seemed too few and far between. I wondered if he felt my distractedness as he gently pulled back from me.

"We should probably go back inside."

"Breakfast calls, doesn't it?"

He nodded.

I sighed. "I know you like to cook for everyone and all, but sometimes I wish I could have you all to myself uninterrupted."

Brandon took my hand in his as we slowly made our way back to the beach house. "You do."

"You know what I mean."

"Do I?"

I felt my cheeks heat and bit my lower lip.

"Tell me."

"Tell you what?"

"What having me all to yourself uninterrupted means."

Why was this so embarrassing to say aloud? I'd run the scenario through my head countless times. "It means...it means just you and me. No DAO, no ex-girlfriends, no siblings, no anyone other than you and me."

"Thank you, Webster."

I blinked. "Webster?"

"Like the dictionary."

"What do you want me to say?"

"What you're really thinking, baby doll."

He just *had* to use that pet name. Of course.

"Just you and me living in a house by the water. You can have a catering business since you're used to feeding a lot of people. I can write bad poetry and light bonfires. We can spend the evenings lying in a hammock together looking at the stars and the days swimming or training or whatever we want."

I held my breath as I waited for his reaction. He stayed quiet as he mulled over my wishes.

He sighed. "It would be nice, that kind of life. It's one we'll never have, though."

Damn him and his practicality! Couldn't he just play along for a few minutes? Instead of chastising him for pointing out the ugly truth, I just said, "I know."

Neither of us spoke as we entered the house. Just as Brandon suspected, everyone was now awake and milling around. Fang, Melody, and Shaw hovered over the coffee pot, waiting for their caffeine fix to finish brewing. Brandon took two dozen eggs out of the fridge—we'd purchased them at a convenient store in California before we crossed the border—and set to scrambling them for everyone's breakfast. Agatha offered to help him, but he insisted he could handle the meal on his own. Half of our supply of orange juice we'd also procured from the convenient store was gone. I poured myself a glass before I missed out on it all together.

The conversation over breakfast was minimal. Exhaustion still clung to us all. I imagined it would until we rescued Gareth and Ophelia and figured out a way to keep them both away from Marshall. My gaze slipped to him as I thought about him. He still gave me the creeps. Despite being blind, deaf, and mute, he was capable of completing an extraordinary amount of tasks on his own.

'*Sable, your eggs are getting cold,*' he chastised. I decided I would never be used to him hearing what I was thinking and responding to it in my mind. A shiver ran down my spine as I acknowledged him by shoving a forkful of eggs into my mouth. His chuckle rumbled through my consciousness like soft thunder. I tightened my grip on my fork to refrain from clawing at my prickling scalp.

CHAPTER 16

I'd never been on a submarine before, but I was glad I wasn't claustrophobic or else I would've freaked out. It wasn't a big roomy submarine like the ones in the movies. There was enough space for us all to move around in the *Roman Candle* without bumping into each other, but just barely. Fang had the worst time, being that he was the tallest and the broadest of us.

Marshall had determined that the location of our captured comrades was an underground settlement in international waters. Apparently, this was just one of many of these types of trade posts where things—and people—were bought and sold on the black market. Not just anyone had access to this underground atrocity. This was just for the one percent of people who controlled the world's finances.

I couldn't imagine Commander Goldbrook being privy to that kind of money, but how was I supposed to know what kind of money the leaders of secret government assassin agencies brought in in a fiscal year?

There were eight beds in each room of the sleeping quarters, stacked into bunk beds for maximum space utilization. Our submarine had sixteen beds in all. Bunk rooms were assigned by gender. I was the only one sleeping on a top bunk in the girls' room. Leilani slept beneath me.

I stared at the cold steel ceiling. A million different scenarios played through my mind about the impending rescue mission. It saddened me to realize that the thought of buying and selling human beings didn't shock me much anymore. There was a time in the not too distant past, but that seemed like it happened forever ago, where my comrades and I were up for auction in our nation's capital. I had to swallow the fact that this abhorrent practice happened far more often than was publicized on the news.

What if Ophelia and Gareth had already been sold to someone else? Or would Commander Goldbrook want to trade them for a more powerful Diseased? According to Marshall, Ophelia was the Holy Grail of our kind. Gareth's ability was nothing to sneeze at, either, but Locators were more common than Seers. Shaw said Ophelia and Gareth both had highly developed Gifts. That would make them highly profitable on the black market. I hoped Commander Goldbrook's asking price was too high for anyone to pay so we had more time to find them.

The plan was for Marshall and Gus to try purchasing them from him. Marshall wanted to try trading them, but the only bartering chips at his disposal were the rest of us. Shaw was unwilling to lose more of us since he was already losing one of us if this mission was completed successfully.

Most people coveted Ophelia's Gift, but not me. That would be some kind of hell to have everyone trying to use you all the time. I wouldn't want to know the outcomes of every situation before it happened. Plus, if someone changed their mind about one little detail, the whole outcome could change. Really, the Seeing skill was unreliable, if you asked me. But I knew Ophelia was exceptional in her abilities. Even if someone changed the course of destiny, she was never wrong.

We'd been in this submarine for three days. I was dying for some fresh air. The only other person who seemed to be suffering from cabin fever was Melody. That commonality between us I could deal with. The fact that Brandon was both of our first loves and that neither of us would ever stop loving him bothered me, but the sting of that shared emotion eased more and more as the romance between her and Kelly blossomed. At least one of my love connections worked. When all of this drama was over, I was determined to find a way for Chloe and Leilani to be able to be together.

I sighed and buried my face with my pillow. If only we were sailing on the *Kandis Amelia* until we reached the black market location…

I imagined myself doodling a birthday cake of flames in the air since it was my birthday. That would contaminate the stale air of the submarine, even though there was no smoke produced from fire simply appearing on my skin.

"Sable! Good heavens child, don't suffocate yourself!" Agatha cried.

I pulled the pillow off of my face and grumbled, "I'm already suffocating in here."

"How about I tell you a story to take your mind off of being stuck in an underwater blimp?"

I sat up and looked down at her. The top of her head barely reached the bottom of my bunk. "What kind of story?"

"Well, you climb down, I'll go get Brandon, and we'll talk. I think he'll be interested in this story, too."

I watched her as she bustled out of the room. What kind of story was she going to tell Brandon and me? I climbed down from my bunk and sat cross legged on the lower bed of the unused bunk. Just as I settled in comfortably, Agatha returned with Brandon. He and I smiled at one another as he sat on the floor next to my seat on the bed. Agatha settled across from me, like we were at a slumber party together.

She took a dramatic breath before she began speaking. "I thought the two of you should know this before I told Drake. After all, it affects the two of you the most."

"Agatha, what are you talking about?" I asked.

"I'm talking about white hot fire and electricity. You both are familiar with the concept of true love, yes?"

Brandon and I nodded at her.

"I thought you might be. There are legends in every culture about true loves ending in tragedy. The Gifted are no different."

"There's folklore for Gifted people?" Brandon inquired.

Agatha smiled. "Everyone's got stories about their history. Now, the particular story of love and loss in our world has to do with two young lovers who destroy each other. The most passionate loves are fiery and can burn those involved. In most cases, this burning is figurative. With you two, this is a more literal issue."

I choked on the air in my lungs. "You mean we're going to burn each other to death?"

"There's a possibility. But it doesn't have to end that way. There are true loves between Gifted people who don't have this risk. So you're probably wondering why you two have it."

"Is it because of our Gifts?" Brandon mused.

"If only it were that simple. There is a force beyond explanation by any language that unites people. Seldom is this connection potentially fatal, but there are cases like yours where this is a possibility. You have to have my

Sight to see it, but even when the two of you are simply in the same room, you glow. It starts as a quiet hum that grows and grows until it explodes into blinding white light. You've seen that part for yourselves. The key to this overwhelming culmination of energy is for you two to work together. You can manipulate this energy just like you can fire and electricity, respectively. If you learn to harness it, your potential is limitless. This also makes you an invaluable asset."

I blinked. "So what does all of this mean?"

"You know Drake will protect you. I don't know if Marshall realizes the power you two hold as one. I would hope he doesn't but I assume he knows. His Gifts are very finely tuned. I never underestimate him and have advised Drake not to either."

"You know Shaw is going to want us to develop this skill further. Do you know how we're supposed to?" Brandon asked.

"You'll know when to begin," she answered mysteriously. Then she rose from the bed and left us with a wink over her shoulder.

I collapsed back onto the bed. "What the hell was that supposed to mean?"

Brandon squeezed in next to me. "I don't know. I'm not sure if I like it."

"I don't get what it's supposed to mean. So we can't make out anymore until we can train or we're going to kill each other?"

"That would definitely be tragic."

I shoved his arm playfully. "That's such a guy thing to say."

"You're the one who brought it up."

"Touché."

"I guess Shaw will come to us about it when Agatha tells him."

"I wonder how he'll take the news that we have to determine when we're ready to develop our potentially fatal super power. You know how he likes to have control over everything."

We let the weight of that realization settle in. Would we need to accelerate the rate of growth of this power to increase our chances of survival? If the power was as explosive as Agatha warned it was, would it be dangerous for us to push its limits?

Brandon ran his thumb gently across my forehead. "Don't worry, we'll figure this out."

"Figure what out?"

"All of it."

I captured his hand with mind and placed a light kiss on each of his knuckles. "How are you always the calm in the center of the storm?"

He chuckled. "That seems pretty ironic, considering I control lightning."

"You know Chloe and Melody and Kelly see you that way, too."

"I guess so."

I stared at his face for a while as we lay together in silence. Every one of his features was etched into my mind, but I liked tracing over them anyhow. The flecks of sapphire in his ice blue irises kept them from looking white.

His lips were full, the bottom one just a hair bigger than the top one. The cut of his jaw and his nose and his cheekbones were sharp beneath his tanned skin. His temples were hidden behind soft black curls that were identical to the ones above the nape of his neck.

"What are you thinking about?" he whispered.

I noticed he did that sometimes when he didn't want to break the silence.

"You," I whispered back.

"What about me?"

"Oh, you know, this and that. What about you?"

"What?"

"What are you thinking about?"

"Lots of things."

"Such as?"

"You know, things like how we'd be in trouble if Shaw found us like this. Or how we'd be in bigger trouble if Chloe found us. More importantly, I'm thinking about making every person on this submarine blind."

I traced my fingers along his eyebrows, cheekbones, and lips while I spoke. I just couldn't help myself. "Really? And why would you want to go and do something like that?"

"It seems like more and more now we're finding ourselves embarking on these dangerous missions. The odds seem to me like the probability of us burning each other up pales in comparison to us getting killed on one of these operations. So I'm thinking I'd rather take my chances on burning with you than dying at the hands of someone who wants to enslave or exterminate us."

His words gave me chills, and not the good kind. "Brandon, what exactly are you saying?"

He stayed silent for a long while before answering me. "I've been blindly following along with Shaw's mission to protect the Gifted and stay out of sight for almost eight years. I never questioned his motives or his methods. He took care of me and Chloe when he didn't have to."

"Are you saying you don't believe in Shaw's cause any more? You're not thinking of doing things Marshall's way, are you?"

"No, no, nothing like that. It's just…I guess what I'm trying to say is that I need to start carving my own path in this life. I don't really know what it is or how I'm supposed to do it. All I know is that the thought of having to figure it out without you with me literally causes my chest to constrict. I've watched you almost die four times now. That's four times too many. How long will it be until our luck runs out?"

That question haunted me every day. How many more times would we escape uncertain doom? My fingers shook as I ran them through Brandon's hair.

"Sable, don't cry. I'm sorry. I didn't mean to upset you."

I felt the tears running lazily down my cheeks. "I'm not crying."

I pulled his face to mine with too much force for us only being inches apart. My lips crashed against his in urgency. My father used to always tell me *carpe diem* when I was troubled by something. Seize the day. This was the perfect time to heed that advice.

As our kisses became more earnest, our limbs entwined like we were trying to save each other from exploding, to keep the pieces of ourselves from breaking apart and disappearing. I lost track of where our hands were roaming, when our lips parted and explored each other only to find their way back again. The familiar warm feeling spread through me as green flames licked their way from my flesh to his.

"Brandon—"

"I love you, Sable."

Ragged breathing made our words sound raw. "I love you, too. I won't leave you. We'll burn together."

"We *are* burning together."

The flames became brighter with every kiss and every caress. Electricity charged the air. The lights in the *Roman Candle* began flickering, yet the inside of the vessel became increasingly brighter.

"We're going to cause a power failure," I rasped.

The light was so bright it was like staring directly into the sun.

Shaw's disembodied voice came crackling over the intercom system. "Attention everyone. We are swiftly approaching our destination. Meet in the control room for further instructions."

Brandon and I broke away from each other. The room seemed pitch black in comparison to the blinding light from a few seconds ago. His chest heaved beneath my palms. I knew Shaw expected us to report to him immediately following his announcement, but I couldn't drag myself out of the moment.

"We'll make it through this. Ophelia and Gareth will be fine, we'll figure out how to keep them both. No matter what happens, we're going to make it out of this together," Brandon assured me.

I nodded, desperately wanting to believe him. My hands slid up his chest and clasped themselves together behind his neck. I rested my head over his hammering heart and closed my eyes. Just one moment more of this solitude, that was all I needed. One more moment of peace before we risked our lives again to rescue our family. I prayed luck would be on our side one more time.

CHAPTER 17

The black market was housed in a building that looked like a skyscraper was dropped into the ocean. It was difficult to wrap my head around forty floors of illegal trafficking looming before my eyes. Shaw, Marshall, Gus, and Agatha were going to venture inside and try to find Ophelia and Gareth and barter for them. Fang went along as the muscle. The rest of us were instructed to stay in the *Roman Candle* and wait for them to return so we wouldn't be captured. If they didn't return in twelve hours, then we were supposed to get the hell out of dodge. Brandon was to be Shaw's successor and carry on his cause. He accepted his charge stoically, but I saw the fear in his eyes. It was hard enough to lose your parents once. If Shaw didn't come back, Brandon, Chloe, Kelly, and Melody all stood to lose a father again.

It was silent inside the submarine. Every minute felt like an hour as time dragged on. Muffled sounds of people bringing in or departing with goods kept the *Roman Candle* from feeling like a coffin. I played solitaire on the floor of the female barracks with a deck of cards Fang brought from Las Vegas. I'd lost count how many times I'd played since half of our crew left to complete their task. I played all different kinds of solitaire—traditional, pyramid, twenty-one, spider, and free cell, among others. As I was setting up another round of pyramid solitaire, Melody sat on the floor across from me.

"Still playing cards?" she asked.

I nodded without looking up from my spread.

"Want to play euchre?"

"What's that?"

"It's a game Agatha taught me to play, but we need a couple more players. How about we have a girl's game?"

"Did I miss something?"

"What do you mean?"

"Pardon my skepticism. I mean, you're never nice to me, except when you tried helping me fix Chloe and Leilani up. And I figured that was more for their sakes than mine. So what exactly are you doing now?"

Melody picked at the ends of a lock of her golden hair. "Maybe I just wanted to try something new for a change."

I blinked. "Why wouldn't you want to commiserate with someone who's going through the same feelings you are?"

"What feelings?"

I felt my cheeks heat. "I know you guys are freaking out about the possibility of Shaw and Agatha not coming back."

She blushed. "Actually, you and I have more in common about that than I do with the others."

That wasn't the answer I was expecting. "How do you figure?"

"Well, Kelly, Brandon, and Chloe all lost parents and found a new one with Shaw. I never knew my birth parents. Agatha and Shaw are the only parents I've ever had. And I know you don't consider them as your parents. So you've lost the only parents you've ever had. I don't know how you've dealt with it. I would completely lose it if my parents were gone. Were they awful to you or something?"

I chose my words carefully. "No, my parents were pretty standard. They encouraged me to be more social, they made sure I did well in school, they disciplined me. The only terrible thing they've ever done to me was send me away to the asylum. At first, I felt too betrayed and angry to mourn the loss of them. When I accepted the fact that they were just scared and doing all that they knew to do to protect themselves, I found forgiveness. At that point, I was already so involved in this life of running and warring that thinking about my life before Brandon brought me to the *Kandis Amelia* was like remembering a movie I'd seen a thousand times. I have fond memories of them, but I've never missed them."

Melody brushed the tears pooling in her eyes away with the back of her hand. "That makes sense, I guess."

Then she stood and walked away. Did I say the wrong thing? I thought it was better to be honest about my feelings. She wanted me to tell her everything was going to be all right, but I couldn't. Life wouldn't ever be the same for her if Shaw and Agatha didn't come back. She might learn to adapt to life beyond them, but the truth was that a part of her soul would always be empty because of their absence.

In the afternoon, Leilani and I decided to make sandwiches for lunch. It was a crude offering in comparison to Brandon's gourmet meals, but it was the best either of us could do. I figured Brandon could use the break. He and Kelly had spent the whole morning assuring Chloe and Melody that everything would be fine and that soon we'd be finding a more permanent place to hide from the DAO. No one believed them, but everyone wanted to.

The time kept dragging by with no sign of our comrades returning. No one disturbed our submarine, but life went on around us as people left and arrived at the black market. There was no way to ease the tension in the air. I tried sleeping to eat away at some of the time, but I couldn't relax enough to get any rest. At least I wasn't obsessively checking the clock. Chloe was preoccupied with that activity.

At the eleventh hour, the outside noise had quieted significantly. From what Marshall told us, the black market was open all day every day. The six of us gathered in the control room to watch the minutes tick away. I sat on the floor next to the chair Brandon sat in and squeezed his hand with mine. He squeezed mine back, but he didn't look at me. His eyes were trained on the clock. A muscle ticked in his jaw. That was the only sign he showed of how scared he was. Leilani was the only one who didn't know him well enough to sense his fear. Not that she needed to. Fear permeated through us all like a toxic gas released in the air.

At ten minutes until the hour we were supposed to leave, a loud banging sounded and footsteps rang out loud and quickly on the floor. My jaw dropped when they came through the doorway.

I gasped. "Ophelia?"

Before I realized what my body was doing, I was on my feet sprinting toward her. We hugged each other tightly and started crying. I held her back at arm's length and looked her over. She wasn't quite as emaciated as she'd been in the asylum, but she was definitely worse for wear. Then I spotted Gareth behind her and I hugged him, too. He appeared startled at first, and then he returned my embrace.

"Where are the others?" Brandon asked. His voice was tight when he spoke.

Gareth hung his head. All the air left my lungs.

Something akin to a scream escaped from Melody's throat. I knew all too well that that was the sound of heartbreak.

"Shaw and Agatha traded themselves for our release. Fang escorted us here with Marshall and Gus. They were explaining the terms of one of us having to go with him. Then Fang snapped and started beating them down. He screamed at us to run to the *Roman Candle* and that he'd be right behind us, but—but he..." Ophelia trailed off.

"We couldn't find him. We waited for a half an hour, but we had to come here. There was no way to know if someone was coming after us or not," Gareth finished for her.

Everyone sat in stunned silence for a few moments. The elation of Ophelia and Gareth's safe return was taint-ed by devastation of losing Shaw, Agatha, and Fang. Melody broke the silence when she began sobbing into Kelly's shoulder. Tears ran down Chloe's face, too.

Chloe quickly dashed away her tears with a flick of her wrist. "Well, big brother, what do we do now?"

"We leave and find somewhere safe to plan our next course of action." His voice was completely devoid of emotion. He'd turned into the commanding soldier that Shaw had trained him to be.

Brandon, Kelly, Chloe and Leilani set to work pre-paring the *Roman Candle* to leave the black market. Mel-ody and I tended to Ophelia and Gareth, making sure they had something to eat and clean clothes to wear. I was surprised that we were all able to shove our tears down to be able to perform the various tasks we needed to in order to make our getaway. There was no conversation aside from giving orders and responding to them.

We returned the submarine to Marshall's friend who we'd borrowed it from. He seemed unsurprised how the course of events unfolded. I wondered if he could see the future, too. From there, we returned to the beach house on the Pacific coast. Everyone was dog tired, but none of us slept. We all sat in the living room staring at each other until after the sun rose.

"Does anyone have an idea about what we should do now?" Kelly asked. His voice was raw from not being used for a while.

"We'll talk about it after we've all gotten some rest. You did good work, everybody," Brandon answered.

One by one, everyone moseyed to their rooms. Ophelia and Gareth had rooms waiting for them. Shaw had outfitted the rooms with new wardrobes for them in good faith that we would find them and bring them home. I just wished that for once, we could all come away from a standoff together.

As I stood to head off for my room, Brandon caught my hand.

"What is it?"

"I don't know what to do," he confessed.

I sat back down next to him. "We'll figure it out together. You don't have to orchestrate this rescue mission single handedly. No one expects you to."

"Shaw would've known what to do."

"He's had a lot more practice at this than you have. You're only seventeen. I know it's easier said than done, but don't put so much pressure on yourself."

"How do you always manage to say the perfect thing?"

I kissed his cheek softly. "I don't really."

"You're better with words than I am."

"You don't have to be a good speaker to be a good leader. Go try to get some rest. I'm going to check on Ophelia, okay?"

He nodded and I headed off to Ophelia's room. Her door was open, but I knocked, anyway.

"Come in," she called.

I came in and sat on the foot of her bed. She was sitting at the head of the bed cross legged with her arms resting on them, her hands palms up. She was meditating. I waited for her to finish since I didn't want to interrupt. When she opened her eyes, a fog seemed to lift from her violet irises. She was coming out of a vision.

"See anything interesting?"

She sighed. "It wasn't anything helpful."

"Too bad."

"We'll find a way to bring them all back safely. Don't worry."

"That's what I told Brandon. He's less optimistic."

"He's uncomfortable leading everyone. It was something he was born to do, but right now the charge seems alien to him. He'll find his stride and make Shaw proud. Telling him that won't make him believe it, though."

"I don't know how he doesn't see it. Any time Shaw isn't standing there with us, Brandon is the one who takes control and tells us what we need to do."

"The way he sees himself and the way everyone else sees him are two completely different Brandons. His safety net is missing, so it's natural for him to feel uneasy."

I sat down on the edge of her bed. "How are you doing?"

"I've been worse, but it was definitely no picnic. Commander Goldbrook was trying to keep us well enough to make a good profit on the black market, but leave us weak enough so we were unable to fight back."

"I'm surprised that he wouldn't want to keep you. Marshall seemed pretty upset when Shaw wouldn't let him keep both of you."

"Commander Goldbrook is more interested in collecting muscle than he is with psychics. Not that I'm complaining. I can't tell you how unbearable it was to know that Shaw was going to offer himself up in exchange for us. That vision came to me not long after we were captured. I saw Marshall's proposition about keeping one of us, too. Gareth was going to go with him if Shaw's plan was successful. He thought it would be too dangerous for Marshall to get his hands on me. Then Fang had to go be all stupid and heroic—"

I hugged her. "I know. I wonder if Shaw planned for that, too. He told us that he was taking Fang along in case things got ugly, but I wonder if that was the plan all along."

"I don't doubt it."

"I'm still glad to have both of you back safely."

"Me, too. This is probably the worst birthday ever for you, huh?"

I didn't bother asking how she knew, so I just smiled uneasily. "It's definitely the most eventful. But it's also the best because I know my best friend is safe."

"We'll make up for it later."

"It's fine, really. You should get some rest."

She yawned. "I am exhausted."

"Goodnight, Ophelia."

"Goodnight, Sable."

I left her to get some rest. As I predicted, rest didn't come so easily to me. I tossed and turned and didn't sleep for more than fifteen minutes at a time. Before frustration consumed me, I decided to go sit on the balcony.

It seemed so strange that it was just days ago that Shaw sat in the very spot drinking coffee and reading the newspaper and that he wouldn't be doing it in the morning. Why did he go to so much trouble to protect us? Did he really see us all as his adoptive children or was he just ensuring that the younger generation of Diseased carried on and had the ability to create more Diseased in the fu-

ture? Maybe it was a little of both. Would I want to subject a child to this life? I'd never given much thought to
having children before. I always assumed I'd end up as
an old maid.

The stars twinkled above the ocean in the moonless
night. A warm wind blew across the water creating little
swells. I traced the tiny white caps with fire. Before I
came to live with Shaw, I used to write whenever I felt
stressed. Now I doodled in the sky with fire. It was too
dangerous to have anything written down. You never
knew how the DAO. would use something against you or
the ones you cared about.

What would Shaw do in this situation? I bet Brandon
was wondering the same thing. Poor Brandon. I couldn't
fathom how that felt to have the pressure of living up to
the legacy of someone who taught you everything you
knew. Like Ophelia, I was sure he would rise to the occa-
sion. I just wished he would believe it himself.

CHAPTER 18

Brandon

I paced back and forth along the stretch of beach behind our rental house. Activity swirled around me as people played fetch with their dogs, children ran from the water's edge to their parents and back again, and vacationers enjoyed the hot summer weather. Sable was watching me from the balcony. None of that mattered. Nothing mattered except that Shaw and Agatha were gone. Shaw was the closest thing I had to a father now. I left my father before as a child, which was painful. Having my new father abducted from me was so much worse.

I wanted to scream and cry and punch things, but I had to keep my composure. Everyone was looking to me for answers. I was the rock in the chaos. How could I fake being strong for everyone else when I'd never felt so weak?

I'd run out of cigarettes a while ago. All I could do now was pace and try to make sense of what was going on in my head. I had to stay in control. I couldn't break down. It was too important for me not to.

Melody and Kelly joined Sable on the balcony. Their voices were as clear to me as if I were standing next to them. My resolve to show no cracks in my fragile façade of calm strengthened.

"How long has he been doing this?" Melody asked.

"I don't know. I woke up after he came out here, but I know it's been a while," Sable answered.

Kelly sighed. "He's been up all night."

"I don't doubt it," Sable agreed.

"I'm surprised he's not—" Melody started.

"He ran out a while ago," Sable interrupted.

"Since when do you two finish each other's thoughts?" Kelly wondered.

"We don't. It's just that we both know him really well," Sable explained.

"He should eat something," Melody mused.

"Did you?" Sable asked.

"No. My nerves are too jarred, you know?" Melody replied.

"You should try and eat something, even if it's just a piece of toast," Sable encouraged.

"I tried to tell her that," Kelly pointed out.

Sable sighed. "I bet none of us feel much like eating. Are the others still asleep?"

"Yes," Kelly said.

"Should I—should I go down there and talk to him?" Sable asked timidly.

"Maybe. I don't see how it would make anything worse," Kelly suggested.

I stopped pacing when I saw Sable walking toward me. I waited for her to reach me and then turned around and walked the other way. Her steps fell into my pace. She didn't say anything or try to touch me. I didn't do or say anything either. If I tried to reach out, I would shatter.

We walked another few passes before I decided to take her hand in mine. After all, this Bond thing was supposed to make us stronger, right? The well-worn path I'd created in the sand became longer on each side as the sun rose higher in the sky. I just had to focus on one step after the other, one breath after the other. Maybe she was holding me together.

As we turned to face the pier again, she laid her head on my shoulder. I stopped walking and brushed the hair out of her face. I offered her a tight smile as I lifted her chin with my finger.

"You look like you fell asleep outside." My voice was raspy when I spoke. Too many smokes in too short amount of time.

"After being stuck in the submarine, I needed some fresh air."

"Me, too."

My strides slowed when we resumed walking. Instead of turning around at my usual stopping point, we continued on toward the pier. I decided that if she was with me, I could go a little farther. She squeezed my hand and I squeezed hers back.

We stopped at the end of the pier and looked out at the ocean. A couple of people zipped past on jet skis. I sat our adjoined hands on the pier's railing and let out a long sigh.

"A penny for your thoughts?" she asked.

She deserved to know the truth. Would she think less of me if I fell apart? "Sable, I don't know how I'm supposed to do this."

"Do what?"

Hysteria bubbled up inside me. "Save everyone! I'm not Shaw, and I don't even have him here to advise me on what I should do. I don't even know where to start—"

She pressed her lips gently to the corner of my jaw. "The rest of us are here to help. Gareth can help us locate them and we'll come up with a strategy from there. You don't have to do this alone."

I squeezed me eyes shut and he breathed a long heavy sigh. "You're right."

At least, I hoped she was.

"Brandon—"

My need for her in that moment overwhelmed me. There was nothing I could say to articulate it right, so I grabbed her by the back of her neck and crushed my lips against hers. The sense of urgency I felt must have been infectious because she went from gingerly kissing me to devouring me in the blink of an eye.

Vaguely, I was aware of the people on the peer staring at us. Did we just look like a couple of horny teenagers who couldn't stand going five minutes without mauling each other? Probably. Could they sense my desperation?

I shouldn't use her this way, I shouldn't taint her love for me like this. My rational voice was drowned out by the frenzied panic that consumed me. She was my absolution, the only thing I had to cling to so the storm raging in my head wouldn't wash away my sanity.

Her fire raced through my veins as she melted into me. She tugged gently at my bottom lip with her teeth and I groaned.

With shaky hands, I pulled my face away from hers. "Not here."

Without giving her time to ask what I meant to do, I grabbed her hand and started dragging her behind me. She had to jog to keep up with me. I should've slowed down, but my guard was slipping and everything inside was spinning out of control.

We ended up underneath the house Shaw rented amongst the stilts. Sable had to crouch a little to fit and I almost had to bend in half. We were shielded from the view of everyone else on the beach. As I turned to face her, I practically tackled her. I didn't mean to, but I let the sensations I felt dictate what I did. I stared into her eyes. Confusion and desire fought for dominance in her expression. I didn't give her time to decide, but I hadn't needed to, either. Her fingers twisted in my hair as she pulled my face to hers.

I wasn't exactly aware of my actions. The only things that registered in my mind were that we were pressed together, the softness of her, and a growing heat in the air. Shocks fired through my blood and caused my body to spasm every time they sparked.

Somewhere in the back of my mind, I pled silently to her, '*I need you.*'

'*I'm here,*' she answered.

More of those currents zoomed through me as pale green flames engulfed us. The house could've flattened us, but I didn't care. All I could think about was her, reaching inside of her and never letting go.

My hands snaked up past the hem of her shirt. Her skin was white hot beneath my fingertips. I gasped at the intensity of the sensation. The need to pull her into me was overwhelming. We couldn't be any closer, physically. Where was this coming from?

Without warning, I broke away from her, which shocked me as much as it did her. She ran her hands down my clammy arms as we caught our breath. The farther I was way from her, the more intense the tugging sensation in my gut became, like I was internally tethered to her. It was almost like my soul would explode out of me at any moment.

"What the hell?"

"Is there a solar flare?"

"Where's that light coming from?"

"It's burning my retinas!"

"Someone make it stop!"

People on the beach were yelling and screaming and

their voices blended into an incoherent panic. What light? What were they talking about? All I could see was Sable. She looked like she was glowing, but she always seemed like that to me.

Wait—she really was glowing! She stared up at me with a stunned expression on her face. I gingerly raised one of my hands in front of my face. I was glowing like her, too.

"Brandon?" she asked in a shaky voice.

I opened and closed my mouth a few times before giving up on words and just shrugged. What was happening to us? That pull in my stomach was taut. I was anchored to Sable, and I knew she was anchored to me, too.

I heard someone clear their throat. My head whipped to the side to discover Ophelia crouched down and smirking at us.

"Well, it looks like you've finally discovered the hidden power Agatha mentioned you had."

CHAPTER 19

Sable

"D id you see this coming?" Brandon demanded.

Ophelia sat down on the sand. "Of course I did."

"Why didn't you tell us?"

She shrugged. "It's something you had to discover on your own. Just because you can see the future doesn't mean you can go blabbing about everything you know. There are some things that, instinctively, you know you have to let nature take its course. Sometimes, knowing the outcome and trying to change it or hurry it along causes irreparable and unnecessary damage. This was one of those things."

Brandon shifted to get off of me. When he was a little more than a foot away from me, a scream ripped from my throat. It felt like a sharp hook was inside me and tearing through my flesh in a desperate attempt to free itself.

Somewhere in the back of my consciousness, I heard Brandon groan. He collapsed back on top of me and the pain instantly stopped.

"Take it easy," Ophelia instructed. "You're Bonded, so you have to wait until the glow fades before you put too much physical distance between you two. Just try and calm down and the Bond should dissolve quicker."

"How do you know all this stuff?" I panted.

She looked down at the ground and shifted her weight as if she was uncomfortable. "I knew Shaw and Agatha would be taken before Gareth and I were kidnapped. I knew they would trade themselves for us, so I tried to warn them. She just smiled sadly at me and explained how the Bond worked because she said she had a feeling she wouldn't be nearby when it presented itself. Sometimes, I think she can sense the future, too."

Ophelia's voice was rough with unshed tears by the time she finished speaking. Was that what she was talking about when she said trying to change the future made things worse sometimes? I wanted to crawl out from underneath the house and hug her, but the Bond was still in place. My whole body vibrated with the intensity of it.

"Baby doll, just breathe," Brandon soothed.

I hadn't realized how tense I was until he said it. He kissed my temple as I slowly exhaled. The Bond slackened the more I relaxed. Ophelia and Brandon waited patiently until I moved away from Brandon on my own without wincing. I crawled out from underneath the house on shaky limbs. Ophelia helped me stand. Brandon stood, composed as ever, his momentary lack of confidence abandoned.

We followed Ophelia back into the house, brushing the sand off of ourselves as we walked. I glanced behind me at Brandon as we entered the house. A steely resolve hardened his blue eyes like ice. His posture was rigid. He was assuming his role as commander. It pained me that he still felt he had to bear the burden alone.

Our remaining cohorts were gathered in the living room, waiting expectantly. Ophelia settled next to Gareth on the couch. Immediately, his hand found hers. Had their capture brought them closer together? I'd have to ask her about it later. I sat down on the floor in front of Kelly, who sat with Melody curled into his lap. Chloe sat next to them, and Leilani occupied the armchair. Brandon stood in front of the entertainment center, just like Shaw would have if he'd been here. His absence, along with Agatha's and Fang's, were a heavy weight on all of our shoulders.

"All right. We need to come up with a rescue plan." Brandon's voice wavered as he spoke.

"Gareth, can you locate them like you did me before?" Kelly asked.

Just last winter, Gareth had found Kelly for us at an underground facility in Canada when he was captured by the DAO.

"I've tried, mate. Someone's put a block on the lot of them. We're going to have to do this the old fashioned way. Put our ears to the ground, maybe make a deal with the devil. We've pissed them off. When Ophelia and I escaped, that's the third time someone in our little band of heroes here has bested them. Commander Goldbrook isn't going to keep letting us make an ass out of him," Gareth answered.

Murmured agreements passed between us all. Commander Goldbrook definitely wouldn't just hand them over to us because we found him out. This wasn't a cheesy cartoon about some kids who mostly lucked into solving the mystery at the end of thirty minutes of slapstick comedy. The task at hand was daunting, to say the least.

Melody threw up her hands. "How do we even know where to start?"

No one spoke for a long time. Hope was a slippery thing to grasp when the situation was so bleak. Sure, we'd all been involved in some pretty dangerous situations. Ophelia and Gareth more than the rest of us. Despite that fact, at the end of the day, we were eight teenagers trying to take on a secret government agency to save the most skilled members of our group. Our leader, our medicine woman, and our military man were gone.

Brandon, Kelly, and Chloe had the most combat training. Melody and Leilani weren't far behind. Gareth and Ophelia had spent most of their lives locked up by crazy people who experimented on them. Then there was me. I'd lived like the non-Gifted most of my life. I'd been living this life less than a year.

The only thing keeping me from having a panic attack was the knowledge that Brandon was just as freaked out about this as the rest of us. He knew we weren't much of an army to take on this kind of mission. I didn't know if everyone else realized he felt that way, and if they did, if it made their own sense of panic increase. Maybe it was different for me because I was in love with him. Someone had to be there to share that load with him. That person was me.

"How do we even know where to start?" Melody repeated.

"Good question," Brandon mumbled.

"We could go back to the black market," Leilani suggested.

"It's too dangerous!" Chloe snapped.

Brandon scrubbed his hand down his face and sighed. "It might be our only choice."

"How will we know who to talk to?" I asked.

Kelly shrugged. "I hate to admit it, but we could actually use Marshall right now."

"We have to tread carefully," Brandon warned. "Ophelia and Gareth, you'll have to use your psychic intuition. We need to talk to people who seem like they would never deal with the DAO. However, you never know who would take a cash bribe from Commander Goldbrook and his goons."

"Maybe we should go incognito," I proposed.

"I can give us all makeovers," Melody offered.

"Good idea," Brandon approved. "There's a laptop upstairs, right, Melody?"

"Yes."

"Go order everything you'll need and have it over-night delivered here. I want to get moving on this opera-tion as quickly as possible."

"Brandon, you need time to prepare more than a rough outline of the plan," Chloe cautioned.

Brandon squared his shoulders as he addressed his sister's concern. "What I don't figure out in the next two days, I'll figure out on the way down to the black mar-ket."

Determination radiated from him as he followed Melody up the stairs. One by one, we were each called up to confirm with Melody what we'd be willing to do to alter our appearances. I noticed a lot of colored contacts and temporary hair dye were being ordered.

After my turn was finished, I went outside and sat under the house amongst the stilts in the place Brandon and I discovered our Bond. Now that we had a semblance of a plan in place to attempt yet another rescue mission, my mind had time to wrap itself around the concept of the Bond. What were we able to do with this new Gift? How many other people were Bonded? Was it always a Gift lovers shared?

If we couldn't rescue Agatha, would I ever know the answers to the ever multiplying questions popping into my head?

My thoughts about the Bond morphed back into un-answerable questions about our missing comrades. If we were one being, our brain, heart, and muscle were miss-

ing. How could we function without such vital compo-
nents? I wondered if Brandon was thinking along those
lines. All the questions swirled around my mind and
fused together like ingredients in a blender until all I
could hear was the grinding and screaming of the motor. I
pressed the heels of my hands against my temples in a
vain attempt to quiet the noise.

'*Sable...*'

A whisper slithered through the chaos in my head.
Surely I was just imagining it.

'*Sable, listen to me...*'

The voice sounded familiar. I strained to separate it
from all the white noise.

'*SILENCE!*'

In the blink of an eye, the noise vanished. A relieved
sigh escaped me.

'*Now, can you hear me?*'

"Yes."

'*Where are you, Sable?*'

"I'm not sure I should be telling you that, Marshall."

'*Very good! I wondered how long it would take you
to figure out it was me. Clearly, I have chosen the correct
person—*'

"What's the point of this? Where's Fang?"

'*I don't believe you'd find the sound of his agony
pleasing.*'

My hands balled into fists, wrinkling the fabric of
my shirt. "What have you done to him?"

'*Mind your temper or I'll release the voices I have
caged in your head. You wouldn't want that, would you?*'

"I imagine you want something from me. What is
it?"

'*I'm afraid your friend has put us in quite a situation. While his intentions to sacrifice himself to save the
lot of you were noble, I suppose, he caused quite a scene.*

We were noticed by the wrong people, if you catch my drift.'

"Commander Goldbrook got you, too."

'Precisely.'

"Are Shaw and Agatha with you, too?"

'That I cannot say. While my mind can reach out to another's, I am unable to physically see, as you know. I have been separated from Gus, but Fang is beyond the wall from me.'

"You're deaf, too. How do you know he's next to you?"

'I've nearly lost the ability to hear others' minds with the volume and rage of his mental anguish. I can also feel the vibration in the floor and the walls every time he lashes out physically.'

The air left my lungs and I my stomach twisted in anguish. What was the DAO doing to him?

'To answer your next question, I don't know where we are. I do know that you're a clever little thing and you'll figure it out.'

"Who said I'd help you once I found him?"

'You know there's a war brewing. At this point, it depends on who will deliver the first blow. Don't let it be them, Sable, or you will be sorry. I understand that Shaw and those closest to him don't agree with my methods, but we have to stand together as the Gifted against those who've labeled us as Diseased. The sands of time are slipping through the hourglass at a rapid pace. How many grains will you allow to fall before you move to action?'

"Marshall, what are you not saying?"

The silence left in the wake of his ominous warning was more deafening than the torrent of questions preluding his arrival. Before I could stop it, a howling scream ripped from my throat and tore into the night.

CHAPTER 20

S able? Sable, where are you? Sable?" a male voice
called from the darkness.

"Marshall, so help me God, leave me the hell
alone!" I shrieked.

"I told you she was under the house, mate," another
male voice called from above me.

"She's delusional and looks like a feral cat. I'm not
going near her." A female voice this time.

"Should we get Brandon?" the first male voice questioned.

"No. He's got enough shit to worry about without
dealing with his girlfriend having a psychotic breakdown.
I say we leave her where she is until she figures out to
come back in the house," the female voice sneered.

"Chloe, we can't just leave her sitting under the
house," the first male voice chastised.

"Gareth found her first, let him come drag her out,"
Chloe countered.

"Kelly, you can yank her out of there, can't you?"
Gareth asked.

"Maybe Ophelia should come and sit with her,"
Kelly suggested.

Kelly's, Chloe's, and Gareth's disembodied voices

disappeared and were replaced with the oppressive silence again.

After what felt like an eternity later—although rationally it was probably only five minutes—Ophelia settled next to me in the sand beneath the house.

She combed through my hair with her fingers while she spoke. "What's up, buttercup? Having nightmares?"

"Living nightmares."

"About Marshall? Kelly said something about you screaming about Marshall."

I shuddered. "I hate when he talks in my head. It's like he's prying into my thoughts with knife-tipped fingers and he can see everything I know and everything my subconscious protects me from."

"Are you sure you weren't dreaming?" Her tone gave away that she wanted desperately to believe I was indeed imagining it.

"They're all trapped. He doesn't know where. He's worried about the Gifted being divided in the war. He says it's coming soon. We're not ready." By the end of my rambling, my voice diminished to a whisper.

Ophelia wrapped her arms around my shoulders and squeezed them gently. "I can't pretend like I know what to do, but we'll just have to figure it out when the time comes."

"I don't want to tell Brandon," I sobbed. I buried my face in her shoulder as hot tears streamed down my face.

"It's okay, we don't have to tell him. It will be our little secret," she cooed.

I released myself from her hold and wiped my eyes with the backs of my hands. "What are we going to do?"

"Right now, we're going to go inside and get you cleaned up. You're going to try to get some sleep. Then tomorrow we assume our new identities and start looking for the missing members of our family."

I followed her out from underneath the house and brushed the sand off my clothes as I stood. My limbs wobbled under my weight. Ophelia held onto me by my waist and helped me inside.

The scent of chicken soup with hints of mint and lime filled my nose upon entering the house. Brandon must've been cooking. I allowed Ophelia to lead me upstairs to the shower. She told me she would pick out something for me to wear to bed while I got cleaned up.

Only after I dried my hair and combed it out did I notice the note taped to the bathroom mirror. It read, *Feel a little luxurious tonight!*

I didn't have to wonder what Ophelia meant by that suggestion for long. A black satin chemise trimmed in black floral lace hung on the back of the door. Where the hell did that come from? If it was one of Ophelia's, it wouldn't fit my slender build nearly as well as it would cling to her curves. My cheeks burned hotter and hotter the more I thought about it.

Well, my choices were to either make a mad dash to my room in the chemise or in the nude. I chose the chemise. The so-short-it-was-a-miracle-you-couldn't-see-my-butt-hanging-out-of-it chemise. I cracked the door open and listened to see if I could determine if anyone else was upstairs. The TV downstairs blared music from a music video countdown show, so I knew Melody was down there. Odds were good that Kelly was down there with her. The odds weren't so good that Chloe was with them. There were no footsteps on the stairs. I took a deep breath and tiptoed toward my room. The sooner I could throw on a pair of boxers and a tank top, the better.

"Sable?"

My skin was so hot that I couldn't fathom how I wasn't engulfed with flames on the spot. My brain screamed for my feet to run, but I stayed rooted in place.

Slow footfalls creaked on the floor behind me, coming closer to me with each one.

"Ophelia, I'm going to kill you!" I hissed under my breath.

Brandon's fingers gripped my shoulder. Electricity pulsed in the pads of his fingers and sent little shocks cascading across my skin. I shivered.

His hand slid down my arm and closed around my wrist. His breath hitched.

Footsteps sounded at the bottom of the stairs. I engulfed a panicked gasp.

"Come on!" Brandon gritted out and pulled me into his bedroom. The door snapped shut behind me just as Chloe appeared in the hallway.

I stared at Brandon. He stared back at me. His lips parted like he was going to say something, but then he closed his mouth without a sound uttered.

A knock sounded on his door. "Brandon, I think we should go over strategy."

"Not now, Chloe." His voice sounded strained. His eyes never left the little black satin cloth wrapped around my torso.

"What's wrong with you?" she yelled through the door.

"Nothing! We can talk in the morning," he retorted.

Chloe stalked back down the hallway, grumbling loudly about him being an arrogant ass as she went.

We stood staring at each other. My eyes never left his. His eyes moved up and down me like an elevator. What was he thinking? I felt like such a tramp. Who wore stuff like this? Sure, I had corsets, but I always wore them overtop of other shirts or with sweaters over them. Like this, I was just so…exposed. How could anyone feel confident and sexy like this? I bet Melody could.

I wrapped my arms around my middle.

Sure, that's going to make him quit staring at you, I thought.

I swallowed the lump in my throat. "Brandon, say something."

After a few long, tense moments, he managed a slow, "Wow."

I hesitated. "Is that a good wow or a bad wow?"

His hands twitched at his sides.

"Brandon?"

Before I had time to think, he scooped me up in his arms and had me pressed against him so tightly it would've stolen my breath if his kiss hadn't stolen it first. Even though my eyes were closed, I could see the green flames licking over us both. The air in the room thickened like it did right before a storm ripped the sky apart.

My fingers buried themselves in the curls at the nape of his neck and I tugged his head back. He groaned as he allowed me to break the kiss. The green flames blazed and swirled around us but didn't burn anything they touched.

He kept me pressed against him with one arm while he ran his thumb over my star tattoos.

"The flames—they're so bright," I mumbled.

"They pale in comparison to the fire burning in your eyes."

I dislodged myself from his grip and sat on the edge of his bed. He sat next to me, but he left space between us. Usually, when we were kissing, nothing else in the world mattered. This time, I couldn't keep my thoughts from nagging me. There was so much else going on right now, so much at stake. How could we be doing this when a war was about to begin?

"Are you okay?" he asked me.

I shook my head. "I guess I just feel kind of lost right now."

He sighed. "I know what you mean. Chloe's right, we should be talking strategy right now."

"She probably is."

Neither of us moved. When I couldn't stand the silence any longer, I laced my fingers together with his and brought our hands to my lips. I kissed each of his knuckles, the tips of his fingers, and the inside of his wrist. Somewhere, my brain finally shut itself off and I acted on natural instinct. My lips pressed against his shoulder, made a trail along his collar bone and up his neck and across his jaw. Every time my lips landed on him, a groan of appreciation sounded low in his throat. When I landed at the corner of his mouth, he took my chin in his hand and tilted my head up so I was looking into his eyes.

He took a deep breath before he spoke. "You know I love you, right? I mean, I'm not just saying it because that's what you're supposed to say to your girlfriend. I just need you to know, in case I don't get the chance to tell you after tonight, how truly in love with you I am."

"I know."

And I truly did know. I couldn't really explain how I knew. It was a feeling deep down in my soul. That same feeling that told me that I was in love with him, too.

My fingers locked together behind his neck as I kissed him again and again. His hands trailed up and down my spine, my ribs, my hips, my thighs. I lay down on his bed and pulled him down with me. We touched and tasted and explored each other. All the while the flames were leeched of their color.

Then the moment came. He was hovering over me, his eyes asking for permission. The Bond tugged at my stomach. I sat up and rested my weight on my hands behind me.

I whispered in his ear, "No matter the outcome of all of this, I will always be in love with you, Brandon."

I allowed him to press me back into the mattress with his body and I wrapped my arms around him so my hands rested on his shoulder blades. The Bond between us intensified with every kiss, every touch, every sigh. In those moments, I understood what the Bond meant. Two souls became one, literally. Beyond our physical actions symbolizing two people becoming one, I could feel our souls fuse together as our passions peaked.

His every joy and pain became mine and mine became his. As he collapsed on top of me, I vaguely wondered how long the Bond would take to dissolve this time. I couldn't imagine it ever happening. We were too much a part of each other now. We were two halves of a whole. His whole body trembled. Mine did, too.

He rested his head on my clavicle. I pressed my cheek against the top of his head and traced the length of his spine.

"Are you okay?" he asked softly. I felt his warm breath steadying on my skin.

"Yes. Are you?"

"Yeah."

All the energy I had moments before left me just as quickly as it came. I sagged into the mattress with exhaustion. The Bond was still an iron vice squeezing us together. Even if it hadn't been there, I wouldn't have wanted him to move.

To hell with this war, with the DAO, with Gifted and non-Gifted. In this moment, just as we were, cradled in each other's arms, this was where we belonged. This was nirvana. This was love.

CHAPTER 21

My eyelids grudgingly fluttered open. The morning sunlight filtered through the sheers filled the room with a soft glow. Brandon remained asleep on my chest. A smile twitched the corners of my lips up and I pressed a kiss to the top of his head. He stirred at my touch but didn't wake up. All too soon, this reverie would be broken and all the troubles of reality would slap us in the face.

"Chloe, let him sleep!" Ophelia called from downstairs.

My blood turned to ice and my cheeks burned.

I slapped at Brandon's shoulder a little more forcefully than I intended to, thanks to my rising hysteriapanic. "Brandon, wake up. Come on, Chloe's—"

"*Brandon*!" Chloe shrieked.

Too late.

She barged in the door. Her face turned as red as her hair. Brandon shot up off of my chest and banged his head on my chin. My mouth opened and closed as I floundered for words.

"You're both *naked*," she hissed.

"Why are you staring at your naked brother then?" Brandon retorted.

Death would have been a preferable alternative to the hell I was going through at this very moment. Chloe's outrage and horror was written all over her. Brandon's shamelessness was all the more mortifying. I scrunched myself under the blankets until I could barely peer over the edge of it.

"You tawdry little—" Chloe started.

Brandon cut her off. "Get out."

"This discussion isn't finished."

"There is no discussion. I said get out."

"You're using the wrong head, Brandon. Here I was thinking you were all torn up about having to be the big fish around here. Little did I know you just needed time to get your rocks off."

"Hey, it's hardly different from what I walked in on you and Leilani doing. At least, I had the decency to be in a room with the door closed!"

Wait, Leilani and Chloe hooked up? If I weren't still in the middle of this massively awkward situation, my interest would be piqued higher.

Chloe turned from red to purple. "You swore to me you'd never bring that up again! My private life is my own business."

"So is mine. Now I won't ask you again. Get out."

Chloe turned on her heel and stomped back downstairs. Brandon sat next to me on the bed and peeled back the covers so he could see my whole face.

He kissed my forehead and sighed. "I'm sorry about that. I didn't mean to argue with her in front of you."

"I'm just shocked you could keep your composure while you were so—exposed."

"Definitely not my finest hour. Seriously, though, are you all right?"

"Do you mean right now or before that little episode?"

He chuckled. "Before."

"I was perfectly content, thank you. And how—how were you?"

"I was fantastic."

I breathed a sigh of relief. "I guess I should go get dressed, and you probably should, too."

I stood and wrapped his blanket around me like a burka. He placed a chaste kiss on my lips and opened the door for me. Thankfully, Ophelia was waiting with my bedroom door open. I darted into my room and she closed the door behind us. She faced the door until I was dressed in an outfit that showed the least amount of skin possible.

When she turned around, Ophelia *tsked* under her breath. "Oh yeah, because that outfit doesn't scream, 'I had sex last night and my boyfriend's sister found out about it.'"

I gasped. "Shut up!"

She laughed and started rummaging through my closet. After a few minutes, she pulled out a different shirt, one with shorter sleeves. "At least wear the T-shirt. Long sleeves can't hide what's already been seen."

I changed shirts and let what she just told me sink in. "Wait a minute. You knew that we—that he and I—"

"Would have sex last night? Yes."

My mouth opened and closed a few times before I could form words. "Couldn't you have given me a heads up or something?"

"And ruin the romanticism of it all? No way! My clue was the negligee, but I wouldn't want to interfere more than that. So, how was it?"

"Ophelia!"

"It's okay, you don't have to say anything. That goofy smile spreading across your face says it all."

I covered my mouth with my hand. "I am not smil-ing!"

"Even though that was extremely muffled, yes, you are."

A knock sounded at the door. "Ladies, please be downstairs in the living room in five minutes. We need to start going over our plan to find the missing three and Melody needs to start working on our disguises. It's going to take her all day."

My stomach flipped when I heard Brandon's voice. How could he so quickly go back to being all business when my insides still clenched and stirred up butterflies whenever I thought about him, about us? I envied him for it.

"Well, sounds like the boss man has information to share," Ophelia said.

"Can we wait just a minute before we go down?"

She giggled and nodded. Was this what it was going to be like all day? Was I going to turn into a lovesick idiot every time I looked at Brandon? Probably. Would Ophelia keep snickering at my reactions to him? Maybe. Would Chloe want to stab me in the chest every time she saw me or heard me speak? Most definitely.

My feet dragged as we descended the stairs. Everyone else was crowded around in the living room waiting on us. Their eyes all bored into me as I sat on the floor as far away from Brandon as I could get without leaving the room. Ophelia sat next to Gareth on the love seat. Brandon stood in front of the television and silently assessed us all.

He cleared his throat before he began speaking. "Today we're going to spend time getting our incognito looks worked out. If there's something you'll have to reapply, Melody will teach you how to do it if you don't know already. In addition to that, I will be securing a submarine to take us down to the black market tomorrow. I want you all to try and relax today because this might be the last time we get to for a while. Melody, go ahead and start working on your first project. I'll go last in case finding transportation takes me longer than I expect it will."

Melody nodded. "Okay, you're first, Chloe."

As Melody's transformations were completed, I was amazed that I could hardly recognize anyone. Chloe's hair was dyed a deep burgundy and her freckles were gone. Leilani's head was shaved and she wore green contacts. Kelly's hair was cut short and his glasses were gone. Gareth had his hair dyed dark brown and stubble was on his face in the shape of a goatee. She'd instructed him to let it grow out since his facial hair grew the fastest. Ophelia's hair was a rich golden blonde and she had brown contacts. Melody also had brown contacts and a fake Medusa piercing.

When it was my turn, I got clear plastic spacers to make my spider bite piercing disappear. My tattoo was covered by concealing makeup. Chocolate curls were stained inky black. Green eyes were lost behind ocean blue contacts.

Melody was cornrowing Brandon's hair, so she decided to sit on the couch with him sitting on the floor in front of her to do it. She'd worked hard on all of us all day. I respected her dedication to the mission.

The US national news played on the TV. More and more stories about the Diseased uprising against their oppressors in this state and that state littered the program. It seemed that the war Marshall had predicted was indeed closer than any of us realized. I tuned a lot of what the newscasters were saying out as I turned Marshall's warning over and over in my mind. Then a name brought me screeching back to the here and now—Doctor Pantiel.

He stood with Commander Goldbrook on the steps of the asylum that Fang, Ophelia, and I were imprisoned in. Everything inside me froze when I realized Doctor

Pantiel was holding onto a bound Agatha in front of him.

"Turn up the volume!" I shrieked.

The few of us who weren't already watching the news bolted into the living room so they could see. Melody held a half-finished braid in her hand and gaped at the screen. Her face was glazed with terror.

"It is no longer safe to live among these Diseased," Commander Goldbrook explained. "You see the upheaval they cause every day all over the globe. The only option we have left is to eradicate them."

"Is that really the only option we have? Can't we contain them or something?" the reporter asked.

"Unfortunately, there are no containments that will keep every class of Diseased captive," Doctor Pantiel answered. "We've been trying to create an antidote to their affliction for years, but there's been no success. This wasn't a problem while the Diseased were kept to themselves and only had random outbursts of criminal activity like us normal humans do. However, now that these parasites have decided to bite the hands that feed them, we have no other alternative but to exterminate the lot of them."

The reporter was visibly uncomfortable now. "Isn't that a bit like Hitler's take on the Jews in World War Two?"

"I can see where you would draw that comparison," Doctor Pantiel obliged. "The difference is that the Jews were not causing harm to anyone. The Diseased are a dangerous breed that cause unprovoked physical harm to those of us whom are unlike them. If they were dogs, they would be euthanized for such behavior."

"But these aren't dogs. They're people," the reporter insisted.

"I would use that term loosely," Commander Goldbrook grumbled.

The reporter swallowed audibly. "Are you intending on implementing some sort of vigilante justice or are you going to pursue this through legal channels?"

Doctor Pantiel smiled cruelly like he did when he performed experiments on me and pulled a scalpel from a pocket in his lab coat. With a quick flick of his wrist, the blade glided smoothly across Agatha's throat. Blood splattered onto his coat, the reporter, Commander Gold-brook, and Agatha.

With a chilling laugh he declared, "I think vigilante justice will do just fine."

CHAPTER 22

Silence. Stunned, bitter silence. Except the alarm blaring from the television. The broadcast was cut off. No one in the room even breathed. Was everyone trying to hold in their screams of outrage and heartache? Or was that just me?

I looked over at Melody. Her eyes were wide and glassy with unshed tears. Brandon held her face in his hands.

I couldn't make out what he was murmuring to her, but I doubted she heard him, either. She stared past him like she was looking at Agatha's ghost in the corner of the room.

"He was right," I whispered.

Ophelia grabbed my hand and dragged me outside.

"Not right now," she growled.

"He was! Marshall said that a war was coming and if I didn't do something soon that—"

"Sable. Listen to me. Marshall is an ass who knows how to manipulate even the best of us. He's had over fifty years to perfect his Gift. Chances are good that he already knew this was going to happen. You couldn't have prevented this. There's no way. Now, I know this isn't fair to ask of anyone, but we need to be strong for Melody,

Brandon, Chloe, and Kelly. They just lost the closest thing any of them has had to a mother."

As if on cue, a gut wrenching wail emanated from inside the house. The shock of watching Agatha be slaughtered on live television was burned away by the anguish boiling inside her. Ophelia grimaced and walked back into the house. I followed suit.

There they were, brothers and sisters by circumstance clinging to each other in their hour of need, all of them trying to be strong for Melody. Her sobs wracked her body as she rocked herself back and forth in her seat. Chloe's and Kelly's arms were wrapped tightly around her. Their eyes were both rimmed with red. Brandon sat at Melody's feet, mumbling apologies. I could feel through our Bond that he was screaming inside. It took my breath from me.

"I swear to you, Melody, that those men will die by my hand," Brandon promised.

"You have to let me help," she choked between sobs.

He nodded. She grabbed him around the shoulders and held him close to her. I couldn't watch them grieving anymore, so I went into the kitchen.

I'd never experienced the death of anyone close to me. I'd never even been to a funeral before. How could you possibly do or say anything to console someone who was so clearly broken from their devastating loss? I'd heard people say "everything will be fine" or "they're in a better place now." How do they know? Even though I had no idea what I should do, I still felt like I needed to try something. I ended up making cucumber sandwiches.

After I set the plate down on the coffee table in front of the mourners, I went back outside. The air in the house was so suffocating. I stared off the balcony into the water and thought about the short time I knew Agatha.

She was always kind to everyone, even to Marshall.

She healed me and pointed Brandon and me toward discovering our Bond. Shaw loved her and she loved him. Did Shaw know she died? Had he been slain before her? Before I realized it, I was retching off the balcony. Thank God I finished before Brandon came out to smoke. I curled into a ball behind a chair. What was I supposed to say?

I watched him fumble with his lighter. His hands shook so badly he couldn't get his cigarette lit. He punched the railing and growled. His shoulders shook as he silently cried. I'd never seen him so openly vulnerable. Probably because he assumed he was alone out here.

I crept out of my hiding place, took his cigarettes and lighter out of his hands, and lit one for him. I hated that taste in my mouth, but I knew he'd feel a little better if he had one.

"Thanks," he mumbled as I handed the lit cigarette back to him.

"Don't mention it," I said softly.

He took a long drag and stared out into the water. It reminded me of the time we sat on the deck of the *Kandis Amelia* like this before we went to rescue Kelly and Chloe from the DAO. It was our first rescue mission, which we completed by sheer dumb luck. I had a feeling our luck had finally run out, but I kept that to myself. No need to put another nail in the coffin housing our morale.

We sat in silence long after he finished with his cigarette. As the night wore on, I heard everyone slowly make their way to bed. The breeze was chilly coming off of the water. I hugged my knees to my chest in a vain attempt to keep myself warm. Brandon never seemed phased by the cold. He was probably too numb.

The sun broke over the horizon and we watched in silence as it climbed higher into the sky. People started filling up the beach and playing in the water. Still we never moved. Somewhere in the back of my mind I knew it was a miracle I was still awake, but I didn't want to leave him alone.

"Brandon," I croaked. My throat was dry from inhaling the salty ocean air all night.

He turned his head to look at me. Every pain and worry in the world haunted his eyes. My heart shattered.

"We need to get ready to go to the black market, right?" I suggested.

He sighed. "Right."

He stood and popped his stiff joints before heading back inside.

I yawned and followed him back in. My back and legs screamed in protest when I straightened them. I was definitely going to be sorry later for sitting on a hard wooden floor all night.

After a quick shower and wardrobe change—I was dressed in black jogging pants and a matching hoodie—I came down to the living room. Everyone looked so different it was hard to tell who was who. One person stuck out like a sore thumb among us. Melody sat in the place I'd last seen her in last night. Her eyes were swollen and red and had deep purple half-moons beneath them. I had an idea that she hadn't moved since the night before and she'd long since run out of tears. She breathed in raspy pants. Even though the tears were gone, she was still crying. Seeing her in that moment made me wish I could trade places with Agatha so Melody could have her mom back.

Although my own mother wasn't dead, she might as well have been. When I'd told Melody that I didn't really miss my parents, I lied. I tried really hard not to, but it was something I couldn't just turn off. Most of the time I could block out the memories of my life before finding out I was Diseased. Sometimes, though, I would dream about my parents. The hollow ache in my chest caused by the absence of them would make me wake up crying. I would never wish that kind of pain on anyone. Well, maybe I would wish it on Commander Goldbrook and Doctor Pantiel.

"Um, we need to be gone from here in half hour," Brandon said quietly.

Everyone except Melody gathered up our possessions from the house and packed them into suitcases. That's how we lived since we lost the *Kandis Amelia*. Had it really only been three months since then? Nothing was ever marked, in case we lost them in travel and whatnot, so we couldn't be tracked. We'd been losing a whole lot of things lately.

When it was time to load up into the Jeeps Shaw rented when we first came to this beach house, Kelly scooped Melody in his arms and we piled into our respective vehicles. The first was occupied by Kelly, Melody, Chloe, and Leilani. Gareth and Ophelia rode in the second one. Brandon and I should have been with them, but we drove the Jeep that Shaw, Fang, and Agatha should've been in.

We rode in silence to the marina the submarine was housed in. I could practically see the wheels in Brandon's head turning. Just like everything else painful in his life, he shoved it down inside and locked it away, solely focusing on the mission at hand. The Bond pulsed with a deep ache in the pit of my stomach.

His resolve wasn't as solid as he probably would've liked. Somewhere in my subconscious, I mentally chastised him for the unhealthy habit. I shook my head and *tsked* myself under my breath.

"What?" Brandon asked.

"Nothing."

He nodded and kept his eyes on the road. What was

he was thinking about? Probably, he was trying to strategize. Not much of that had been done.

"Hey, Brandon?"

"Hmm?"

"You know, you don't have to think of everything ahead of time. Sometimes you can do things without having it all worked out first and make things up as you go."

We pulled into the marina and Brandon parked the SUV. The others were caught at the last stop light still. Brandon leaned his head back against the head rest and closed his eyes.

"But Shaw—"

I took his face in my hands and made him look at me. The vulnerability there made my heart ache. "Shaw is a great man, but you and he are two different people. He was training you to be a strong leader, not to be a carbon copy of him. Do what your intuition tells you is right. No one is expecting you to be Shaw. I mean, none of us know what to do either, but that doesn't mean you automatically should. Cut yourself some slack."

He pressed his forehead against mine and sighed. "What if I fail?"

"Then we all fail together, and it would be because Commander Goldbrook bested us. It wouldn't be because you dropped the ball. We're only seventeen, Brandon. Change is coming, and, whether it's good or bad, we'll face it together."

"We're only seventeen…" Brandon's eyes grew wide. "Sable! Oh my God, your birthday was a whole two days ago—"

I couldn't help but smile. "That's not really important right now—"

"I'm so sorry—"

"Look. When we get Shaw and Fang back, you can make me a huge birthday cake and go as crazy as you want to. Right now, we have other things to take care of."

He kissed my cheek as the other two SUVs parked beside us. "You really are the most wonderful person, you know that?"

I winked. "I try."

For the first time in what seemed like ages, he cracked a smile as he got out of the vehicle.

ഓഓഓ

Our new submarine, aptly named *Little Guppy*, was about half the size of the *Roman Candle*. As I sat down next to Brandon, I wondered if Fang would even be able to stand upright in this thing. The picture in my head of him stooped over as he tried to move around in here made me smile. Then tears pricked the backs of my eyes. I missed him terribly.

Kelly, Melody, Chloe, and Leilani sat at the banquette in the galley. Melody moved like a zombie and had lifeless glazed eyes, like her life ended when Agatha's did. Did Shaw know she was gone? It seemed like the sort of information the DAO would use to break him with. But Shaw was so stubborn, he'd refuse to believe anything they said. When we got him back and told him it was true…

I swallowed the bile in my throat.

Ophelia and Gareth were sitting on a bed opposite from the one Brandon and I sat on. They explained to him what they knew about the black market, which wasn't very much. Commander Goldbrook had them blindfolded most of the time. What they did remember was walking a long way from the docks and when they arrived at their destination, Commander Goldbrook tried to sell them to a man named Giuseppe Stavropoulos for five million dollars apiece. Apparently, the man would only pay one million for both of them. They said it made Commander Goldbrook angry. They were almost back to the docks when Shaw, Agatha, Fang, Marshall, and Gus happened upon them.

So far, our only strategy was to move around in two groups of four and see who solicited us. We would trade our information for theirs, although I wasn't exactly sure we had any information that anyone in the black market would find useful. Brandon, Gareth, Chloe, and I would make up the first group, which left Ophelia, Leilani, Kelly, and Melody in the second.

We were all pinning our hopes on our ragtag group of teenagers being able to pull off another miracle. I kept reassuring Brandon our plan would work and we'd be able to find where Commander Goldbrook was holding Fang and Shaw prisoner. Inside, I wasn't nearly so confident. I hoped Brandon couldn't feel through the Bond that I was lying.

CHAPTER 23

I stepped onto the dock gingerly like it would crumble away when I touched it. Of course, that didn't happen. The structure was just as sound as any other well maintained dock. When we all squeezed out of the *Little Guppy*, I stared at my comrades and tried to memorize their faces. Melody really had done an excellent job disguising us all. Everyone was dressed in nondescript jeans, T-shirts, and sneakers so we wouldn't draw attention to ourselves.

Before we split off, Brandon gave us orders not to, under any circumstances short of our lives being threatened, use our Gifts. We shook hands and hugged before Ophelia's group made their way to the black market entrance. Our group would wait ten minutes before we went in. In the meantime, we busied ourselves with keeping up the appearance that we were making sure the *Little Guppy* was securely fastened to the dock and that we hadn't picked up any stray barnacles or ocean plant life on our way down. Then on Brandon's cue, we made our way into the black market.

The noise level was incredible. We practically had to yell at each other to be able to be heard above the racket. There were different sorts of smells permeating the air. It was an overwhelming blend of salt, metal, sulfur, bleach, and something akin to smoked barbecued meat. There were so many things to see, I practically made myself dizzy from my eyes darting back and forth. People were selling weapons, food, animals, and other people, along with an array of other goods and services. One woman had a fortune telling booth—which Gareth told me was a fraud—with thick jasmine incense smoke wafting from it. The women I thought were prostitutes were actually women being sold as sex slaves. I had to swallow back vomit a few times.

We moved through little winding paths between shops and booths and carts in the wide enclosure. It was almost like we were salmon swimming upstream. Chloe's shrewd gaze scanned the crowds for anything that seemed like it might be useful. Brandon kept looking back to make sure he hadn't lost any of us and conferring with Gareth to see if he found any of his surroundings familiar.

I just looked like a tourist who gaped at everything she passed like this was an African safari or something.

An unease that wasn't my own unsettled me. Right. The Bond. It was Brandon's nervousness I felt. I peered at him with a sidelong glance. If it weren't for the Bond, I doubted I would've been able to tell he was worried at all. His face was a mask of calm and calculation. If this had been a few months ago—hell, if it had been even a week ago, I would've taken his cool exterior to mean he had everything under control. Of course he knew what he was doing. This was Brandon we were talking about. But now? Now I knew better.

As I studied his face a little longer, I realized I would've known of his lack of confidence even without the Bond. I could see it in the set of his jaw, the way his hands kept bunching the fabric of the pockets in his jeans, the way his irises looked like electrical sparks would pop out of them at any second. Gareth couldn't tell, I knew. Could Chloe?

Crack! Crap. I'd been too lost in thought to notice the ceramic vase that was almost as tall as me blocking my path and ran right into it. It broke into large sections when it toppled onto the ground.

The olive skinned shop owner scowled at me. His hand rested on the hilt of the knife sitting in front of him. "I hope you're intending to pay for that, little girl."

"I uh—I don't—I'm sorry—I don't have any money," I stammered.

Brandon laid a hand on my shoulder and squeezed hard. He was pissed, too. Whether it was at me or the shop keeper or both of us, I couldn't tell. "Is there a problem here?"

"Are you responsible for this girl?" the shop keeper demanded.

"No, but I couldn't help but notice you threatening a kid. Is that really necessary?" Brandon countered.

"What do you care if something happens to her, then?"

"Like I said, I don't like seeing girls being roughed up. She apologized to you, didn't she? You have lots of other valuables here worth far more than that vase. I'd even wager that you picked that up from a furniture store and now you're trying to pedal it here like it's some sort of treasure," Brandon challenged.

The shop keeper twirled the knife between his fingers. "I'd watch what you say, unless you'd like to lose your hand like your young friend here will."

Well, he wasn't threatening my life, but I didn't like the idea of losing an appendage because of an accident. I let my fists glow with a low burning flame.

"Pick one," I dared him.

His eyes grew wide and he dropped the knife. "You might want to remove your hand from her before she burns you, friend."

I winced as a jolt of electricity shot through me. I could hear the static of it popping in my ears. Thankfully, my knees didn't buckle from the intensity of it. Brandon was showing restraint, lucky for me.

"I think I can handle myself," Brandon said quietly.

"Both of you get away from my wares," the shop keeper hissed.

Brandon and I extinguished our Gifts at the same time. He let go of my shoulder and snatched up my wrist instead. Before I could move of my own accord, he was dragging me away from the scene. Gareth and Chloe were hot on our heels.

"Way to not get noticed, star gazer," Chloe spat.

"I'm sorry," I mumbled.

Brandon whipped me in front of him and held my face firmly between his hands. "For the love of God, will you *please* pay attention to what you're doing? We can't afford another episode like that. Do you want us all to get killed?"

I blinked stupidly at him. This felt worse than the time he punched me in the eye when I first started combat training with him. The worst part was that he was completely right. I was unfocused. I couldn't afford to be that way, especially here. There were other people counting on me, even if I wasn't particularly responsible for anything other than myself. I fought back tears as I nodded once.

He must've felt my shame through the Bond because he closed his eyes and let out a heavy sigh. Then he brushed his thumb over my spider bite piercing before his hands dropped to his sides.

As we started making our way deeper into the black

market, Gareth fell into step beside Brandon, Chloe followed behind them, and I brought up the rear. I stopped focusing so much on our surroundings and trained my eyes on my comrades. Hopefully, I wouldn't run into anything else this way. It was stupid of me to just check out like that and put my friends in danger.

The anger I felt toward myself was intensified by Brandon's anger, but the edge of the emotion was tempered by his overwhelming sense of relief. Was he relieved we got out of our little scrape without drawing too much attention? I was. How long would it take to get used to feeling his feelings aside from my own? Was he affected by my feelings, too? Now wasn't the time to ask.

I stopped short when a tall, thin man who reminded me a little of a praying mantis appeared in front of us. He wore a dusty sand-colored hooded robe so only his face and his hands were visible. Brandon had to tilt his head back slightly to meet the man's eyes.

"Gifted children, come with me." His voice was soft, but I could hear him through the noise as clearly as if everything around us was silent.

"Who are you?" Brandon asked.

"Conductor, now is not the time to speak of these matters. Just know that I am your brethren. My colleague has gathered the others of your tribe. We have important information to discuss," the man explained.

"Our tribe?" That description sounded odd to me.

"Who are these other members you speak of?" Brandon questioned.

"The Seer, the Shifter, the Poison, the Light, and the Shield," the man replied.

I made a mental checklist and deciphered whose name went with each Gift—Seer was Ophelia, Shifter was Kelly, Poison was Leilani, Light was Melody, and Shield was—

"*Fang!*" I screamed. The name ripped from my throat of its own accord. I pushed past Chloe and almost knocked her over in my haste to get to Brandon. "We have to go with him!"

"He might be lying—" Brandon warned.

"Then have Gareth look for him. Let him see if it's true. If Fang is here," I pleaded.

Gareth touched my bicep. Sadness swam in his eyes. "Even if Fang is here, that doesn't mean the others are with him. And I don't have anything to track any of them with."

People started moving around our little knot like water passes around debris in a stream. Some people made disgruntled remarks as they went by, and others shot us skeptical glances, but most just kept going on about their business without paying us any attention.

I anchored my hands on my hips as a show of defiance. Brandon was supposed to lead, but I had to see if Fang was indeed all right. I had to know who was lying to me, this man or Marshall. "Fine, if you guys want to play it safe, go ahead. I'm going with this guy."

"We don't know if we can trust him." Brandon sounded calm, but his words were as sharp as a razor.

"When Chloe was kidnapped, you didn't hesitate to go find her, did you? Fang is my brother and I won't pass up an opportunity to find him, even if it isn't safe," I countered.

Chloe sighed and rolled her eyes. "Well, someone has to make sure you don't get killed. I'm in."

Brandon's eyebrows shot up in surprise. "Chloe you're—you're going with Sable?"

She nodded. "We've been searching for leads for God knows how long. This is the closest thing we've found to it. If Fang is with these people, he might know more about where Shaw is. It's not the safe thing to do, but it might be the only chance we have to get some answers."

Brandon looked over at Gareth. They shared a long glance at each other. Brandon was silently asking Gareth if he thought they should go or not. Gareth just offered an almost imperceptible shrug.

Brandon pinched the bridge of his nose and closed his eyes. "Fine. We'll go."

A heavy weight I felt in my stomach dampened my elation. I'd gotten my way, but at what cost? I said I silent prayer to whoever would listen that this would turn into something good instead of us walking into a death trap.

CHAPTER 24

We followed closely behind the robed man as he led us on a winding path through the black market. Brandon's waning irritation trickled into me through the Bond. The frustration became miniscule when he took my hand in his. Despite his mixed feelings, I knew enough that this small gesture was his way of trying to be supportive. I knew the odds were better that we'd all get kidnapped and sold off into slavery than this man being truthful about meaning us no harm, but I couldn't make that matter as much as it should.

Brandon squeezed my fingers gently. I squeezed his back. How long had we been walking? I started to get anxious. I dug my nails into my palm to distract myself.

Brandon winced. "Sable, don't worry so much."

I bit my lower lip. "Can you—can you feel my physical pain through the Bond, too?"

"No, but I can feel your nails cutting into my palm."

I yanked my hand out of his. "Oh my God, I'm so sorry, Brandon!"

He brought my hand to his lips and kissed my knuckles before winding his fingers back through mine at his side. "It's okay. I've had worse."

That was true. I just hoped "worse" wasn't what we were walking in on.

There wasn't much of any conversation between any of us as we followed the stranger through the black market. Since this place was so far underwater and lit artificially, there was no way of tracking by sunlight how long we'd been walking or in what direction.

As if sensing my impatient nature, the man called over his shoulder to us, "We're nearly there."

"Nearly there" ended up being four hundred seventy-six paces. I counted out of boredom and an attempt to control my building unease. Brandon's added worry through the Bond didn't help me calm down any.

That's when I heard his voice boom out above the noise of the bustling market. "Miss Sable!"

Fang! But where was he? I couldn't see him. I jumped up in a vain attempt to locate him in the crowd. It was a stupid thing to do, really. Fang wasn't exactly the kind of guy to blend in with crowds, given how tall and broad he was and the scar that marred the length of his face. Then my feet were no longer touching the ground and the air in my lungs was squeezed out. I threw my arms around Fang's neck and buried my face in his shoulder. Tears oozed down my cheeks.

"Don't you ever scare me like that again!" I wheezed.

Fang set me back down and held me at arm's length. "That was never my intention, Miss Sable."

Brandon smiled. "Good to see you again."

Fang looked at Brandon and nodded.

Chloe and Gareth exchanged pleasantries with Fang.

The robed man waited patiently during our reunion. When Brandon looked at him expectantly, he turned on his heel and led us the few yards remaining between us and the rest of our comrades.

Three other men in robes identical to those of our guide's waited with Ophelia, Kelly, Leilani, and Melody. We exchanged brief smiles of relief that we were all accounted for. But now that we were all here, what did these mysterious cloaked men want with us?

As if on a silent cue, all four men pushed the hoods from their heads and revealed their faces. One look at them had me wishing they would've left their disguises intact. Each man looked identical to the next. All paper white skin, their blue veins beneath creating a living marbling effect of the skin's surface. Their eyes had a letter X carved over each one, which were then sewn together with a thick black cord. Their lips were thin and purple. Were these men freezing to death?

The one who guided us to this tent gestured for our attention. "Your patience with us is much appreciated. We cannot reveal much information about ourselves. Like you, we are also hunted—"

"Why?" I interrupted.

He gave me a sad smile. His teeth were black. They looked as if they were made of onyx as opposed to rotting bone.

"Our blood carries in it all the knowledge of the universe, past, present, and future," he obliged in a low voice.

Brandon folded his arms and rested them on his torso. "Then you know where Shaw is."

"Your assumption is correct. We also know how this war of Diseased will end," one of the other robed men informed us.

"I don't mean to sound disrespectful, but what are you?" Melody asked.

"We are what you would refer to as an alien race. There is no word in your native tongue that translates to our proper names," our guide answered.

"So are you going to tell us anything, or are you just trying to impress us with your supposed vast knowledge base?" Chloe challenged.

The alien standing closest to her chuckled. "You use hostility to hide your fear. Your Gift is rather appropriate in that regard. Drain the life from those who you fear so they no longer pose a threat to you. It is rather intriguing how well each Gift suits the bearer of it."

"Please, we don't mean to press the issue, but I'm sure you understand how vital it is for us to find Shaw. Without him we are lost," Ophelia implored.

Our guide shook his head. "There is much unrealized potential in you all. You have begun this uprising, yet you claim no responsibility for it. Your destiny is great and terrible."

"I don't understand. What uprising did we start?" I questioned.

"There will come a moment when all in your world will be watching you. An act of rebellion will ignite other Gifted into action. The Bonded will lead the charge to absolution or elimination," he explained.

The Bonded? That meant Brandon and me. I swallowed as a shiver of fear raked up my spine. Brandon pulled me into his side protectively. His expression was brave, but I felt his terror and disbelief barely contained by his façade of steady composure.

The alien standing next to our guide wheezed, "Your medicine woman understood this. Her sacrifice was made in good faith that you would prevail in your charge."

Agatha thought we would win the revolution. She said Brandon and I would be important, but this responsibility? The weight of expectations sank uncomfortably in the pit of my stomach.

Leilani sighed. "If we're going to have any chance at being successful, we need Shaw."

Our band of supposed heroes murmured in agreement. Shaw was the mastermind of battle strategies and the like.

Our guide spoke again. "Our time together must draw to a close. You may ask of us three truths and then I will guide you back to your aquatic vessel. We must go back into hiding, and so must you, Gifted."

"What is this, like three wishes from a genie?" Chloe snorted.

"Enough," Brandon admonished her.

She anchored her hands on her hips defiantly and pressed her lips into a hard thin line.

"Who decides what we get to ask?" Gareth wondered aloud.

"Well, it seems like Brandon and Sable are supposed to run this show, so perhaps they should be the ones to decide," Kelly offered.

The others nodded in agreement and looked to Brandon and me expectantly.

"Where is Shaw?" Brandon asked.

"He is being held in the very place you found the Phoenix," our guide answered.

Wait, we had to go back to the Crazy Cannon Place? Memories of being experimented on like a lab rat swamped my mind. I almost died there twice. My stomach twisted painfully.

"Why is the Bond so important?" Brandon continued.

"Through the Bond, you are capable of so much more than any mere Gifted could ever hope to be. It is effective even when you are separated, but together, when your Bond is used correctly, you have the potential to be unstoppable," our guide explained.

"Why us?" I whispered.

Brandon twitched at my question. I really hadn't

meant to say it aloud. My cheeks heated with embarrassment. The Bond clued me in that Brandon was irritated. He obviously wanted to ask something different.

"My child, could you please be a bit more specific?" our guide inquired.

I blinked up at him. "I mean, why were Brandon and I—and the rest of our comrades for that matter—tasked with this? Surely there are other Gifted just as capable, if not more so. Why are we the ones who responsible for the fate of our race?"

He shook his head. "Little Phoenix, there is more depth to you than you can imagine. The reason is not as important as the necessity to accept your role in the revolution.

"Now, I will escort you back. Our safety here quickly dwindles."

We followed behind our alien guide wordlessly until we reached the *Little Guppy*. Before we boarded the vessel, the Pharaoh nodded to Brandon and me in turn before losing himself in the throng milling around the black market.

Fang went to lie down before we set off for the world above the water's surface. The others asked Ophelia questions about what the Crazy Cannon Place was like. She'd spent the most time there of all of us. I should've helped her answer them about what went on in that dungeon of Hell. But I couldn't. I still had trouble digesting everything that happened there to begin with.

My usual refuge from feeling so trapped was to go outside. Even while I was imprisoned at the Crazy Cannon Place, I imagined I could squeeze through the cell window that Fang punched his fist through to let the sea air in to permeate the stale air within the basement containments. Then I could sit on the beach and gaze out at the Atlantic Ocean. On the *Kandis Amelia* I would fall asleep on the deck all the time instead of in the barracks below. Now I was confined in a submarine. It would take hours for the *Little Guppy* to break through the Pacific Ocean's surface.

Strong arms banded around my middle and the scent of lemongrass and anise filled my nose.

"Breathe, Sable. Just breathe," Brandon soothed.

I turned and buried my face in his shoulder and let tears I hadn't realized I was suppressing fall until I was full on sobbing. Brandon eased us to the floor and cradled me in his lap. He tried to screw up enough courage for both of us, but the traitorous Bond told me that he was just as afraid as I was.

CHAPTER 24

Brandon

Everyone sat on the patio of our temporary beach home. All of our disguises were discarded and everyone looked like themselves again. Sable fussed over Fang even though he was fine. It turned out that he was able to hide in the black market after he was separated from us. He took refuge with the aliens and they agreed to offer him scantuary since they knew we would come back for him. Sable's overwhelming relief of his return made her buoyant, but it made me feel even more exhausted than I already was. I still wasn't exactly sure how the Bond worked, but whatever it did, it wore me out a lot.

The adrenaline from the day had waned and the exhaustion I felt was mirrored on the faces of all my companions.

"So what's the deal with this asylum place?" Melody asked.

"It's Hell on Earth," Ophelia replied.

"Didn't Brandon bust you guys out of that place on his own? It doesn't seem like it would be too difficult to spring Shaw from there, too," Gareth mused.

"Commander Goldbrook wouldn't be foolish enough to bait us with Shaw in a place that would be easy to liberate him from," Leilani retorted.

"That's true," Fang agreed.

"So your prior experience with the place wouldn't help us at all?" Gareth questioned.

"I was undercover in that place for months before I accidentally shorted out the electric system," I admitted.

Chloe gasped. "That wasn't intentional?"

I shook my head. Memories of that day flooded in my mind, unbidden.

An emaciated-looking Sable, lying on a metal table, her eyes wide and wild. The needle coming closer and closer to puncturing through her skin. The plunger waiting to be pressed, dispersing the toxin that was meant to kill her...

My stomach roiled.

"But—but you never lose control! What happened to you in there?" Chloe spluttered.

I sighed. "They had Sable in this room, and they were going to kill her, and I just—"

"You were dating Sable in the asylum?" Melody interrupted.

"No, he wasn't," Sable clarified.

"So you're telling me you freaked out over a hot piece of ass?" Chloe hissed.

"Chloe—" Kelly said in a warning tone.

But the warning wasn't enough. Before I realized what was happening, Sable leapt over the patio table and slapped Chloe across the face so hard that the sound echoed into the night.

A red handprint bloomed on Chloe's cheek and she placed her fingers gingerly over the mark. Then she seemed to come out of her daze and lunged for Sable. Chloe's fingers twisted in Sable's hair as the heel of Sable's hand connected with the tip of Chloe's nose. Chloe howled in pain, but didn't release her grip on Sable's hair. Instead, she yanked down on it and ripped a chunk out of Sable's scalp. Then the two of them were punching and kicking each other so fast I couldn't separate out whose limbs belonged to whom. Fang managed to yank Sable far enough away from Chloe that they couldn't touch each other. To make sure she wouldn't perpetuate the brawl, I pulled Chloe into the house.

I turned the lights on and looked her over. Her nose was gushing blood and she had a black eye. There were scratches covering her bare arms. Her wild fiery hair was a tangled mess. I steered her into the kitchen and grabbed a chair from the dining room table. After I eased her into it, I went into the bathroom and grabbed a hand towel. I wet it down in the kitchen sink and wrung it out before I wiped the blood off of her face and arms.

Through the Bond, I'd felt a surge of rage like when Sable first smacked Chloe. I focused on keeping my breathing steady so the negative emotions wouldn't consume me.

As I rinsed the blood out of the towel, I asked, "Why did you have to say that in front of her?"

"You know why," Chloe muttered petulantly. Her bottom lip was swollen.

She was right. I did know why. Her whole life, Chloe said snotty things to people when she was afraid. I just wasn't exactly sure what she was afraid of. It could be that she was afraid of going back to the asylum. The stories I told her about the place were frightening enough without having experiencing them firsthand. She could be afraid that Sable would mess me up worse than Melody had when she was ripped out of my life. Or it could be that she was scared about Shaw dying just like Agatha had. Maybe it was a combination of all three.

It was a strange thing to feel simultaneously sorry that my sister sustained the injuries she did and proud that my girlfriend had flourished so well in her combat training.

"Yeah, well you still shouldn't have said it," I admonished her.

"You don't always have to take her side," she hissed.

"Where am I now? Who's not in this room? I could be with her, trying to calm her down instead of being in here with you, cleaning you up like—"

"Like when we were young," she interrupted.

A memory of cleaning up Chloe's cuts and scrapes after a brutal day of training when she was fourteen flashed into my mind. She insisted on learning to fight in heels that were so high and so small around that it made me dizzy thinking about having to balance on them, let alone roundhouse kick someone with them on. I asked her why she bothered. She smiled at me and said she wanted to be beautiful *and* lethal. I told her she was both of those things without the heels and she hugged me tight.

Now I hugged her, but was careful not to press on any of her wounds. She rested her head on my shoulder and slung her arms across my back.

"You should probably apologize to her," I murmured into her hair.

She huffed and pushed me away from her. "I don't have to apologize for anything."

"Chloe, you're going to have to get used to her sticking around. Besides, you and Leilani are hitting it off pretty well, aren't you?"

She turned on her heel and walked toward the patio. "That's none of your business."

I shook my head and threw the towel in the sink before I followed after her. "It's not really. That never stopped you from sticking your nose into my personal business."

She whipped around to face me and slammed her hands onto her hips. "So what is this, an eye for an eye?"

"No, but I do want to see you happy."

Her shoulders slumped and her face fell. "You don't have to worry about that."

I grabbed her hand. "Of course I do. You're the only sister I have. Why wouldn't I worry about you being happy?"

Tears brimmed in her eyes as she looked into mine. "Are you happy, Brandon?"

"With Sable? Yes. In general, no."

"Aren't you—aren't you afraid of getting hurt again?"

"There are more pressing matters to worry about right now. Do I think about it sometimes? Yeah, sure. Who wouldn't? But I love her. I love being around her and talking to her. When everything is so dark, she makes them a little brighter without even trying."

"Do you love her like you loved Melody?"

"No, it's not the same. It's hard to explain. I cared about Melody a lot. We had a lot in common and we were really good friends. When she left, I was really upset about it. With Sable, it's so much deeper than that, which I guess is what makes it scary. The risk is so much higher, but the reward is so much greater. I want that for you. You should find your bright spot in the darkness."

Chloe stared at me for a while before pulling away. I knew she was considering what I'd told her. Was she so hostile towards Sable this whole time because she was being protective of me, or because she was trying to defend Melody's place? I doubted she would know the answer if I asked her.

A wave of frustration hit me through the Bond. I was

beginning to regret all the times I wished I knew what was going on inside someone else's head. The weight of carrying someone else's emotions and your own was taxing, to say the least.

I found Sable sitting on the beach. The surf lapped lazily over her feet. In the moonlight, her pale skin almost glowed. Little flames burst and died out quickly nearby her. She must be setting fire to the seaweed that washed up near her. I felt her trying to contain herself, but the hold on her thinly veiled anger was weak.

I took a seat next to her in the sand. She glanced sideways at me, but said nothing. Her star tattoos looked like a blurry shadow beneath her curls. She flexed her fingers, made a fist, and flexed her fingers again. I watched her repeat the action over and over in time to waves slithering onto the beach. If she hadn't been taught to control her Gift, would she be engulfed in flames?

"I'm sorry about my sister," I said in a low voice.

"You don't have to apologize for her. She's not your kid." Her voice sounded thick and she spoke slowly.

"Can I—can I see the damage?"

Sable looked at me face to face. I swallowed a mouthful of bile. In the fight, Chloe ripped one of Sable's lip rings out.

I reached out to touch her face. "Sable—"

"Don't."

That one word stung as much as a hard slap in the face. She knew it did, too, because I instantly felt her remorse through the Bond.

I reached out to touch her face again. She didn't rebuke me this time. Her eyes closed and they squeezed closed tighter as I brushed my thumb beneath the injury.

"Can it be pierced again?" I asked gently.

She sighed. "I don't know. It hurts like a bitch."

"I'm sorry."

"I've had worse."

I hated when she said that. She was right, but every time she pointed it out, I always remembered the times it was worse. I wished I could scrub those images out of my brain, but there were some things you couldn't just forget witnessing.

"I mean I'm sorry about all of it. Chloe shouldn't have said those things about you. She's just scared, you know?"

"Well, I wish she would quit expressing it so violently," Sable muttered.

"It definitely would make my life a little easier," I joked.

She smiled begrudgingly. I felt her trying to cling to her anger. I kissed her on her cheekbone next to her tattoo. She laid her head on my shoulder. Even without the Bond, I knew that meant she wasn't mad at me anymore.

While I had her in a better mood, I asked her, "So I guess this means that we won't be kissing for a few days?"

She swatted me on the shoulder. "Is that all you can think about right now?"

I shrugged, which made her laugh. I loved hearing her laugh. It was a light and airy sound that made me feel lighter, too.

"I can't kiss you for a while."

I gave her an exaggerated pout, which made her laugh again.

"That doesn't mean you can't kiss me, though—"

As I leaned in to kiss her jaw, I heard someone clear their throat behind me. Sable offered them a tight smile.

"Brandon, are we going to decide about how we're going to make it to the asylum to break out Shaw?" Melody inquired.

I sighed and raked my fingers through my hair. Then

I stood and offered Sable my hand and helped her up. "Yeah, let's go figure this out."

The three of us walked back to the house in awkward silence. Even though Kelly was Melody's new object of affection, Sable still seemed a little on edge around her. Everyone was waiting for us on the patio. Chloe sat with her feet propped up on the table. She offered a stiff nod to Sable, who returned it with a steely glare. Would I always be caught between these two?

"So, we need to make a plan to get to the asylum, which is on the opposite side of the continent from us," I stated.

"The *Kandis Amelia* sure would come in handy right about now," Kelly mused.

"Is there a way we could rent a boat to travel that far? Or maybe we could fly," Leilani suggested.

"If there's a mass hunt for Diseased right now, I think an airport would be dangerous," Ophelia pointed out.

I nodded. "I agree. What I can try to do tomorrow is see if I can buy us a new boat. Hopefully these funds Shaw gave me access to are enough to do that."

"And if it doesn't?" Chloe challenged.

"Then we'll come up with a different plan tomorrow," I stated.

"We can still try to make a plan about getting into the Crazy Cannon Place," Fang supplied.

"I doubt we'll be able to infiltrate their ranks like I did last time. They'll be expecting that now," I said.

Gareth crossed his arms over his chest. "We'll have to break in from the outside."

"Which means we'll need to run reconnaissance when we get there," Fang added.

While the others debated about the best way to scope out the place undetected, I sensed Sable's anxiety heightening. She stayed quiet and listened to the rest of us toss-ing around ideas. Pressure built in my chest as our dis-cussion continued. I thought Sable might be on the verge of a panic attack. As much as I hated her reaction, I knew it was logical to be afraid of returning to a place where you were held captive and almost killed, especially when the people who tried to kill you were still there.

"Okay, let's wrap this up for tonight and we'll finish talking about it tomorrow once we have a better idea about our transportation," I decided.

Everyone bid each other goodnight and headed off to their rooms. I caught Sable's wrist as she was about to walk inside.

"Will you stay with me?"

She blinked at me. "Do you need to talk to me about something?"

"No." I just wanted to hold her. There was nothing else I could think of to do to offer her some semblance of comfort.

"Okay."

I followed her inside and up to my room. When the door was closed, we both stripped down to our underwear and climbed into bed. Even though the tropical climate made the air warm and humid, Sable's skin was freezing. I wrapped my arms around her and pressed her into my side. She nestled her head into my shoulder and I kissed her hair.

"It's going to be all right," I whispered in her ear.

"Yeah," she whispered back.

Her tears rolled off her cheeks and onto my chest. I held her tighter against me and kept whispering reassur-ances to her until she fell asleep. I wanted to cry, too, but I had to be brave for her.

I had to be brave for all of us.

CHAPTER 26

Sable

"I found something we can use, but it's a big purchase," Brandon explained.

Everyone sat around the dining room table, finishing their breakfast. Brandon had left before the sun came up and looked for some way to get us to the Crazy Cannon Place.

"Big as in size or big as in price tag?" Kelly asked.

"Both," Brandon answered.

"What is it?" Ophelia inquired.

"A yacht. It'll hold all of us, and it's comfortable—" Brandon supplied.

"Can we afford a yacht?" Melody interrupted.

"I don't know," he confessed.

"How much is it, Brandon?" I coaxed.

He sighed. "Just over three million."

"You better mean three million pesos, mate," Gareth chided.

Brandon stood behind me and rubbed my shoulders absentmindedly. Anxiety rolled off of him in waves, even without the Bond. "No, it's in US dollars."

"I ain't so sure you can just go buy something like

that by flashing Shaw's credit card without some investigation," Fang pointed out.

Brandon's grip on me tightened. "I feel deplorable even saying this, believe me. But I think we're going to have to use Leilani's power of persuasion to convince the salesman we can handle the expense."

Leilani's eyes grew wide, but she retained her composure. She nodded her acquiesce and excused herself from the table.

Everyone else muttered amongst themselves. This plan was risky. Brandon knew it was. It wasn't the type of perfectly calculated play that Shaw would've made. Brandon was the only thread holding us all together now. So whether or not we agreed with him, we were compelled to follow his vision through.

I didn't really like the idea that we were most likely stealing the yacht, but I knew Brandon really needed the moral support.

That's what good girlfriends did, right?

When we got to the marina, Brandon had us wait with all of our suitcases where the cabs dropped us off while he and Leilani went to talk with the salesperson. The plan was for the two of them to pose as a young couple who liked to flash their cash so the salesman would show them around the yacht.

Then when they were going to buy it, Leilani would kiss the salesman and convince him the sale was solid.

While we waited, the rest of us wondered about what we should name our new vessel. Kelly suggested we name it *Agatha* and the rest of us agreed. Melody grew teary-eyed, and Chloe changed the subject to speculate what our new accommodations would be like.

Every idea we had about it was wrong.

Brandon had Kelly come sail the *Agatha* over to where the rest of us were waiting. The yacht was much smaller than the *Kandis Amelia*, but it was much more opulent. All the woodwork inside was teak. There were televisions everywhere and a deluxe sound system throughout the space. The staterooms had king sized beds with gun lockers behind the headboards and their own bathrooms and laundry facilities. The *Agatha* boasted two galleys, a flying bridge with a barbeque grill on it, and a salon.

No wonder this thing cost so much.

One of the staterooms had three twin sized beds in it, which Chloe, Leilani, and Fang occupied. Gareth and Ophelia, Melody and Kelly, and Brandon and I each shared a stateroom with our significant other. After everyone settled in, Kelly took to the flying bridge and steered the *Agatha* out to sea.

I sat on one of the leather benches nestled into the bow and enjoyed the spray of the ocean on my skin. It felt like a lifetime since I'd been on the *Kandis Amelia* doing this exact same thing, although the *Agatha* was smaller than the former naval vessel, so more of the sea spray could be felt.

Ophelia sat down opposite me with a grim expression on her face.

"Hey," I coaxed. "What's wrong?"

She sighed and stared out at the crystalline water ahead of us. "I have a bad feeling about this."

"About the yacht?"

"No, about going to the Crazy Cannon Place."

My chest seized and I almost choked.

"Did you have a vision about it?"

"No. But nothing good can come of going back to that place."

"But we have to go get Shaw out of there," I protested.

She regarded me shrewdly. "I know. But don't you

think there's a reason that Commander Goldbrook wants us to return there? As horrible as it was last time we were there, I can't begin to imagine how awful it will be this time."

I got up, sat down next to Ophelia and grabbed her shoulders. The fear in her eyes turned my blood to ice. "I'm scared, too. Petrified, really. But we have to go back and get Shaw. He rescued us, and now it's time to repay the favor. Do you remember when we were there before and how determined you were to get Shaw to let you stay with him? What else can we do?"

She sighed. "You're right, but I can't help feeling like something horrific is going to happen."

I didn't want to admit how much her spoken fears ratcheted up my own. There was no way to know what Commander Goldbrook and Dr. Pantiel had planned for us. Surely they knew we'd be coming to the rescue. A cold sweat chilled my skin.

"There's not really any place on this yacht to train," I mused.

"I don't think more training is the answer. Sure, we could always use more training, but I think we need more work on our Gifts. You and Brandon need to figure out what you can do with that Bond besides blind people," Ophelia said.

"Well, we know how the other one is feeling," I supplied.

"That's cute, but not helpful in combat."

"True. How do we figure out what else this Bond is capable of?"

"When do you notice it's at its strongest?"

My face burned with embarrassment. "Just when we're messing around, I guess."

Ophelia ignored my admission. "Well, we need to test the limits and see what we can get out of it."

I nodded in agreement. How were we supposed to do that, though?

"I guess I should bring this up to Brandon," I suggested.

"We should wait until we're pretty far out to sea, just in case," Ophelia pointed out.

☙☙☙

Brandon and I stared at each other while everyone else stared at us. Neither one of us knew how to start activating the Bond. The small amount of information Agatha left with us didn't seem useful at this point. We knew we were supposed to be some kind of weapon, but we were already separately. I sensed Brandon's agitation through the Bond. He was frustrated because he couldn't make the puzzle pieces fall into place. I was anxious because everyone was expecting something to happen and all we came up with was a whole lot of nothing.

"What are you guys thinking about?" Kelly asked.

"Nothing really. Honestly, I don't even know where to start," I confessed.

Gareth waggled his eyebrows. "Maybe you should think about snogging. That usually seems to the trick, doesn't it?"

Ophelia elbowed him in the ribs and hissed, "That's not helpful!"

Brandon arched an eyebrow at me. Was he considering thinking about us kissing to cause a reaction? I shrugged slightly. It was better than blankly staring at each other.

I closed my eyes and recalled how kissing him made me feel. The warmth of it spread from my core out to my limbs, but there wasn't anything powerful in it. There was a lack of intensity to it. Maybe we did need to kiss to make this happen? But we couldn't stop in the middle of a fight to make out to get our superpowers running. Superpowers? I smiled and shook my head at my momentary absurdity.

"Maybe we need to do some more brain storming about this before we waste another hour of our lives watching these two stare longingly at each other," Melody griped.

"That would probably be for the best," Brandon agreed.

"Well, I'm turning in for the night. Don't you kids stress yourselves to death, there's no use in it," Fang advised before leaving for his cabin.

Brandon sighed. "Everyone else should turn in, too. Tomorrow is going to be a long day of training. This undoubtedly will be the toughest situation we've dealt with yet."

Everyone bid each other good night and headed below deck. Brandon and I stayed put. When the others were out of sight, Brandon flopped down onto one of the benches at the bow.

"What I wouldn't do for a pack of smokes right now," he grumbled.

"You know, that really is bad for you."

"Yeah, I know."

He adjusted his position on the bench and held his arms open. I curled into his side and laid my head on his chest.

"I can't for the life of me figure out how we're supposed to activate this internal secret weapon," I mused.

"Me either."

"Maybe our brains need a break."

I felt him shrug his shoulders beneath me. "Couldn't hurt. So what should we do instead?"

"Well, I haven't looked at the stars in a while."

"That's funny. I look at them every day."

He gently traced his thumb over my tattoo.

"It never ceases to amaze me how romantic you can be."

"I don't know that I've ever been accused of being romantic before."

This I could not believe. "Surely Melody told you?"

"Do you really want to get into it about her and me right now?"

I shifted my position so I could get a better view of his face. He tried so hard to keep his guard up, but I saw the exhaustion and the stress lurking in his eyes. I sat up and he did, too. Then I sat on his legs so our faces were level and brushed his hair out of his eyes.

"Hey," I said softly.

"Hey."

Even though it hurt, I kissed the corner of his mouth, then the hinge of his jaw, and his temple. There was nothing more that I wanted than to offer him some assurance that things would work out. We sat in silence, staring at each other. I knew better that there was nothing I could do or say to make things easier, to take the pressure off of him a little.

"Sable?"

"Yeah?"

"If you hadn't ended up here with us, if you were still at home with your parents, what would you have done?"

"Be a loner."

He laughed. "That's not what I meant. Like I would've been a chef. What would you have done?"

I thought about it for a while. It wasn't something I'd considered much before my parents shipped me off to the Crazy Cannon Place.

"I don't know. Go to college, try to find myself or

something. End up working some minimum wage job somewhere and moonlight as a poet."

"You write poetry?"

"I used to. I haven't since, well, all of *this* happened."

"If you could now, would you?"

"It's hard to say. But probably not. Honestly, there wasn't really anything I was passionate about before."

"You seem to be pretty passionate about matchmaking," he teased.

"I like making people happy, that's all."

"You make me happy," he said quietly.

I smiled.

"It's such a rare thing for you to smile like that. I love it when you do."

The warmth I felt earlier remembering how it felt to kiss him returned, and I kissed his lips softly. He pulled me closer to him and mirrored my softness with a tenderness of his own. Then he leaned us back so we were lying down again. We whispered sweet nothings to each other between kisses. I wasn't looking at stars, but he was.

CHAPTER 27

The air was so cold I could see my breath. Goose bumps covered my naked skin and purplish blue veins stood as a stark contrast to my paleness. I blinked as I took in my surroundings. My naked body was chained to a metal table. Even though the air was frigid, it was damp. The room was made of unpainted cement blocks with no windows. Bright fluorescent lights covered the ceiling. I was hooked up to medical monitors that measured my pulse, my oxygen levels, and other graphs and charts I didn't understand. To my right was a metal tray covered in surgical instruments. An IV pole sat unused in the corner of the room opposite the door the nurse entered through.

I didn't see the nurse come in. She wasn't here a minute ago, was she? Pale yellow scrubs lay neatly folded between my spread legs.

How did I end up in the asylum again? Weren't we still sailing around the coast of Mexico heading for the Panama Canal? Where were my comrades? I broke into a cold sweat as panic gripped me.

There was no sense of Brandon through the Bond at all. Was he dead?

I tried to scream, but no sound came out. My throat

was raw anyway. A cruel sneer spread over the nurse's face. She grabbed a syringe filled with pale blue liquid and sat down next to me.

"Now, where to administer this? If the point is for you to die from the injection, I don't see why I couldn't just stab this into your black heart. But the doctor must conduct his research. When he gets his answers, he can purge the world of the disgusting filthy Diseased. There's no cure for you. You're all too far gone. And now you think you can make yourself into some weapon of mass destruction? Not on Commander Goldbrook's watch. Thank God for him and for the DAO. Now just hold still. This is probably going to hurt. I hope it does."

I tried screaming again but there was still no sound. The needle bit into the flesh of my thigh and the liquid injected into me felt like ice water. That was probably exactly what it was, liquid ice meant to extinguish my Gift of fire. This was how they meant to kill me. This is how I was going to die. This was what Brandon had saved me from before—

"Sable! Wake up!" Brandon yelled as he shook my shoulders.

The sun blinded me as I ripped open my eyes. I sat up and heaved in some cleansing breaths as I took stock of where I was. We were still on the deck of the *Agatha*, although I was on my ass on the floor instead of on the bench where I'd fallen asleep with Brandon.

"Oh my God," I panted.

Brandon's eyes were wide with terror. I knew his fear was secondhand, since his overriding emotion through the Bond was concern.

"Sable—"

"It's fine. I'm fine."

"You were screaming in your sleep."

"I'm sorry, I didn't mean to wake you up."

"I was already awake, but that's not the point. What happened?"

"They had me. They were killing me. I was *dying*—"

Brandon sat next to me and wrapped his arms around me and kissed my hair. "Shh, it's okay. You won't die in there. I won't let them kill you, I promise."

How was I supposed to face my greatest fear? I had to, I had no choice. I needed to be brave, but it eluded me. Every day we came closer to the asylum. Every hour there were less and less miles between me and the place where I learned what I was, where I was almost euthanized.

It was a different thing when you were in the middle of a fight. You knew you could die as a casualty at any moment, and that was frightening. But when you're faced with someone who meticulously planned out how you would meet your demise, it was terrifying.

Brandon tucked my hair behind my ears and wiped away the tears I hadn't realized I'd cried.

"I'm sorry," I whispered.

"You don't have to apologize for being human, baby doll." He stood and bent over to kiss the top of my head. "Just take a few minutes to relax and I'll be right back, okay?"

I nodded and put my head between my knees. I really needed to figure out a way to get my shit together. How was I supposed to help Brandon be strong if I kept falling apart?

"Miss Sable?" Fang scooped me up in his arms and sat me on a bench. Then he sat on the one opposite me.

I sniffled. "I'm such a mess."

"I've seen you look worse," he mused.

In spite of myself, I giggled. "I'll bet."

"Tell me what's goin' on in that pretty little head of yours."

"I'm so scared of going back there. The first time we were there was awful enough. Now that Commander Goldbrook and Doctor Pantiel know we're coming for Shaw, coming for them...Fang, someone's going to die. *One of us is going to die.* We've been so lucky until Agatha that no one's died. That we've escaped so many of these ludicrous situations. Everyone's luck runs out at some point. It's only a matter of time before ours does completely."

He sighed a heavy sigh. "I won't lie to you, Miss Sable. We *have* been lucky. If I didn't know better, I'd say they've been letting us off easy. Maybe they're still trying to study us, see what we're capable of. And if they couldn't recruit us, they got to study us some other way. Know thy enemy. I reckon by who they took and where they took him to, they know us pretty damn well."

"This isn't really making me feel more secure," I whined.

"There is no security in war."

"I guess not."

"But I do know we ain't going down without a fight. If we're going to die, we're going to do it fighting. That's all we can do."

Fang leaned over and tipped my chin up with his hand so I looked into his eyes. "Even though I don't know much, I do know that you are a strong young woman, and it's going to take more than a couple of assholes to take you down."

I sprang off my seat and launched myself at him. He caught me and I squeezed him tight. I kissed his cheek. "What would I do without you?"

He smiled. "You'd figure something out, but I'm glad you don't have to."

"Me, too."

"Come on, let's go down to the galley and have some

of that breakfast Brandon's whipping up."

Brandon was cooking? It seemed like forever since he had.

I followed Fang to the galley and the scent of maple syrup and nutmeg hit me. The rest of our comrades sat around the table eating bacon, eggs, and cheese on French toast. Fang put three of the sandwiches on his plate and sat on the edge of the bench seat next to Ophelia. A plate of French toast topped with strawberry and banana slices and powdered sugar sat on the breakfast bar.

Brandon stood in front of the stove frying up more bacon. I wrapped my arms around his waist and kissed the back of his neck. His body tightened at the contact.

"Thanks for my favorite breakfast," I murmured in his ear.

He tilted his head to the side and rested it briefly on mine before returning his attention back to cooking. "I thought it might cheer you up."

"It does."

"Go eat, we're going to have a long day."

ⅇↃⅇↃ

Ophelia, Brandon, and I spent hours trying to unlock the mysteries of the Bond while everyone else did spar training. I kept trying to think of scenarios that would create some sort of reaction in the Bond, but nothing worked.

I thought about the intimate moments Brandon and I shared, I thought about all the times we'd been imprisoned, all the times we almost died. I tried to think about what would happen if Brandon died, how I would feel about it.

If I dwelled in those dark places too long, I felt like I

was suffocating. Between my own frustration and Brandon's mental fatigue filtering into me through the Bond, I was completely wrung out.

"Since you've noticed the Bond, does it only flare up like that when you guys are being passionate?" Ophelia inquired.

"I guess that's the only time it's happened, but it doesn't happen every time we kiss," I explained. Wow, this conversation was embarrassing!

"I wonder if maybe the Bond only works outwardly when both of our emotions are running high," Brandon mused.

"If that's true, then what are we supposed to do with it when it happens?" I questioned.

Ophelia rested her chin on her fists and her elbows on the table. "Sable, I've been thinking that maybe the Bond started with you."

"How do you mean?" I asked.

"I think it started with the green fire when you went to rescue Chloe and Kelly from the DAO. I don't know what triggered it, but I really think that was the beginning of it. Then when your ribs were healing, you forged the Bond with Brandon. When you destroyed all the glass containment cells with white hot fire, it grew. And when you and Brandon were under that house, the Bond anchored itself in the two of you," she reasoned.

Brandon shrugged. "It makes sense to me."

"Clearly, Sable's Gift has been enhanced by the Bond. I wonder if yours has, too, Brandon."

"I've never really tried to push the limits with it."

"Maybe we should experiment with it," she suggested.

"How are we supposed to do that without electrocuting everyone?" I wondered aloud.

Ophelia stayed quiet for a minute before she spoke

again. "We could start on a smaller scale. Your fire doesn't burn him, right?"

I nodded.

"Maybe his electricity won't affect you."

Brandon shook his head. "I'm not willing to take that risk."

"We have to try *something*." I definitely didn't want to be electrocuted, but we needed to start narrowing down our options somehow.

I took Brandon's hand in mine and let the fire consume them both. Then I let the flames take over me so I became a burning pillar. Ophelia watched us in contemplative silence. I focused my energy on forcing the inferno into Brandon's body. Much in the way I had to push my limits when I learned to spread the fire from my hands to the rest of me, the force required was extraordinary. As the flames reached his shoulder, my body began to shake.

Brandon sat still and watched with wide eyes as his chest and torso began to glow.

Every fiber of my being was stretched taut. I had to force my eyes to remain open to gage what was happening. Slowly the flames crept down to his feet and all that remained untouched by fire was his head.

"Brandon—give me—your Gift," I growled through grit teeth.

He shook his head vehemently.

"Just—do it!"

The orange glow in the room was met with bright white as Brandon's electricity exploded from him. It traveled much more quickly than my fire. The current raced up my arm and seized my insides. Every single cell in my body rattled with the fusion of Gifts. The invisible cord in my gut that tethered us together in the Bond pulled at me. My lungs wouldn't fill with air. A roaring sound in my ears deafened me. Dark spots winked in and out of my vision. Just when I was sure my heart would explode from the pressure, everything went black.

CHAPTER 28

Brandon

Ophelia, take her pulse!" I commanded. If I wasn't so nerved up, I would've done it myself.

Sable lay slumped back in her chair and her skin looked white as a sheet. When the fire rushed back into her and out of me, it felt like I'd been hit by a truck.

Ophelia pressed her fingers against the side of Sable's neck. After a tense few moments, she nodded. "She's okay. Her heart rate is normal. The strain must've been too much for her. Just take her to bed, she should be fine."

I breathed a sigh of relief. Anxiousness gave way to exhaustion. Sleep sounded like the best thing in the world. I gathered Sable up in my arms and carried her from the salon to our stateroom. My arms shook under her slight weight.

There was nothing more in that moment that I wanted to do than lie down with her and sleep, but I had to report our findings to the others. Being the unspoken leader sucked a lot sometimes.

I was pretty impressed with myself that I was able to turn the covers down and get Sable under them without dropping her. Before I left, I kissed her on the cheek and hoped this meeting wouldn't take too long.

Ophelia must've assumed I'd want to talk to everyone since they were all assembled in the salon when I got back. Looking at everyone's drawn expressions, I knew that they trained just as hard as we did. If there was one thing I was grateful for it was that no one lacked motivation to keep themselves in the best shape they could. The down side was that that motivation came from survival instincts, but it was there all the same. At least everyone else would want this meeting to be over quickly, too.

I stood in the front of the room and folded my arms across my middle. "Okay, guys, I'll try to keep this brief. As you know, Sable, Ophelia, and I are working hard on figuring out if this Bond can afford us some sort of advantage. We learned that Sable and I can pass our Gifts to each other while retaining our respective Gifts. Right now, it takes a great deal of strain to execute and to carry, but I'm confident that with time, we'll be able to find out what we're capable of doing with it."

"Unfortunately, time isn't exactly on our side with this," Melody pointed out.

The others nodded and murmured their agreements.

"I know. We need to take a little break, seeing as how Sable's dead to the world right now. When she wakes up, we'll go back to working on it. Kelly, how many more days would you say it will take us to reach New York?" I asked.

"A week at the most. If I taught some of the others how to drive the yacht, we could possibly shave that down to five days," he answered.

"Okay, who wants to volunteer to learn to drive the yacht?" I inquired.

Fang, Gareth, and Melody raised their hands.

"Good. I don't mean to be a slave driver, but we

don't have any time to waste. Hopefully nothing bad has happened to Shaw yet. Our drivers will take six hour shifts each. When we're not eating or sleeping, we're training. While we're eating, we're strategizing how to get in and out of that place with the least amount of damage to us. We have to. Any questions?"

No one answered.

"Good. I'll allow tonight for us to get rested up since the next few days are going to be really taxing. Kelly, you can teach the volunteers how to drive the yacht in the morning."

Without bothering to see if anyone followed me or not, I headed for my stateroom. Fatigue made my footsteps heavy.

Sable was still asleep when I closed the door behind me. I left my clothes in a heap on the floor and yanked on a pair of basketball shorts before climbing into bed. Careful not to wake her, I smoothed a lock of Sable's hair out of her face. She wore a pinched expression. It was probably another nightmare about being trapped back in the asylum. As much as I didn't want to admit it, the probability of her nightmares coming true were pretty high. I enfolded her in my arms, still making sure I didn't disturb her sleep, and hugged her close to my chest. At first, her breathing was shallow and she twitched every now and then. When she finally calmed enough that she was sleeping normally, I allowed myself to succumb.

❧❧❧

The sunlight coming in from the portholes woke me up. I blinked a few times to clear the last remnants of sleep away. Sable was still in my arms, curled into my chest. This training was going to be rough on her. Really rough. I loved that she threw herself completely into everything she was learning. No matter what, she would push herself beyond her breaking point.

I remembered when she first started her training on the *Kandis Amelia*. Shaw tasked me with making sure she could do some damage in physical combat. I was hard on her, I had to be. Part of me expected her to quit, and I tried to push her until she did. I wanted to see what it would take to get her to crack. Even when she was frustrated and plateauing, she kept driving forward until she exceeded my expectations. It was something I loved about her.

Before I could decide if I wanted to wake her up or let her sleep, she stirred. Her eyelashes fluttering open felt like feathers brushing against my skin. She stifled a yawn and rolled her head from side to side. Then she looked up at me and gave me a soft smile.

"See? I'm not dead," she croaked. Her voice was scratchy from sleep.

I laughed. "No, you're not."

She shifted so she didn't have to crane her head to look at me. "You tell the others what happened?"

"Yeah. They didn't really say anything. I don't think anyone knows what *to* say."

"That's true."

She sat up and stretched her arms over her head. "So, what's on the agenda for today, Captain?"

"Training. Every day until we reach New York."

I watched her as she gathered clothes from the closet. Her movements were graceful like a panther. When I first met her, she was one of the clumsiest people I knew. A small spark of pride lit me up inside. I'd trained her well. She paused at the bathroom door and turned to face me again.

"I assume you paired up everyone with their sparring partners last night. Who's mine?" she asked.

"We're not sparring. You and I are working on this Bond. When we can transfer our Gifts more easily, then we need to figure out how we can use that. What advantage will it give us? How much power will that afford us?"

She smiled at me and gave me a salute. "Whatever you say, Shaw Junior."

I waited until she closed the bathroom door to allow myself to smile at her comparison. Shaw probably wouldn't have drawn that comparison himself.

Before I let myself go too far down that toxic thought process, I dragged a T-shirt over my head and went up to the galley to fix breakfast.

I pulled ingredients out of the fridge to make spinach, Canadian bacon, and Swiss cheese omelets. It surprised me how much food I could fit on the yacht. It helped that there was a fridge and a freezer in the galley that was supposed to be the crew quarters but housed my sister, Leilani, and Fang instead. After I poured the whisked egg and cheese mixture into a hot frying pan, I switched on the percolator to make coffee for Melody and Fang. I liked the flavor of coffee in other things, but not so much on its own.

At least cooking was second nature to me so I could think about an infiltration plan while I worked. From what I remembered about the place, the basement where the Gifted were kept wasn't accessible from the outside. There were only two entrances into the asylum. One was the front doors beyond the wrought iron gates and one was out of the kitchen where the food for the patients was delivered.

The kitchen door was probably the safest point of entry, but you had to pass the main entrance to get to it. Sneaking in undetected was the problem. What I wouldn't give for someone with the Gift of invisibility!

The only time I'd ever seen that though was in fictional super hero stories.

The sound of footsteps distracted me from my musings. Melody padded into the kitchen. I knew better not to say anything to her until she'd had her coffee. I nodded at her to acknowledge her and she grunted in response. She poured herself a cup of coffee. I continued cooking breakfast.

Kelly, Chloe, Fang, Leilani, and Sable had found their way to the galley by the time I finished fixing everyone's omelets. Ophelia and Gareth weren't too far behind. I put a carafe of orange juice on the table while Sable set out place settings for everyone. Everyone made small talk in between bites of breakfast. No one made any mention of strategizing, which was okay with me. I wanted to have some semblance of an idea to present them with before I brought the subject up. I hoped at lunch time, I would have a clearer idea of what to do.

As everyone was finishing up their meal, I decided it would be a good time to let them know the few time tables I did have figured out.

"Okay, here's how I want training schedules to work. You're all going to have to swap sparring partners depending on who's training with Kelly to drive the yacht. Kelly, I want you to spend two hours with each volunteer to train them. When you're comfortable with the idea of them taking the reins on their own, I want Gareth on first shift, Melody on second shift, Kelly on third shift, and Fang on fourth shift. I'll let you know what times the durations of those shifts start and end later on today. Sable and I will be working on the Bond and how to best utilize what information we gather about it. I'll report our findings to you during dinner.

"You can eat lunch whenever you're hungry. There's stuff for sandwiches, so help yourselves. I'll cook breakfast and dinner for everyone daily. If there's any questions about anything, we'll be in the salon. Someone hop on dishes, and everyone else find a sparring partner and get training. Kelly, you can start training Gareth first."

I put my plate in the sink and headed toward the salon. I glanced over my shoulder and saw Sable following me, so I slowed my steps. When she caught up to me, I twined my fingers with hers. She squeezed my hand gently.

"You're doing great, you know," she said.

I winked. "I can make omelets in my sleep."

"That's not what I meant."

"I know."

She stopped walking and stood in front of me. Her free hand found mine and took it so she was holding both my hands. "I was being honest."

I kissed her chastely. "I know. Thanks."

She smiled at me and led me the rest of the way to the salon.

It was much easier for me to pass my Gift onto her than it was for her to reciprocate. Sable was like a lightning rod. I was like water—a great conductor for electricity, but a terrible environment for fire. After her fifteenth attempt to push her fire through me, she collapsed on the chaise lounge, panting. I sat near her feet and waited for her to get her bearings.

Only a few minutes had passed before she whispered, "Again."

I put my hand on her shoulder. "You've earned a break longer than two minutes. Just relax a little."

She shook her head violently. "The others, they're counting on us! We have to figure this out!"

Her anxiety crashed into me through the Bond. The pressure for hers and everyone else's survival weighed heavily on her. She was trying to take some of the burden away from me, but I worried it would crush her.

"We will, but a ten minute break isn't going to make the difference between success and failure—"

She launched herself at me, and before I knew it, I was lying on my back on the chaise lounge and Sable was sitting astride me. I sat up on my elbows, wondering what she intended to do. She bent down and kissed me hard. Distantly, I wondered what spurred her decision to start making out with me was. But I wasn't going to complain.

I wrapped my arms around her and pressed her body against mine. Her fingers found their way into my hair and entangled themselves there. She was uncontrolled, kissing my mouth, my face, my neck, my shoulders. There was no way to know where she was going, and I didn't care. It was selfish of me to indulge in her but, in that moment, I didn't care if I was being the most selfish bastard in the world. She always made me feel that way, like I was being irresponsible. Another in the long list of things I loved about her.

My hands found their way past the hem of her shirt. Her skin was soft like silk. I groaned low in my throat as she pressed herself harder against me. Fleetingly, I noticed a tightening feeling in my stomach.

I tried in vain to keep control of what I was doing, how far I was going to let things go. She was always my undoing, whether or not it was on purpose. I sat up with her still clinging to me. My lips trailed kisses from her clavicle to her earlobe and she sighed a breathy sort of sound. I unbuttoned her tunic and pushed it off of her shoulders. Her chocolate curls looked darker in contrast to her pale skin. I marveled at her curves while she pulled off my T-shirt. Then we were back to kissing and feeling each other's flesh against flesh.

Our breathing became more erratic and labored, and the tightening in my stomach increased. I pushed her slightly away from me and a pained mewl got strangled in her throat. At the same time, I gritted my teeth in response to the sharp pain in my core. Quickly, I crushed her against me again. My rational mind told me that something was happening with the Bond, but the rest of me didn't care.

"Brandon," she whispered in my ear.

I bit her lower lip.

"Brandon," she said again, more insistent this time.

I broke away from her and stared at her face. We were ensconced in a ball of electrical fire.

My eyes grew wide and I stopped breathing. I couldn't see anything past the flare we'd created. There was only Sable, the fire as green as her eyes, and the lightning.

"How do we do this without kissing?" I breathed.

She shrugged. "We'll have to figure it out."

I held her face in my hands and stared at her. Her tattoo stars were small black blurs lost in the glow of our Gifts.

I pressed her against me again and kissed her until the flames died.

CHAPTER 29

Sable

Come on, Sable. Try harder," Brandon prompted. I nodded and focused all of my energy on sending fire through him.

We were only two days' time away from the Crazy Cannon Place. We still hadn't figured out how to produce the massive ball of energy without getting physical with each other. Everyone trained as hard as they could. The only strategy we could come up with was to charge into the place with guns blazing, so to speak. Of course, that sort of hinged on Brandon and me figuring out how to make the Bond work for us.

The hours we slept were less and less each day. Brandon made whatever meals were the least time consuming and we inhaled them so we could get back to working. One morning, Kelly found us collapsed on the floor in the salon. We'd fallen asleep sometime in the early hours of the morning while trying to push the boundaries.

Fire licked its way lazily down toward Brandon's knees and fizzled out. I growled in frustration. Why was this so difficult? There must be some sort of block that prevented him from accepting my Gift as easily as I accepted his. He released my hand, but I snatched his back. There wasn't time to give up and try again later.

An idea struck me. If I couldn't get him to accept the fire *externally*, maybe I could get him to take it *internally*. I grabbed his face and kissed him hard. After his moment of shock passed, he put his hands firmly on my shoulders. He meant to push me away. I grabbed his wrists and kept kissing him, willing him to understand what I was trying to do. Instead of focusing on the fire consuming my skin and then his, I pictured it like a burning stream running through my veins, permeating throughout from the inside. The heat built rapidly within me until the flames streamed out of my pores.

I opened my eyes and gasped. It worked! Brandon looked just like me, consumed by fire. I broke contact with him and stepped away from him. The fire was still there, just as if it were his own Gift instead of mine. I focused all of my energy on making the fire hotter and bigger. Slowly but surely, the flames grew in height and the color shifted from a deep orange to a pale yellow.

"Brandon, I did it!" I exclaimed.

He held out his arms and stared at them in bewilderment. "How?"

"I just thought about it. The Bond took care of the rest. See if you can control the electric current in me."

I let go of my hold on the fire and it disappeared in an instant. Brandon closed his eyes. His brow furrowed deeper the harder he concentrated. Live wires jolted and zapped in the pit of my stomach. All of my nerves twitched with the pressure of static electricity. White hot lightning shot along the path of my veins.

Another brilliant idea popped into my head. I grabbed Brandon by the arm and dragged him onto the main deck where everyone else was sparring. Naturally, they all stopped what they were doing to see what we were up to. Brandon kept the electricity circuiting through me. I concentrated on manipulating the current like I did when I manipulated my Gift. A little ball of electricity formed in my palm. I focused on expanding it until it grew to the size of a large exercise ball. Then I threw it with all the force I could manage skyward. Heat lightning raced across the low hanging clouds.

I whooped in excitement. Brandon swept me up in his arms and spun me around before kissing me hard.

"What the bloody hell was that?" Gareth inquired.

"They figured out how to use the Bond," Ophelia answered.

I clapped my hands together like a little child. "Brandon, we have to see if we can do that together. Let's see if we can make an electric fire ball. There's no way the DAO can stop us if we can pull it off!"

"We will, but since we made a significant breakthrough, I think we all deserve some relaxation," Brandon decided.

Kelly grinned. "I'll second that."

Fang clapped me on the back. "I knew you'd figure it out, Miss Sable."

I hugged him tightly. "Thanks."

"So what should we do to relax?" Leilani asked.

"Laying out sounds good to me," Melody chimed in.

"Well, someone needs to get back to driving the boat, but whatever else you guys want to do is fine with me," Brandon said.

"I was, but when I heard all of the commotion out here, I had to see what was going on," Melody supplied.

Everyone else dispersed to find a way to unwind. Some wanted to take naps, some wanted to watch television, and others wanted to sunbathe. Brandon went to take a shower. I followed him back to our stateroom. By the time I made it there, I heard the water running in the shower.

I kicked off my sandals and flopped onto the bed. I stared at the ceiling and watched the ever changing pattern the light streaming into the portholes reflecting off of the water made. After a few minutes, I got the hang of the pattern and traced it with my flames. It felt like I hadn't done that in forever.

The bathroom door opened and Brandon stood in the doorway with a towel hanging from his hips. His wet hair stuck to his temples and fell into his eyes. My breath caught in my throat. I'd seen him naked before, but the image was still shocking to me. The dancing light in the room made his tanned skin glow and his eyes appear to be more aqua than ice blue.

"Why are you biting your lip?" he asked.

"I like the view."

The comment popped out of my mouth before I'd had time to register that it might have been too bold a thing to say. Me and my damned mouth.

He blushed. "Is that so?"

I nodded. There was no taking it back now.

I sat up, hugged my knees to my chest, and rested my forehead on them. The sound of the closet door sliding open and closed let me know that he was getting dressed.

He brushed my hair behind my ear. "It's safe to look now."

I smiled sheepishly. He sat down next to me on the bed and leaned back on his elbows.

"Brandon, do you remember the first time we slept together in the same bed?"

"Yeah." His voice was soft.

"It just feels like so much has happened since then."

"It has."

"How long has it been? It feels like years."

"I don't know, maybe five or six months. What's gotten you into such a pensive mood?"

I sighed. "I don't know. Maybe because soon we won't have time to just remember things, to just sit around and think about them. We'll be running on fight or flight instinct, living in fear. If we're successful in rescuing Shaw, it's going to start a war. Everyone's already going crazy about Diseased roaming the streets with the non-Gifted."

He grasped my shoulder. I let him pull me backward so I was lying next to him. He rolled over and flipped onto his side, propping his head up with his hand. I rolled onto my stomach and rested my cheek on my folded arms. Then I kicked my feet up and crossed my ankles. Brandon chuckled.

"You know what I remember? About the first night we slept in the same bed. I thought you were so brave and so stupid to come with me on a suicide mission. And I remember kissing you, how it felt to do it without getting interrupted by my sister. Your vulnerability…That was the night I realized you would were my undoing—that you always would be."

I sat up and leaned over him as he turned onto his back. My hair hung in a curtain around us as I pressed my lips to his.

"You know, you can be really romantic sometimes," I murmured.

"Just sometimes, eh?"

I laughed and swatted his arm playfully. "Only just."

"Is that so? You know, you've mentioned that before."

Before I could respond, he flipped us over and pinned me against the mattress. I screeched and fell into a fit of giggles. Brandon smiled as he rained feather light kisses on my face and throat.

He sighed. "I'll miss that laugh."

The thought was sobering. My smile faded as I thought about what would happen in a day and a half.

As much as I wanted to pretend we were living a normal life and had a normal relationship, we didn't. We would never be that couple who went to the prom together or out to the movies on a Friday night with a midnight curfew. Ophelia and I would never have a sleepover where we gossiped about boys or our classmates. We'd never go to the mall together and walk around for hours when there was nothing else to do. The Gifted never had a shot at that. If we didn't die this time, we would always wonder if our friends would make it out alive the next time. Our days were always numbered.

"Hey," Brandon said softly. "It's going to be okay."

"I didn't mean to be such a downer."

I knew he felt my sadness through the Bond.

"It's all right," he promised. "Are you really that certain we're not going to make it out of this?"

I sighed. "I hope we do, but I'm being a realist. Even if we make it out of the Crazy Cannon Place, who's to say that we won't die the next time the DAO comes for us?"

"Well, what if we were non-Gifted? Say we went to a party and got hit by a drunk driver on the way home. Nothing in life is certain, Sable. If you dwell on the negatives, the positives will be more difficult to achieve. I know the odds are stacked against us, but I have to believe we'll all make it out alive."

His eyes shined from unshed tears. All I was doing was talking about his family dying. When did I become so depressing? I put my arms around him and pulled him against me. Then I pressed my lips against the hollow of his throat.

"I'm sorry," I murmured.

"You don't have to apologize," he assured me.

"You know how much I love you, don't you?"

He kissed my temple. "I know. I love you, too."

"Losing you is the scariest thought to me."

"I know from experience exactly what you mean. I've almost lost you three times, and I died a little inside each time."

"Brandon?"

"Yeah?"

"Will you just hold me for a little while? Please?"

"Of course."

He lay down next to me and I nestled into his chest as he put his arm around me. I ran my fingers through his hair, traced his eyebrow, his jawline, the seam of his lips. He caught ahold of my hand and kissed my knuckles and my wrist. I listened to the sound of his heart beating and felt his chest rise and fall with each breath.

ᖇᖇᖇ

I hadn't realized I'd fallen asleep until I woke up. Brandon offered me a small smile as I blinked the sleep out of my eyes.

I yawned. "How long was I out?"

He shrugged.

"Did you fall asleep, too?"

"No."

"So you just…watched me sleep?"

He nodded.

"Sounds boring."

He chuckled then. "Have you ever watched me sleep?"

"Yes."

"Was it boring?"

"Not to me."

"Well, there's your answer I guess."

"So what should we do now?"

"I have to go cook dinner."

"Okay."

We walked hand in hand out of the stateroom until we got to the galley. I kissed Brandon on the cheek and left him to his work.

I wandered out onto the deck and found Ophelia, Leilani, and Chloe sun bathing. When I noticed Chloe and Leilani holding hands, it gave me warm fuzzy feelings inside. If we got out of the asylum, we were going to have to figure out a way for them to work things out.

"Hello, ladies," I said.

"You finally ripped yourself away from Brandon, huh?" Ophelia teased.

"Please, don't make me puke," Chloe groaned.

Leilani chuckled.

I flopped down on one of the benches with a dramatic flourish. "It was hell, but I managed."

"Was he making you plot to overthrow the evil overlords at the Crazy Cannon Place?" Ophelia asked.

I shook my head. "No, we just sort of talked about a bunch of stuff."

"Is 'talking' your new code for making out with my brother?" Chloe asked acidly.

I studiously ignored her. There was still a sizeable part of me that wanted to beat her face into the floor for ripping my piercing out. For Brandon's sake, I behaved myself.

"It's weird to think that by this time tomorrow, we'll be casing the asylum," Leilani noted.

"Yeah, it is," I agreed.

"We'll get Shaw back," Chloe assured us.

Ophelia nodded. "Of course, we will."

I stared at Ophelia and she gazed back at me. She

seemed to keep the same unspoken fear in her eyes as I did. We'd be lucky if we'd have a snowball's chance in Hell to make it out of there unscathed. Maybe Leilani was more realistic about our chances since she used to be a part of the DAO. Maybe the rest thought that we'd trained long enough and hard enough to make it through.

What would our odds be if the Bond was a reliable weapon for us? I still felt like we were going in blind. It left a lead weight settled uncomfortably in my gut.

Almost as if she read my mind, Ophelia nodded imperceptibly. Did she have a vision about the rescue mission? She'd known about Agatha's death before it happened but wasn't able to say anything about it beforehand. Was this the same situation?

When Brandon called us into the galley for dinner, I had to force myself to choke it down. What would've normally been a delicious meal tasted like sawdust in my mouth. Something was wrong, even though I couldn't place my finger on it yet. I hoped I figured it out before we arrived in New York.

CHAPTER 30

Ophelia gripped my hand in hers. Fang had a hand on each of our shoulders as he stood behind us. *Breathe in, breathe out. You can do this.*

The Geraldine S. Cannon Hospital for the Mentally Disturbed—more commonly referred to as the Crazy Cannon Place—was every bit the stereotype I remembered it to be. A crumbling brick structure covered in creeping vines contained behind a rod iron fence. Like the last time I'd been thrust into this place, there were no people walking the grounds. Unlike the last time I was here, I could hear the screams outside the building.

If my blood wasn't already running cold, it was surely frozen solid now. A memory popped unbidden into my mind…

❧❧❧

I was submerged in a bath of ice water. Doctor Pantiel was testing to see what the lowest temperature I could handle was. There was a high risk of me dying, a risk that was worth taking, according to my captors. Shockingly pale blue eyes stared at me through the small plexiglass window in the door. Their color was the polar opposite of the deep blue veins visible beneath my frigid skin.

I felt my blood literally turning to slush. It forced its way through my inflamed veins, causing its own kind of burning. The fire in me burned hotter in a futile attempt to keep my body warm. My inner temperature was always warmer than the average person's by seven degrees. I wondered if even a non-Gifted person could handle these arctic temperatures. Shouldn't I have frostbite by now?

The nurse behind me kept rattling off numerical stats concerning my blood pressure and pulse to someone else I couldn't see. My teeth had stopped chattering a long time ago. I was too cold to even manage that action. Goose bumps covered my skin, creating rock-hard nodules all over my body.

Wouldn't it just be easier to die? Honestly, what was I hanging on for? My parents had left me in this God-forsaken place, I had no one on the outside who cared about me. Fang seemed nice, but who knew how much hold he had left on his sanity? Or Ophelia?

Black spots winked over my vision. I took a deep breath and let it out slowly. This was the end now. No more tests, no more torture, no more pain...

༄༅༄

I couldn't stop shaking. Ophelia squeezed my hand harder. I flicked my gaze to hers. Were my eyes that wide, too? She was one of the bravest people I knew. When I'd met her here, she'd been an emaciated-looking girl with a sense of determination I didn't quite understand.

She and Fang were the only reasons I survived the asylum. The fact that this place scared her as much as it did me was no comfort.

I tried feeling Brandon's emotions through the Bond, but I was too consumed by my own. Silently, I apologized to him for my crippling fear. Whether or not he understood, I'd never know.

More flashbacks from the last time I was here scrolled through my mind like a sadistic flip book. The rubbery eggs, the stale air in the basement, the gruel, the showers with the fire hose, more experiments—

"Miss Sable, we'll make it out alive. We did it once, we'll do it again," Fang assured me.

I attempted at a smile but only managed a grimace.

We waited for Brandon's signal to sneak into the kitchen one by one. It was some sort of bird call I would never remember. Was it a blue jay? Maybe a sparrow? Fang promised to let me know when it was my turn to go. Brandon, Leilani, and Gareth had already made it inside. Next would be Chloe, then Melody, Kelly, Ophelia, and me. Fang would bring up the rear. I worried about him being alone, but he assured me his Navy SEAL training would serve him well if trouble found him.

More screams of pain blasted through the campus. Were they only housing the Gifted here now? What did they do with all of the other patients? Maybe they were shipped to other mental hospitals in New York. Were the Gifted who were forced to be a part of the DAO all captive here now? They could still be being used as an army. Did they hate all Gifted people as much as they hated my little family, or was it just us? The way Agatha was just slaughtered on live television let us know they definitely loathed the lot of us.

After what felt like forever and no time at all, Brandon sounded my bird call. Fang tapped me on the shoulder and waved me in the direction of the kitchen door. My legs were uncooperative lead weights. They simply wouldn't move.

You have to do this for Shaw. He saved you, now it's time to return the favor.

The bird call sounded again, more insistent this time. Fang must've sensed my reluctance because he scooped me up and flung me over his shoulder. "I'm sorry, Miss Sable, but we have to go."

I bounced up and down lightly on Fang's shoulder as he snuck into the Crazy Cannon Place. When we made it across the lawn and safely into the kitchen, Fang returned me to my feet. I let out a breath I hadn't realized I'd been holding in. Brandon looked at Fang and me and narrowed his eyes. I knew what that meant. I was supposed to come alone, and so was he. We deviated from the plan. Brandon didn't like that, not when so much was at stake.

The night before, we sent a crew out to case the asylum and Brandon hatched the plan. We were to sneak into the kitchen one by one. While Brandon ushered us in, Melody would steal pale yellow scrubs for each of us that the patients wore and bring them back to the kitchen. We would change clothes, discarding the ones we came in. Then we would spread out in three teams to search the upper, ground, and basement floors. At dinner, we would meet in the cafeteria and report our findings. After dinner, we would find Shaw and remove him and ourselves from the premises.

It was a simple enough plan, but there was a lot of room for error. We would be more likely to be successful in smaller groups, but we would also be easier to capture if we should get caught. Brandon, Leilani, and I were Team One. Gareth, Chloe, and Kelly made up Team Two. Fang, Ophelia, and Melody comprised Team Three. Team One was in charge of the basement, Team Two was to search the ground and second floor, and Team Three was to search the upper floors.

Once we were all changed into scrubs, we split off.

Brandon allowed himself a chaste kiss on my lips and hurried down the basement steps. I fell into the middle and Leilani brought up the rear. The smell of mildew and decay permeated the air. So did the sound of screams and moans of pain.

The basement must've housed more Gifted than it had when I was here. A shiver ran up my spine. The farther down the steps we climbed, the tighter the knot of anxiety in the pit of my stomach became.

I tried to steel my nerves for Brandon's sake as well as my own, but my efforts were in vain. Every cell we tiptoed past had at least one prisoner in it. Most had two or three. People of all different kinds were locked away. Men, women, and children. All different nationalities, all different ages. People seemed to be imprisoned together at random. Probably whichever cell the orderlies could stuff the Gifted in before the prisoners became violent.

The shrieks and moans of the imprisoned assaulted my ears. I tried to block them all out, but it was an impossible task.

"Turn around before they find you!"

"Help me out of here, I'm begging you!"

"We're all dead, it's no use!"

"Mommy! Where's my mommy?"

I retched.

"Sable, don't give up on me yet," Brandon hissed.

I nodded and mouthed, "I'm sorry."

He pinched the bridge of his nose and sighed before returning his attention to searching cells to find Shaw. Leilani patted me on the shoulder. I gave her a brief smile of gratitude before following behind Brandon.

Would I always be such a crap soldier? Wasn't this the sort of situation we'd trained for? I was frightened when we were trapped in Nevada. Then I focused all of my energy on finding a way out of my cell. There was nothing like that to distract me now. Maybe I would've done better being on my own. Or maybe I would've just stood in a corner, paralyzed by my fear. I had to think of something else.

Find Shaw, find Shaw, find Shaw...

"Brandon, don't you think they would lock Shaw in a cell that was the farthest away from the entrance to the upper floors?" Leilani pointed out.

Well, at least someone was able to think rationally right now.

Brandon considered her idea for a minute and then nodded. "Good thinking. We'll head for the back and work our way forward," he instructed.

"How will we know which one Shaw's in? The ones in the back of the compound don't have windows in the doors like the ones in the front do. All they have is the grates where they shove the trays of gruel through," I said.

Leilani sighed. "It's probably not a good idea to go poking around in all of these cells, either. Someone could give us away on accident, if we haven't been already."

"Maybe we could just listen at each door and see if we can tell that way," I suggested.

Brandon folded his arms across his waist. "That's as good an idea as any. If we don't find him by the time we get to the windowed doors, we'll back track and try a different method."

As we crept through the halls, a particularly loud scream came from one of the doors with a window. It was against my better judgment, but I had to know what was happening. I peered through the window and found myself watching an experiment in one of the exam rooms.

A middle aged man with ashen skin was strapped to a metal exam table. The memory of the frigid steel caused me to break out in a cold sweat. He was handcuffed to a young woman who had similar features to him. Her eyes were shaped like his, as were her lips, but her figure was slight where the man's was more rotund. He had a squared jaw while hers was more pointed. Both had olive-toned skin and jet black hair. Were they related? Was that lady his daughter?

The man had so many needles protruding from him, he'd been turned into a human pin cushion. But the only sign of pain he felt was in his eyes. The young woman he was bound to was covered in blood. Every place on the man's body where a needle was stuck, a small wound appeared on the woman. That explained the blood, but made the fact no less gruesome.

A nurse held a metal rod with a glass handle in her palm. The metallic end sparked every few seconds. She touched the electrically charged end to the pins stuck into the man. Simultaneously, his and the woman's bodies convulsed. Tears spilled from the man's eyes as the woman screamed in agony.

The nurse just scrawled notes onto the papers on her clip board.

Brandon grabbed my hand and yanked me away from the door. "Sable, come on!"

"Brandon!" I sobbed as we ran. Vaguely, I noticed Leilani wasn't with him.

He whipped around, his expression angry. It immediately softened when he looked at my face. He crushed me against him and kissed my hair.

"Sable, you scared the hell out of me! Leilani and I were running and, all of a sudden, you weren't there. She said she'd keep looking for Shaw while I went back to find you. What in God's name were you thinking?"

"I'm sorry—I just—those poor people—"

He raked a hand through his hair, "Baby doll, we can't help them now. I promise you that we'll bust all of these people out of here soon. Right now we can't. We're not prepared. We have to move, come on."

He wiped the tears from my eyes before grabbing my hand and running in the opposite direction. My legs moved automatically. I was still back in that exam room with that man and that woman. How could anyone be so cruel and cold that they would treat other human beings that way? But I already knew the answer. Those people didn't see us as their equals. We Gifted were less than them because they were afraid of what we're capable of. Maybe they were even jealous because they didn't have Gifts like ours. They were sick bastards, all of them.

Somewhere we found Leilani and the three of us ran together. Brandon still had an iron grip on my hand and dragged me along. I felt his determination in his body, not from the Bond. There was too much else for my brain to process besides working out what emotions were coming from the Bond and which ones were naturally mine...

I was strapped to a cold metal table. The only thing I could move was my head. My blood was being circulated through a machine that was supposed to clean it. Every so often, the nurse would make me produce a flame to see if my Gift had been extracted.

"It's really too bad there's no way to harness the fire and extract it from her. It would come in handy later to use on some other Diseased. When we draw her blood, it's just the same as yours or mine. Maybe one day we'll be able to determine the cause of her internal combustion and understand how she doesn't manage to burn away from the inside out," Doctor Pantiel rambled on to the nurse in the room.

She mumbled some sort of agreement as she scrawled notes onto her clip board.

At least this test wasn't life threatening. It was exhausting, sure, but some people went through dialysis all the time, didn't they? If I'd been in a normal hospital, I might've considered sleeping through this process. Not here. You couldn't trust anyone here.

"Sable? Are you still with me?" Brandon asked gently.

I nodded, an automatic response. Was I?

He studied my face for a few moments, skepticism evident in his expression. I don't know what his conclusion was, but he pulled me along anyhow.

Leilani pointed out which cells she'd checked already. There were only two halls left, which meant there were thirty-two cells left to inspect. When I was here before, I never realized the basement was this big. Then again, I'd never gone exploring the place like I was now.

The anguished cries of the imprisoned seemed to intensify the deeper into the compound we ventured. I just wanted to press my hands over my ears and run away. How could the nurses and the orderlies possibly stand to listen to all this despair all the time? All I could think of to do to distract myself from everything was to hum. I could pretend all I wanted, but there would never be anything capable of drowning out the overwhelming sounds of agony.

CHAPTER 31

The sound of coughing cut through my rendition of "Breathe No More." Maybe it was because it was such an ordinary sound, I don't know. Just before I could start humming again, the cough sounded again. Something was different about it.

The sound was forced!

I grabbed Brandon's arm and he paused. He looked at me over his shoulder and raised his eyebrow.

"The coughing," I whispered.

"So?" he demanded.

"Just listen. There's something off about it," I explained.

We waited and listened. The cough sounded again, louder this time, but in the same rhythm. How did I not notice before?

I slapped Brandon's arm. "It's Morse code!"

Leilani's forehead scrunched up. "What?"

"The coughing! It's Morse code!" I insisted.

Brandon eyed me skeptically. "What's the message?"

I strained to hear just the coughing. It sounded again.

Brandon's face twisted into an alarmed expression. "Sable, what did it say?"

"He said—he said to run and not come back for him. He wants us to let him die here—" I choked out.

Brandon's eyes grew wide and Leilani paled.

"He can't mean that," Leilani whispered.

Brandon punched the wall next to him. A small plume of dust wafted from the crumbling cement block. "I refuse to leave him here to die!"

"What do we do?" I inquired.

"Where did you hear the coughing coming from?" Brandon commanded.

"A few cells back, I think," I answered.

We hurried back four doors from where we came. Brandon threw open the grate that was used to slide trays of food into the cell. We took turns peering in, but all we could see was darkness. I wedged my hand through the grate and produced a flame in my palm. Then I slid my wrist over so Brandon could see inside.

I gasped as a cold rough hand grasped mine.

"Shaw?" I whispered.

"Weren't you fools listening? You have to run! Find the others and leave this place. Commander Goldbrook won't let you escape this time. He and Doctor Pantiel mean to kill all of us. It's too late for Agatha and me, but you can still get out of here. Brandon, my son, you have to take care of them. You have to keep them fighting for their lives. The DAO will come for you. You cannot let them eradicate you. We are not their monsters. You can show them. Now go. *Go!*" Shaw's voice was crazed.

"We're not leaving without you! We can't—we won't!" Brandon insisted.

"We just need a plan," I agreed.

"We won't abandon you, Shaw," Leilani chimed in.

"There will be no one to protect the Gifted who are still free if you get locked up in here with me," Shaw pointed out.

I shook my head. "How can we possibly manage to protect the world? We're just a handful of people!"

"One person can have the capability to change the world, Sable. They simply need the courage to make their voice be heard," Shaw retorted.

"We can't do this without you," Brandon protested.

"Even if I perished one day due to simply being an old man, you would inevitably have to carry on without me," Shaw countered.

"That doesn't mean we have to lose you today," Leilani said.

Through the small window in Shaw's cell, I could see the colors of sunset in the distance. It would be dinner time soon.

"Brandon, we have to go meet the others," I said as I pulled my hand from Shaw's and slipped it out of the grate.

He nodded. Before he closed the grate, he promised Shaw we'd be back for him. We didn't wait to hear his response.

ಬಿಎಬಿ

We sat around a circular table. All nine trays of liver and onions with succotash were untouched. Most people I saw in my peripheral vision sort of just pushed the offending meal around on their trays. While I people watched, Brandon explained that we'd found Shaw in the basement. He left out the part about Shaw telling us to leave him behind and making a break for it. Leilani and I didn't chime in. On the one hand, I saw Shaw's point. He wanted us to carry on with his legacy and let the world know that Gifted people weren't the monsters the non-Gifted feared. We just had different talents than others.

I understood Brandon's side, too. Shaw was the only

father any of us had left. He was the one who taught us how to fight, how to control our Gifts. Shaw gave us a better understanding of ourselves and took care of us when no one else was up to the task. And I knew Brandon lacked the confidence to lead us. Shaw knew Brandon was capable, just like I knew. Better than I knew.

"So how are we going to do this?" Chloe asked.

"I could short out the power and we could sneak him out," Brandon suggested.

"They'll be expecting that since that's how we escaped before," Ophelia pointed out.

"And there's no windows down there that are big enough for us to fit through," Leilani remarked.

Brandon sighed. "I wish we had some syringes filled with your saliva, Leilani."

"Yeah, I'm sure the orderlies have all been warned about us and what we can do," she mused.

"It didn't seem like there were too many of the staff waltzing around here. We just saw a bunch of people locked in their rooms. Everyone was pretty docile," Gareth reported.

"Maybe they were drugged," Leilani suggested.

The screams of the people in the basement still shrieked in my head as if they were trapped in a glass jar and the volume kept increasing until the glass cracked. I dug my nails into the skin behind my ears. Again I had the overwhelming urge to press my hands over my ears and flee.

But something Gareth said stuck out to me. There wasn't anyone walking around in navy scrubs. No one else mentioned running into them, either. And we didn't see any.

There was no way that we'd all just lucked out. When I was imprisoned here before, there were nurses and orderlies on rounds all the time.

"Wait—" I squeaked. I wanted to throw up all over again.

"Sable, what is it?" Kelly asked gently.

"They know we're here," I whispered.

"What did you see?" Chloe demanded.

"Just think about it. What are the odds that we could run around here all day without causing suspicion? It's not like they let the patients have free reign here. They're under lock and key until it's time to eat or until it's time for therapy. Commander Goldbrook isn't that stupid," I explained.

"I think we need to get back to the *Agatha* and figure this out," Melody advised.

Fang nodded. "I agree."

"How are we going to get back out of here?" Gareth wondered aloud.

"The same way we came in," Brandon decided.

We waited until most of the dining room was cleared out before we made our escape. One by one, we slipped out of the kitchen under the cover of darkness and swam back to the *Agatha*.

Fang, Brandon, and I left at the same time. Brandon was anxious about my epiphany. That much I could feel through the Bond. Did that mean I was relaxing? This didn't seem like an appropriate situation to let my guard down. Maybe it was because we were on our way back to the yacht, where we would be safe for at least one more night.

The whole time we were swimming, I couldn't stop thinking about how this was too easy. What was the reason for them letting us in and out like that? My worry ratcheted up as Brandon's unease flowed through the Bond.

A hand hung over the side of the yacht to help me up. I took it and allowed myself to be hoisted over the side of the boat. When I was on the deck and on my feet, I realized I was staring into a stranger's face. I opened my mouth to scream but the strange man covered it. An arm banded around my waist and I was pulled tightly against my captor. We'd been ambushed. Orderlies were waiting for us. As I frantically looked around, I realized that the rest of my comrades were bound and gagged, some with gunshot wounds. Thankfully, none of them seemed to be fatal. That meant Commander Goldbrook wanted us alive.

Brandon and Fang appeared as I was being forced to my knees and my hands were being bound behind my back. The zip ties bit into my flesh and rubbed my wrists raw quickly. I couldn't see much from my peripheral vision, but it seemed like the boys were putting up one hell of a fight. Gun fire sounded, followed quickly by a sickening thud. I screamed through my gag until I choked. Someone punched me in the back of the head and I landed on my face. Stars winked in and out of my vision. I blinked to clear them away. Then I twisted around to see who the most recent victim of a gunshot wound was. A small pool of blood grew steadily from Fang's thigh.

Tears ran down my face. Hysteria welled up inside me as I fought an oncoming panic attack. A waft of cigar smoke stung my eyes and my lungs. Someone yanked my hair so my head whipped backward. An upside-down vision of Commander Goldbrook appeared. I felt my eyes grow wide. There was no escape now. We should've listened to Shaw and run.

Commander Goldbrook's lips twisted into a sneer as he blew another puff of smoke into my face. "That's right, little Phoenix. Welcome home."

About the Author

Marissa Bauder is a long-time lover of reading, particularly young adult novels. Now she is writing her very own stories, published by Black Opal Books. When she doesn't have her nose stuck in a book or in her Kindle, Bauder can be found jamming out to tunes with her kids; snuggling up with her cat, her dog, and a warm blanket; or indulging in some hot chocolate and reality television. Bauder has lived all over the continental United States, but currently resides in southeastern Ohio with her family.